GEORGE ELLIS

Knight of War and Dawn

The Eighth Castle, Book 1

Contents

Prologue	1
Maldovar	5
Skullcrusher	13
Phaedra	19
Council of Six	26
Little Galantra	32
The Falls	39
Snakebit	46
Grayfork's Army	56
Maiden Voyage	60
The Hunt	68
Legacy	75
Unbalanced	80
Promised Knight	90
Pity Sword	98
Relic	106
Worktown	110
Gang of Five	119
Trials	123
Freedom	136
Harbinger	144
Crossroads	149
Soldiers	159
From the Depths	168

The Silver Castle   175
Advance Warning   183
Final Days   188
Reguirs   194
The Girl & the Serpent   204
Politicians   212
Kragon's Lair   215
Arthur   226
Bloodlines   234
Last Rites   239
Battle   242
Hillhome   254
Aftermath   262
Secrets, Revealed   265
Epilogue   271
About the Author   276
Also by George Ellis   277

Prologue

Queen Amira herself appeared in the doorway, prompting an audible gasp from the representative of Lockewell.

It was one thing for Tufthorn to send a representative to the Assembly, something it hadn't done for nearly a century, but it was another matter entirely for the queen of the desert herself to show up.

"Cold as a crypt, is it not?" she said, tossing a casual smile at the group of men who sat at the long stone table. That they were all men did not surprise her. She was accustomed to being the only female voice in the room; she rather enjoyed it. Her green eyes shimmered as she sat at the head of the table, or at least what seemed to become the head of it once she graced the spot with her presence. "I've come with news of the prophecy."

The men gaped at Amira, cowed by her bold assertion.

"And here I thought this would be as boring as all those assemblies my father told me about," a smooth voice replied. It belonged to Spiro, a slender, handsome man in a brown cloak. He took a sip of his wine as he appraised the queen, no doubt aware of her magical powers. Spiro was the only one not sitting at the table. He was leaning against the far wall so he could be closer to the window. The air was ripe with the stench of men that hadn't bathed in weeks, if ever.

Spiro represented Fidora, the forest kingdom. Along with men from the other realms—Lockewell, Clem, Skybane, and Maldovar—he was keenly interested in just why Amira had deigned to attend. Tufthorn, the most isolated and reclusive of the six modern kingdoms, never sent anyone to the Assembly to represent its interests.

"I have not come to squabble over lands or discuss new trade agreements," Amira said, reading the room. "Nor do I particularly want to be here, the charming company and aroma notwithstanding."

That rankled the men, especially Wraggus of Clem. The seven-foot-tall beast of a man stood up and pointed his huge finger at Amira. "Maybe you don't know how this works, but we talk in turn, and this isn't yours, woman. So, why don't you just sit there in your brothel robe with your magic tricks and wait until …"

Suddenly, the big man lost his voice. More specifically, he couldn't breathe. He clawed at his neck as he dropped to one knee, ripping off his leather vest in vain, trying to free the blockage in his chest and throat. Amira tilted her head and watched Wraggus's ugly, pockmarked face turn as red as the shock of hair sticking out of his shiny scalp.

"I can continue with my tricks, if you'd like," she mused. "Or I could skip all that and just say what I've come here to say. It's up to you."

"I have no love for the brute either, my lady, but you did surprise us all with your entrance, as pleasant as it was to behold," Spiro interjected. "Perhaps poor Wraggus simply misspoke due to shock. I'm sure he's normally a fine fellow.

Isn't that right, Wraggus?"

The big man's face was now blue, and he was just conscious enough to jerk his head in the affirmative. Amira gazed at him a few seconds longer, then turned to Spiro. Wraggus was immediately able to breathe again. He coughed hoarsely as the other representatives relaxed, easing the tension.

"You are right. Spiro, is it?" she asked, knowing the answer full well. "My manners have escaped me. Perhaps it's my brothel attire! This meeting of the boys club has its customs like any other gathering, I'm sure, but I'm afraid I must insist on sharing my information now, not after Lockewell sets the price on slaves for the coming decade. Does anyone object?"

Spiro bowed his head. "The lady from Tufthorn has the floor."

Nobody objected, certainly not Wraggus, who had climbed back into his chair. He stared straight ahead, stewing, not wanting to make eye contact with Amira. Sir Alan Grayfork, the knight from Lockewell, took visible offense but offered no real objection.

"Thank you. As I said before, I have news of the prophecy."

"Which prophecy?" Sir Grayfork asked, annoyed.

"*The* prophecy," Amira countered. "The only one that matters. A Flyer has returned, and he will take his place as the ruler of all realms."

"Bullshit," Sir Grayfork growled. "The Flyers have been gone for centuries. Even if one returned, he couldn't claim a two-bit village in Lockewell, let alone all six kingdoms."

"Seven," Amira corrected, referring to Stoneridge, the abandoned castle of the Flyers. "And not only can he do it, but he will. I suggest you tell your king and his princess, Lord Bruner."

With that, she turned to Lord Bruner of Skybane, the land of the Fins. Centuries earlier, the island kingdom had been a natural rival to Stoneridge and its Flyers. Despite that, according to the prophecy, a princess of Skybane would unite with the Flyer upon his return to join forces and assume the throne above all others.

"I think I'll let the king tell her himself," Lord Bruner quipped nervously.

Maldovar

Jamie was up before the sun again. That made it nine days in a row. He kept track of such things, much to his aunt Berta's chagrin. Berta loved the boy like he was her own, but his astounding memory was one of his least charming qualities, if you asked her. It made him more difficult than any fifteen-year-old had the right to be.

The frail woman removed Jamie's plate from the kitchen table almost the instant he finished his last bite of eggs. She took the fork from his hand, as it was more efficient than waiting for him to put it down.

"I'll need you to get flour from the market today, after you milk the cow," Berta said. "I've put the copper pieces in your satchel."

"You'd think that old cow would've figured out how to milk herself by now," Jamie responded, chewing a muffin he'd managed to swipe off the counter before Berta could store them away.

"Maybe she doesn't want to put you out of a job," Berta said.

Jamie snorted as he forced himself out of the chair, still groggy, and searched the floor for his boots. Berta kept one eye on the boy as she cleaned the kitchen. He was already taller than her and was beginning to resemble his late father with his emerald eyes and dark, curly hair. More than once, she'd caught the girl from the farm over the hill flirting with him as he worked in the field.

It was a far cry from a couple of years ago when he was tormented by older kids about his penchant for reading and drawing. He wasn't such an easy target now, though he was still an avid book lover, a habit of which Berta was extremely proud. She didn't have the means to educate him properly, but she'd worked hard to make sure the boy knew how to read and write. That he took to it so well gave her hope for his future.

Berta knew the time would come when she'd have more to worry about than a besotted neighbor girl or some bullies at the market. Jamie was different. And she had promised his parents she'd never let people know exactly how different he truly was. Oh, there was a chance he was just another farm boy living in the outer edges of Maldovar, but the older he got, the more she doubted her ability to keep the truth from him, let alone the outside world.

"What?" Jamie asked, feeling her eyes on him.

Berta pushed those thoughts from her mind for the moment. It could be dealt with another day. "Just missing your parents," she said.

Jamie nodded his understanding. Aunt Berta often mentioned his parents and how much she missed them. In her stories about them, Jamie's father was a shoemaker, and his mother managed the farm. Jamie believed those stories. Why would he not? It never dawned on him that his aunt was actively hiding his past from him.

"Two pieces of copper is how much flour again?" he asked,

testing her.

"Don't even think about it," she scolded, one step ahead of him. "Now give me a kiss before you go."

Jamie did as he was told, hugging his aunt for good measure. He was careful not to squeeze too hard; the boy was aware she wasn't in the best of health, though he dared not ask what was ailing her. He knew she would deny it. Not asking helped him deny it as well. Despite his deep desire to travel across the world to the lands of distant castles, he also knew his aunt was the only person he had in this world. The thought of losing her was too hard to stomach.

He could use another muffin, though, he reasoned, as he snatched it from the counter on his way out the door.

"I saw that!" Berta yelled after him, a smile on her face. It felt like forever ago when Jamie's mother, nearly a decade Berta's junior, was the one swiping treats from the kitchen as she scurried about. But that was another life. That kitchen was twice the size of Berta's entire house, which made sense, as Berta and her sister had grown up in a noble manor, not the shoebox of a home that she now shared with Jamie.

The market was an hour's walk from home if Jamie didn't stop along the way. He did. Taking a sip of the fresh milk in his canteen, he sat on the dewy ground, his back against the trunk of a wide oak tree. He looked down at the valley below. Jamie had no love for this country, the very southern tip of Maldovar's realm. He often wondered if anyone of consequence had ever lived this far from Genora, the capital city. There were more goats than people here. Still, his lack of pride for his home province did not extend to the scenery this morning. As the sun crept onto the horizon, it cast a gentle orange glow on the green hills of Tarlintown. He would be sketching in black and white, but he appreciated the vibrant colors nonetheless.

As he took his pencil from his satchel, he heard a rustle behind him in the bushes. He whirled and held out his drawing instrument, hoping the source of the noise wasn't a bobcat; he'd had a nasty encounter with one of those the previous summer and barely escaped with his life.

"Gotcha!" Lily giggled as she appeared from behind the oak tree. She laughed at the pencil he was holding like a sword. "What are you gonna do with that? Ooh, you could draw me?"

Four years older than Jamie, Lily knew she could play with him. She stepped forward, teasing. "Would you like to draw me?"

"I don't have time for this today," Jamie said, gathering his things so he could be on his way.

"Don't be like that," Lily pouted. "I just saw you there looking all sad and lonely and figured you could use company. Where are you headed?"

"The market."

"Perfect! Me too!"

It wasn't that Jamie didn't like her; he'd had a crush on her ever since he became interested in girls. Her father was the problem. The man was crazy. He'd once threatened Jamie at knifepoint after Lily had mentioned his name casually at dinner the evening before. It was clear to Jamie that if he so much as looked at Lily the wrong way, he could be in mortal danger.

"I won't tell my dad," Lily said, sensing his apprehension.

"You better not," Jamie replied. And he meant it. Lily's father was rumored to be descended from Clem warriors. He certainly looked the part at three-hundred-plus pounds and six-and-a-half feet tall.

Careful to keep a few feet of distance between himself and Lily, Jamie walked with her to the Tarlintown market, which consisted of about a dozen carts set up in a field. Produce. Household items. Meat. The exact wares for sale varied depending on the day, but you could always find the staples. After he had promised to stop by Lily's house sometime to try and gain her father's approval (a half-truth at best), Jamie perused Mr. Wayling's inventory of tools and knives. Jamie had no copper left after purchasing the flour, but he dreamed of one day being able to afford a proper knife, or even a short sword to defend himself. He had no illusions about Wayling's weapons being of the highest quality. They were just the best Tarlintown had to offer. A local blacksmith, Wayling's claim to fame was that he once crafted a scabbard for perhaps the greatest swordsman to ever live, Sir Galantra himself, and the crusty old codger never missed an opportunity to mention it.

"There he is! When are you gonna tell your aunt to marry me?" Wayling joked. Or maybe he wasn't joking. Jamie could never tell. "If I give you a deal on a blade, think you could put in a good word?"

"I could," Jamie replied.

Wayling cackled at that. "Maybe next time, kid ... or maybe you should actually acquire some silver. You're taking up precious space and scaring off paying customers. Move along. But tell Berta I still fancy her!"

Jamie frowned and started to head off toward the road back to his house. He had to push through the gathering midmorning crowd. As he did, a boy a year or two younger than him bumped his arm, nearly knocking Jamie's satchel off his shoulder. The other boy didn't even pause. He just kept making his way toward Wayling's cart. Instinctively, Jamie checked his satchel to make sure the flour was still there. Pickpockets were common in Tarlintown. Once he was assured the flour hadn't been taken, Jamie was about to close his satchel back up when he realized something else was missing: his pencil set. He turned just in time to see the boy talking to Wayling.

"Thief!" Jamie yelled and darted toward the pickpocket.

The younger boy took off on a dead run toward the woods. Jamie quickly changed direction and ran hard, hoping to cut him off in time. The kid was fast. Faster than anyone Jamie had ever seen, in fact. Then again, fear of being caught can be a great motivator. Taking a wild gamble, Jamie grabbed the sack of flour from his satchel and hurled it at the boy. It exploded in a puff of white against the kid's head, knocking him over. Jamie tackled him before he could get back up.

"Get off!" the boy yelled, his face covered in white dust.

"Give me my damn pencils!" Jamie demanded. Then he saw the writing implements sticking out of the thief's pocket and grabbed them himself. By then, Wayling had hurried over and reached into the kid's coat, retrieving a fancy dagger the boy had taken from his cart. Wayling kicked him roughly in the stomach a couple of times.

"You better disappear before I change my mind and stick you with this myself," Wayling growled, pointing the dagger at the kid. The boy shot Jamie an evil glare, then jogged into the woods. Wayling turned to Jamie. "Thanks."

Jamie was happy to have his pencils back, but he knew he'd catch hell for losing the flour, which was spilled all over the grass and his own clothes. Wayling offered him a hand up.

"C'mere, got something for you," Wayling said.

Jamie dusted himself off as he followed the man back to his cart. Wayling reached under the table where his finished works were on display and produced a long knife with a dark-brown handle. "Take it," he said.

Jamie didn't need the man to offer twice; he grabbed the knife and looked it over.

"Blade's in good condition … I just cracked the handle when I was finishing it. Too much damn wine," Wayling explained. Indeed, there was a small crack in the wood. "Not exactly Galantra quality, but it'll still cut and stab until that crack splits in half. Yours if you want it."

"I'll take it!" Jamie blurted, prompting a gap-toothed grin from the blacksmith.

* * *

Jamie admired the blade as it glimmered in the midday sun. The flaw in the handle didn't bother him one bit. The knife was perfect, in his opinion. The question he kept asking himself was whether he dared tell his aunt about it. There was a good chance she'd either take it away or send him right back to the market to trade it for baking supplies.

No, it was better to keep his new weapon a secret, he decided. He'd just tell Aunt Berta a thief had snatched the flour. She'd believe that. Maybe. She always seemed to know when Jamie was lying to her.

He crested the last hill before the mile-long stretch home and was greeted by the sound of hooves pounding the dirt. He looked up from the blade and saw a pair of horses pulling an iron carriage, heading in his direction. Another horse carrying a hooded rider bolted ahead of the carriage. The dark figure was fifty yards away and closing fast.

Jamie immediately scrambled off the road and into the woods, hoping the rider wouldn't give chase. He'd heard stories of iron carriages and hooded horsemen. None of them were good. Most involved slavers from Clem or Lockewell. A few years earlier, one of Jamie's friends had been killed on this very road, while his older brother had simply disappeared. A roving band of Clem warriors were blamed for the murder and abduction. Jamie cursed the gods for his bad luck.

He stuck the knife under his belt as he plowed through branches and jumped fallen logs. The forest ground was uneven, meaning one false step and he could break an ankle. Still, he kept the pace. Moments earlier, he'd felt like a big man with his weapon, but now all he wanted was to see his aunt again and enjoy one of her baked pies or breads. Hearing a noise behind him, Jamie chanced a look back. Someone was definitely following him.

He turned forward to pick up the pace and ran directly into a thick branch. The world went black.

Skullcrusher

Anke's food tasted like iron again. She put down the turkey leg and wiped the remaining blood from her fingers with an already-crimson towel. Tasting another person's blood didn't particularly bother her; she was used to it as a veteran warrior. But when it threatened to ruin a perfectly good turkey leg, that just pissed her off.

She resumed devouring her dinner and surveyed the Great Hall. *Great, my ass*, she thought. Kragon's Lair was a shithole of a castle. Her predecessor, Garrick the Merciless, whose head she caved in with the business end of her war hammer, thus earning her the title of Skullcrusher, had been as sloppy a ruler as he was a warrior. The castle suffered from years of disrepair and neglect, much like the rest of the kingdom. When she was a child in Sword's Edge, on the border of Clem and Lockewell, Anke loved hearing the tales of glory and triumph from her father, gods be with him now. A full head taller than most of the other men in Sword's Edge, her father Malak was a proud Clem general and had seen many battles, most of which his legions had won. He spoke of honor and bravery, and of a time when all armies, regardless of number or origin, shook in fear at the sight of a Clem brigade across the battlefield. Even in her youth, those days were fading away. Now, they were nothing more than a memory. Clem was still home to some of the most fearsome warriors to carry a weapon, but the clans had not been united in battle for many years. A lawless sprawl of killers and rival factions, Anke's Clem was a far cry from the greatest fighting force the world had ever known.

Anke had only been on the throne for a month, and she already had plans to overhaul the entirety of the Lair and its realm. She would restore Clem to its rightful place among the six realms or die trying.

"A smashing defense, Your Highness," Laroche told her. The thin man sat on her right. He was the only non-Clem in the hall, which was plainly obvious by his fine clothes and ability to read and reason. Anke liked him despite his blatant flattery.

"He had no business in the Circle," she said, eyeing the large fighting circle in the middle of the hall. Her challenger's body was still lying prone where it fell. His head had also been devastated by her hammer.

"They rarely do when you're in there with them," Laroche noted.

Anke's eyes instinctively flicked toward a hulking figure standing in the shadows. Rawk the Fearsome. He had a steel axe slung over his shoulder. Rawk had seen more than a dozen men (and now a woman) kill their way to the throne. All of them were inferior to him when it came to combat. The huge warrior would simply have to step into the Circle, and Clem was as good as his. There was not a soul in the world who could face Rawk in single combat and live to tell the tale, Anke reasoned, except maybe that swordsman from the east everybody was always going on about. Not that he'd give two shits about the Clem throne. Why Rawk never challenged the sitting ruler, on the other hand, was a mystery.

"That reminds me of the old adage: no matter how murderous you are, there's always someone more murderier," Laroche said.

"So, who's more murderier than Rawk?" Anke replied.

"Well, every adage has its exceptions," Laroche admitted. "But thank you for indulging my wordplay." Laroche took another sip of wine, wincing slightly at the taste. Anke couldn't blame him. Clem wine was an acquired taste at best. The feast had gone so late into the evening that they'd run out of wine from Maldovar. They had to tap the local barrels to keep the guests from rioting.

Guests, she sneered to herself. If Anke had her way, there would be no feasts or challenges. She'd rather be in the field of battle, conquering new lands. Alas, it was a time of peace. Just her luck to rule during peacetime. Laroche must have caught the grimace, because he sighed along with her.

"You don't enjoy the challenges?" he asked.

"It's not a matter of enjoyment," she replied. "It's a waste of time. We fight amongst ourselves when we should be out building our kingdom and seeking glory."

"Ah, glory. I don't know much about that," Laroche said. "One of the benefits of being a businessman."

Anke snorted and drank more of her shitty wine from her depressing kingdom. Maybe she'd step down from the throne and go back to being a mercenary. At least that way she'd have more time in combat. Real combat! Not fighting woefully inept challengers every fortnight. Speaking of ineptitude, she spotted the oaf that had represented Clem at the Assembly. He was lumbering toward the raised table where she ate. What was his name again? Ragnar? No, it was more foul than that. Anke had been forced to send the man, as he'd already been chosen by Garrick the Idiot. Not-Ragnar stopped on the other side of the table from Anke, his odor announcing his presence as much as his large frame.

"Skullcrusher," he said, bowing his head slightly.

Anke paused before responding. *What the fuck was his name?*

Sensing the awkwardness, Laroche quickly hefted a mug of wine at the man. "Wraggus!" Laroche exclaimed. "You must be weary and parched from your travels. I saved a mug of Maldovarian wine just for you."

Wraggus snatched the wine and downed it in one glug, a good portion of it dribbling down his bearded chin. Laroche had gambled that the big man couldn't tell the difference between wine from Clem and Maldovar, and he'd been right. Wraggus seemed pleased as he addressed Anke.

"My horse died halfway here, and I had to ride some dumb beast of a mare the rest of the way," Wraggus said, touching the hilt of his weapon. "Just put her out of my misery."

Anke caught Laroche's eye and sent him a silent nod of thanks for the name assistance. If the businessman weren't so damn pretty, she might be interested in fucking him. Pity. She raised her mug to Wraggus. "To your horse. Not the mare."

Wraggus nodded.

"Tell me about the Assembly," she said. "What's the going rate on a slave these days?"

"Best if the spy leaves," Wraggus replied, turning his eyes to Laroche. "Get."

"Laroche is a guest and a valued trade partner," Anke scolded.

"He's a slippery rat and not Clem besides," Wraggus countered. "This wasn't any normal Assembly, and I didn't spend

16

two horses to report back to the likes of him."

"Sounds exciting," Laroche said as he rose, "but I do believe I'll call it a night. Your Highness."

Anke watched Laroche slip out of the hall and was surprised to be so disappointed to lose his company for the evening. Maybe she'd pay him a visit later if the mood struck, though talking to Wraggus was sure to turn her off of sex for a while. The man was vile.

"Go on," she said. "Tell me what couldn't wait until after the feast."

* * *

She would have chosen a different messenger, but the news didn't disappoint. That's all that really mattered. Hell, Anke almost hugged Wraggus, she was so happy. Almost. As she made her way through the musty hall, she finished the last of her wine and handed the empty mug to her manservant Lukas, who was trailing a step behind her. The slender teen boy took the mug in stride and silently handed her the bottle in return. He'd only been serving her a month, and he already knew her well. The nephew of Garrick didn't seem to miss the foolish tyrant. Quite the opposite, actually. He was one to watch, Anke had decided. The kid had smarts and felt trustworthy.

Anke reached the end of the hall and banged on the door. After a few moments, a shirtless Laroche opened it. While no one would ever confuse the merchant for a warrior, Anke was surprised at how sturdy he appeared. *Good*, she thought, *he's going to need it.* Laroche smiled warmly at the wine in her hand, until he noticed her hammer in the other.

"It's not for you," she said lightly, casting a look over her shoulder. "I still have more enemies in this castle than friends."

"I hope you consider me the latter," Laroche replied.

"I don't offer wine and sex to my enemies," she said before motioning to the half-naked young woman standing next to the bed in Laroche's room. "Out."

Anke watched with amusement as the pretty girl quickly gathered her things and scampered past. "See that she gets to her chamber," Anke told Lukas. The boy followed her down the hall.

"I knew you were forward, but this is truly unexpected," Laroche said.

"Or maybe I just wanted her to think I was here for a fuck, so she'd run and tell all the other wenches," Anke countered.

"So, you're not here for a fuck then?" Laroche asked in mock dismay.

"That's not the main reason," Anke said, leaning her hammer against the wall as she closed the door behind her.

Phaedra

The water was pitch black. And damn cold.

Phaedra's search for the trident had led her to depths she'd never experienced before. She tried to focus her vision through the murk, hoping to catch a glint of steel. The young Fin considered diving even further, but the crushing pressure of the deep was already beginning to affect her ability to maneuver. She could only hold her breath for another few minutes, and she would need those to safely ascend back to the surface.

Dejected, Phaedra gave up the search and began to swim back to the ship. She would live with this shame for the rest of her life. Her father's trident had been in the family for generations. It was wielded by Bane the Third himself when he conquered the Great Kraken in Redfish Bay. How could she have been so careless with it?

Phaedra knew the answer. She was a spoiled child, indulged by her father, the king. She had been told as much many times by her mother, and deep down she knew this was true. There were two kinds of princesses in the world: rebellious and spoiled. Somehow, she had managed to be both. Her father's method of spoiling her was to let her act on all her wild urges, resulting in a myriad of problems for herself—and the kingdom she would someday rule. In this instance, she had lost one of the great treasures of her people.

Body aching, Phaedra climbed aboard the *Longfin*, the flagship of her father's fleet. It held a crew of more than fifty, and Phaedra felt all of their eyes on her as she walked barefoot along the deck toward the captain's room. The webbing between her toes retracted while she made her way past the royal guard. Lucian, a few years her senior and her closest friend in the realm, sidled up next to her.

"It'll be okay," he said. "That old trinket was bound to break soon anyway."

Phaedra furrowed her brow, not dignifying the meager consolation attempt with a response.

"Or he'll imprison you at The Falls until you turn eighteen," Lucian said.

"If I'm lucky," Phaedra replied. "Now leave me alone. He already dislikes you enough."

"He doesn't dislike me," Lucian argued.

"Then why did he tell me the next time he caught us alone, he'd castrate you and banish you to the desert?"

"Because he has a delightful sense of humor," Lucian joked, before angling off down a corridor.

Phaedra knocked on the door of the captain's room. Dall, the head of the royal guard, opened the heavy door and grimaced at her. His own ancestors were linked to the trident as well; it was rumored his family had forged the weapon. The fact he was angry with her meant news of her latest misadventure had already reached the king.

"Lord Dall," she managed. "Does he have a moment?"

"For my beloved daughter? Of course!" her father boomed,

motioning for her to enter. Dall stepped out of the room and closed the door, leaving Phaedra alone with her father.

King Bane the Blue, as he was known throughout the realm, was no longer the imposing man he once was. By no means a diminutive person, the king's physical appearance simply didn't match the weight of his presence. He stood less than six feet tall, and the centuries had taken their toll on what the bards had once described as a godlike physique. Now he was just a lean man with a sharp jawline and silver eyes flecked with blue. He was so pale, his skin had a slight blue tint to it. At 320 years of age, he was the oldest person in the known world. At the moment, he seemed much less angry than Phaedra assumed he would be.

"My darling jewel of the sea," he said, motioning for Phaedra to sit down across from him, "you don't smile nearly as much as you used to. I hope that does not reflect on my performance as a father."

Yep, something is definitely off about him, Phaedra thought. *This is bad.*

"I can explain—"

"By the time I met your mother, I was nearly three centuries old," he interrupted. "You know this, of course."

"You've told me the story once or twice, yes," Phaedra said.

"Well, let me tell you it again, only this time, the full story."

"So, you're not mad about the trident?"

The king gazed out the window toward the ocean. For a few seconds, he seemed to be lost in the waves, then finally he cracked the smallest of smiles. "I'm both saddened and excited, Phaedra. What you presume to be your mistake is nothing more than destiny being fulfilled. That trident was bound to be lost—meant to be, in fact—just as I too will someday fade

21

into memory."

He looked at her again. "I don't even remember when I was sixteen. You have youth to spare."

"You're getting a little too philosophical for this early in the morning, Dad," Phaedra said, concerned about where the conversation was headed.

"Three hundred years without a human child to succeed me," he said.

"A human child? You are not on about that again, are you?" Phaedra asked. The king pushed ahead, ignoring her comment.

"Then your mother came along. Followed by you. From the moment you were born, I knew my time was coming to an end. But it wasn't until this morning that I knew how lucky I truly was. How lucky we both are, my angelfish."

Phaedra hated that nickname. "Just what the hell are you talking about?" she demanded.

Her father laughed heartily. "You'll have to work on that temper when you're in charge," he admonished. "I'm talking about what was once a whisper in the wind but now may be the coming storm that sweeps Skybane back into our rightful place at the head of all realms."

"Speak plainly, Father." Phaedra had no more patience for his esoteric bullshit.

"My trident left us on the very day I received word the prophecy will be fulfilled in the coming months and years. *When* is not yet clear. What is clear is that my time is ending, and your reign soon begins."

"What prophecy?" Phaedra asked, confused.

"Ah, I should get to that part of the story, shouldn't I?"

* * *

Above all else, Phaedra was a Fin, a member of the oldest and noblest Skybane family. She did not get seasick. That weakness was not in her veins. So, as she walked across the deck, unsure of her footing and swayed by each minute movement of the boat beneath her feet, she knew she was in real trouble.

Is this what it felt like to be scared? she wondered.

If so, she didn't like the foreign sensation.

Lucian saw her ashen face and meant to approach, but she held him off with a gesture and hurried past, taking a direct path to her cabin.

When she arrived at the door, she caught sight of a sparrow that had positioned itself atop a nearby mast post. The small bird twitched its head in Phaedra's direction, and for a moment, they locked eyes. Phaedra suddenly slammed her hand against the railing, scaring the sparrow. It jolted off its perch and took flight, soaring over the ocean to safety, away from the ship and its ill-tempered princess.

Phaedra watched the bird with disgust.

Once inside her room, Phaedra locked the door behind her and collapsed onto the bed. She closed her eyes and waited for the mix of fear and nausea to subside. Her stomach churned with anger, though she couldn't say exactly why. Or, she should've been happy. Phaedra had expected to be punished for losing a family heirloom. Instead, her father had told her she was fated to rule the world. It wasn't the first time she'd been informed she would someday "marry the one that would unite all the realms." *Fuck that guy*, she thought. For one, she resented the idea that her role would simply be to marry the airborne asshole. He would lead and she would, what, stand by his side? Or maybe ride his back while he flew through the air like some freak?

A knock at the door pulled her from her thoughts.

"Go away, Lucian," she barked.

"It's me, Princess," came the timid reply. "May I enter?"

"Yes," Phaedra groaned. "And stop calling me Princess. I'm your sister."

Phaedra's younger brother, Arthur, shuffled into the room. Eleven years old, he was small for his age. What he lacked in physical stature, he made up for in brains, much to Phaedra's annoyance. *The kid is just weird*, she thought.

"You are both my sister and a princess, and I prefer to use the formal moniker over your name," he said. "It's a good name. Nothing wrong with it. But shouldn't you be happy to be a princess?"

"Are you happy to be a prince?"

"I don't know. Maybe. I don't think about it as much as you think about your role in the family. Perhaps if I were the firstborn, I'd feel differently."

Phaedra forced a smile. "Did you need something?"

"I always need something," Arthur said. "I'm a needy kid, and I fear I'll grow up to be an adult with attachment issues. But this visit is about you and your future."

"You've been eavesdropping again, Artie!"

"Obviously," he replied with no hint of snark.

Phaedra shook her head. The kid was truthful to a fault. She waved her hand at a chair, and he happily sat down.

"What about my future?" she asked.

"I'm worried it will get you killed," Arthur said.

"I'll be fine. I'm going to rule the world!" she exclaimed with disdain.

"That's not my understanding of the prophecy. I believe you're just destined to marry this mysterious Flyer to solidify his kingdom and claim, but there's nothing about you ruling. In other words, I think it's a death sentence."

Phaedra blinked at her younger brother.

"Not to mention all the people that will now try to kill you before that happens," Arthur added. "History is filled with prophecies that never came to fruition because other forces intervened."

"How can a prophecy not happen? That's what a prophecy is. It predicts the future."

"I had a feeling you'd think that. Most people that don't read books share that misunderstanding. It's nothing to be ashamed of," Arthur said. "You're just ignorant."

"Gee, thanks."

"You're welcome."

"So, what do you propose I do, my wise little brother?"

"Disappear at once."

Council of Six

The vote was close, but the measure passed with just enough support from a breakaway faction of the Reds, who joined with the Traditionalists to outnumber the West Maldovarians.

"Thirty-four to thirty-one," Henry Martin growled in disgust. He was speaking to nobody in particular as he stalked toward his office, commonly known as the First Minister's Chamber. The emergency Senate session had just ended, and the body had decided to keep the seat of government in Genora, of central Maldovar, for the next five years, as opposed to relocating it to the realm's western region, where new money and families had been rising in prominence for decades.

It was only a matter of time. Eventually, the West Maldovarians would have their way. Too much power was concentrated in their part of the realm, which bordered Lockewell, an important trade partner. The First Minister reached his office and plopped down into his chair, despondent, knowing his fate was tied to the location of the capital. His family had a long legacy of political strength—he was the third Martin to be First Minister—but all their constituents hailed from central and east Maldovar. As the power of the west rose, the importance of his homeland waned.

"Victory!" Philipa Black exclaimed with a smile.

Henry watched the short woman enter the room. As usual, he wasn't sure what to think of the lower minister or the words coming out of her mouth. Despite being political allies for most of their adult lives, the two weren't close. Black had helped him ascend to his place as the highest-ranking member of the Republic, but Henry still didn't trust her. She was exceedingly clever.

"Yes, quite the cause for celebration. A three-vote margin," Henry groaned. "In five years, we'll all be packing for Hillhome."

"You may be right," Black replied. "Then again, a lot can change in five years. Look at Clem."

She was referring to the constant state of upheaval in the kingdom to the north. Henry snorted at the comparison.

"We are not thugs and corrupt warriors," Henry said.

"Are we not? From your lips to the Senate's ears," Black chided.

Henry laughed. She was right. The Senate was as vicious and corrupt as any Clem clan. Perhaps Maldovar was even worse; all the backstabbing was right out in the open for all to see. More family houses and legacies were destroyed in the Republic than anywhere else in the world.

One by one, the rest of the council filed into Henry's office. The Council of Six, they were called, though Henry hated the name. Yes, there were six of them, but he didn't like the group having a special designation. He felt it was more like himself and five advisors, if anything. Of course, he didn't feel that way when he was just a member of the council. Now that he was in the biggest chair, his views had shifted.

Along with Henry and Black, the other members were Asper Modano, Viceroy Renner, Harper Krull, and Eliana Troy. Only Modano and Troy had been elected. Krull was a military man and had the pompous title of Defender of the Republic. Henry had appointed him years earlier but as of late couldn't fathom why he'd ever made that decision. The man was a dolt. Viceroy Renner was the council's economic advisor, a position he'd earned by befriending a majority of the senators, thanks to the many brothels he owned across Maldovar.

"Best get packing, indeed," Renner said, ripping the scab right off. "I'd be surprised if we made it another five years here."

"No doubt music to your ears," Modano snapped. The two were fierce rivals, constantly vying for the unofficial title of richest man in the realm. "Aren't most of your disease dens in West Maldovar?"

"My dear Asper, you clearly know that is the truth from firsthand experience," Renner replied. "Do you still favor the dominating ones?"

This prompted a grunt from Krull, who rarely spoke in the council meetings but frequently made guttural noises to agree or disagree with various points of discussion.

"Krull seconds it. The motion has passed!" Renner joked.

"Enough bickering," Henry said. "The vote is done. We may yet be looking for new offices, and some of us new jobs, in the future, but as for now, we have more pressing matters to deal with."

"Such as?" Renner asked.

"Such as the new trade terms you negotiated at the Assembly, for starters," Henry replied.

"Are we not pleased?" Renner mused, motioning to the rest

of the council. "I've gone above and beyond as usual."

"For a man who accepted a new tariff on all iron and steel coming from Lockewell, you seem quite proud of yourself," Troy chimed in. At sixty, she was the oldest member of the council and typically spoke in the form of observation, which gave her the ability to remain impartial while making her point known.

"Considering all I had to bargain with was grain and wool, I feel I did exceedingly well," Renner said, referring to the two chief exports of Maldovar: food and clothing materials.

Troy nodded. It was a fair point. There were no illusions around the table about the general state of Maldovar's standing in the world. Once a land of prosperity and freedom, it was now home to corrupt politicians, inefficient farms, and an aging population. Even worse, the political system was starting to fracture. Nobody would consider Henry or his allies flawless and pure, but the West Maldovarians cared about one thing only: power. If they gained the majority and took the First Minister position, Maldovar would become even more divided by class. There were already rumblings among the nobles of suspending or even dissolving the Senate. Henry knew a revolution wouldn't be far behind, and revolutions were very bloody business.

"Perhaps we should just give up then and let our friends to the north sack our lands," Modano said, only half-joking.

"Why would they want to?" Renner responded. "Aside from the fine companions in my establishments."

"While it's encouraging to see the Republic's top advisors insult the very people we're sworn to serve, perhaps we should discuss the other development," Henry said. As usual, he was annoyed with the council.

"Yes, the queen from the desert sure did stir the pot," Troy agreed.

"Who cares about the babblings of a witch?" Renner asked.

"I can't believe I'm saying this, but Renner makes a fair point," Modano said. "The woman shows up unannounced and tries to scare us all with whispers of a Flyer who will rise from the ashes of a long-dead race?"

"She was quite attractive, though," Renner interjected. "I'll give her that."

"What do you think, Eliana?" Henry asked.

Troy smiled appreciatively and ran a finger across her chin, giving his question the proper consideration. "When it comes to the supposed words and wills of the gods, I tend to advocate for a wait-and-see approach. The gods act and we react, the saying goes. That being said, I see no benefit for Queen Amira to claim the fulfillment of this particular prophecy. Who exactly is she trying to curry favor with?"

"That was my thought. Why would she be doing this? And why now?" Henry mused. "Unless she truly believed it."

"I've seen the magic of Tufthorn mages firsthand, so I would never discount it," Black added.

Henry closed his eyes for a moment. On top of the very real issues that faced Maldovar, the prospect of a monarch rising to such power that he ruled over all the realms—including the only Republic among them—was disquieting to say the least. "Did she give any indication who this Flyer might be?"

"Of course not! You can't name someone that doesn't exist!" Renner exclaimed. "This whole thing is a distraction from the fact that Tufthorn wants back into the game. They need goods from the outside. More than a few travelers from the desert have come through my brothels speaking of the difficulties of isolation. They are merely running out of resources!"

"Well, I certainly hope you negotiated a better deal with them than you did with Lockewell," Modano sniped. "Although maybe you're already preparing for the move west."

"Watch your tongue, Asper. It would be a shame for you to wake up without it one day," Renner warned. Threats of that kind were rarely issued in the First Minister's Chamber, but when they were, Renner was usually the one making them, and he was no stranger to following through.

Henry saw a flash of a smile on Black's face. It disappeared as quickly as it arrived, but Henry was sure he'd caught its meaning.

"Squabble on your own time," Henry said. "And we can worry about a promised boy-king another day. Right now, let's focus on shoring up support and rewarding our friends from the Red Party who crossed the line to keep the status quo. Dismissed."

The other members obliged, filing out without another word. Troy was the last to leave and glanced back with a concerned look. Henry didn't always flaunt his power by formally dismissing the rest of the council, but he was in a foul mood. Not only had the vote been much too close for comfort, a more urgent threat had come into focus, one that had been right there in front of him the whole time. Renner and Black were working with the West Maldovarians. Henry couldn't decide what was more troubling: that he hadn't seen it coming or that it might be too late to do anything about it. No less than the fate of the Republic hung in the balance.

Little Galantra

"Shoulda hid that knife in your boot," the boy said.

Jamie opened his eyes to find the ground below him moving at a steady clip. Confused, he touched his forehead and felt a searing pain shoot through his skull. He strained to sit up and get his bearings, soon realizing he was riding in an iron cage on the back of a wagon with another boy.

"You …" Jamie said, bleary-eyed.

"Yeah, me," the boy replied. He was the thief from the market. "If you hadn't made that old jackwap chase me into the woods, I wouldn't be a slave now."

The boy took advantage of Jamie's weakened state and kicked him in the shin.

"Ow!" Jamie groaned. "You're a dirty thief! Wait … slave?"

"Welcome to your new life, farm boy," the thief said, clinking the metal bars of their cell.

The reality of the situation shook Jamie. He would be taken from Maldovar to Clem or, if he was slightly luckier, Lockewell, to be sold like a cow. He'd never see his aunt again unless he escaped. Jamie scanned the countryside and was disheartened to realize he was completely unfamiliar with his surroundings.

"How long have I been out?" he asked the thief, who didn't answer. *"How long?"*

"Just because we're in this cage don't make us friends, farm boy," he replied. "Wanna know how long? Check your pants. Smells like a day or two to me."

Jamie realized his pants were soiled with piss, both fresh and dried. It had been at least a day since he was captured. He pulled himself toward the edge of the cage and spied the man up front who was whipping the horses. He was large, but not large enough to be Clem, and Jamie saw no sign of Lockewell silver on his clothes. He was a bandit, beholden to no realm. Jamie saw the knife Wayling had given him on the seat next to the bearded man.

"You can't reach it," the boy said. "Already tried."

Jamie didn't see any sign of the other rider, the one who had chased him into the woods. "Where's the other guy?"

The thief boy shrugged. Jamie turned back to the man driving the wagon. "Where are we going?"

Without even looking back, the bandit cracked his whip around behind him, and the tip slashed against the bars, snapping Jamie's fingers. The bandit laughed. "Talk again and the next one's in your face."

Jamie sat back, rubbing his now-bloody knuckles. The other boy simply smiled at him.

* * *

They took the road south for two more days. They mostly stuck to the countryside, but twice they had passed through small villages. Neither time did anyone offer help. These villages were even smaller than Tarlintown, where Jamie was from, and the people there were simple farm folk. They knew better than to get mixed up in the affairs of bandits.

During the trip, Jamie and the other boy, Caldred, had been given stale bread scraps and a few sips of water each morning. Jamie's stomach ached for meat or eggs, but he dared not ask for anything; he'd seen the bandit mete out savage punishment when Caldred laughed at the man nearly falling off the wagon when they hit a rocky part of the road. Jamie thought the man was going to kill the other boy, but he merely left him bloodied and unconscious for a few hours.

They weren't exactly friends, but Jamie and Caldred formed a bond, as all people in situations like this did, and there was an unspoken truce among them. They both knew if the opportunity arose, they'd work together to escape.

The hooded rider had not been back, making Jamie wonder if he was off trying to find another slave or had simply gone ahead to their eventual destination. Judging by the direction they were going, Jamie assumed they were riding to Barron, a port town on the tip of Maldovar's Southern Sea. From there, they were likely headed to Clem. He'd heard stories of slave boys being turned into eunuchs and manservants. Rumors of a Clem warrior school of sorts also existed, but that seemed far-fetched. Why would Clem train smaller, weaker men from the other realms to be warriors when their own people were so physically superior?

Caldred slipped him a note. They didn't chance speaking to each other aloud, but the bandit had failed to take a stray pencil from Jamie's pocket. They used a scrap of paper that Jamie kept in his boot. It contained a poem his aunt had written for him that he carried for luck. It was now covered with scrawls of short messages between the boys. Jamie had been surprised to learn the younger boy knew how to write. His skills were crude, and he spelled horribly, but the very fact that Caldred had any knowledge of the written word meant Jamie had misjudged him. Maybe he was self-taught and had stolen a lot of books.

Caldred's latest note confirmed what Jamie had suspected: "Clem. Shippe." Jamie nodded back, not wanting to waste the pencil or paper, as he had nothing more to offer. Suddenly, Caldred touched his ear. Jamie perked up and heard the sound of gulls and crashing waves in the distance. As the wagon rolled over a rocky hill, the small port city of Barron came into view below. To most eyes, the coastal village would not be impressive, but Jamie had never seen the ocean, let alone ships, so he stared at the two boats in the harbor with gape-jawed amazement. One was a simple fishing vessel, he realized, based on the nets hanging from the side. The other was larger and bore a large bear on the sail, no doubt a mark of some Clem clan. Even from here, he could see a huge figure skulking across the deck with bright-red hair. Jamie's eyes tracked from the ship to the town itself, where a cluster of homes and shops surrounded the harbor in a rough horseshoe.

"And here I leave thee at last!" the bandit bellowed in a singsong voice, launching into a tune that he butchered with his rough, tone-deaf warbles. The cage rattled as the wagon bumped along the cobblestones toward the village, the bandit's singing adding an ominous feel to the final stretch of this leg of the journey.

Though he had no desire to be handed over to the Clem ship, Jamie was hopeful for a few minutes outside of the cage. He looked over at Caldred, who was still recovering from his beating the day before, and for the first time, the boy seemed to be fearful.

"The ocean," Caldred whispered, no longer worried about being overheard with just a few minutes left in their ride to the town. "Bigger than I thought …"

Jamie agreed. He watched the waves crash and break. Something inside him knew if he got on that boat, he'd never see his home again. He grabbed his paper and used the remaining space on it to scribble a note to his aunt. He finished writing the note just before the wagon reached the village. He shoved the paper into his pocket as the bandit unlocked the cage and pointed at the ground.

Both boys were still in shackles, feet and hands. Caldred got out first, avoiding eye contact with their captor. Jamie climbed out second and appraised the village, the metal cuffs clinking on his feet as he lifted his legs up and down to give them some much-needed blood flow. It was late afternoon and a few townspeople shuffled to and fro. Jamie had no illusions about any of them helping a pair of unlucky boys like him and Caldred. The man pointed his longsword at them, actually jabbing at Caldred's back, and urged them toward the harbor. Both boys stumbled as they walked, weak with thirst and hunger. The townspeople gaped at them like they were diseased. Hell, they probably looked to be. Jamie scanned the faces for anyone who might have a shred of decency. No such luck as of yet. Still, he needed to be ready. He forced himself to trip and landed on the ground hard, slipping his hand into his boot at the same time. He scrambled back to his feet, but not before the bandit could tag him with a punishing slap of the sword on his arm. Jamie cringed in pain, his hand clasped around the note he'd retrieved from his boot. They were almost at the dock when Jamie spotted a woman walking with her young son, carrying a wrapped fish back from the smaller boat in the harbor. Jamie stumbled and bumped into the woman, careful not to knock her over. At the same time, he slipped the crumpled note into her sack of supplies she was carrying along with her fish.

"Damn it, stay on your feet!" the bandit barked, kicking Jamie forward onto the dock. "At least pretend to be sturdy stock!"

Jamie glanced back to see the woman gathering herself and continuing on her way. By the time he looked back ahead, Caldred was a blur in front of him.

The boy had lunged at the bandit in a last-ditch attempt to escape. He was reaching for Jamie's knife, which was hanging from the man's belt. Jamie barreled forward and tried to knock the large bandit off the dock and into the water but succeeded only in tripping him. All three of them sprawled onto the wooden pier in a mess of arms and legs. Jamie swung his shackled hands into the man's face and struck him on the chin, knocking him back to the deck.

"I'll kill you bastards!" the man snarled, swiping Caldred off him with one arm and punching Jamie in the stomach with the other. Jamie struggled to breathe as the bandit grabbed Caldred by the shoulder and slammed him hard onto the pier. Caldred tried to kick back, but the man swiped his foot away and struck back with a boot to Caldred's head. Jamie once again lunged at the man, who easily swatted him to the side, sending Jamie tumbling once more. Jamie landed hard and for a moment felt like he might pass out, then he saw the blade nearby. His knife had been tossed aside in the struggle. He snatched it and pulled himself to his feet. The bandit was pummeling Caldred.

"Leave him alone!" Jamie cried, getting the bandit's full attention. The man gave Jamie a nasty grin.

"I'm gonna take that knife and kill you with it, boy," the man said.

"Do it then," Jamie retorted, not sure why he was so calm. Maybe he was just sick of being a captive and wanted it all to end.

Jamie readied the knife as the big man charged. A moment before the man reached him, something caught his foot. Caldred, practically dead on the ground, had flashed out his leg and tripped the bandit, who was now reeling toward Jamie with a shocked look on his ugly, bearded face. Jamie had no time to think; he merely jabbed out with the knife as the man collided with him, sending them both tumbling to the pier together.

Jamie waited for the man to continue his attack. It never came. When Jamie looked down at his own hand, he saw the handle of the knife still tight in his grasp. The blade was buried in the dead bandit's right eye. A sense of relief washed over Jamie as the adrenaline began to subside. It was soon followed by a gnawing ache in his stomach when he realized he had just killed another person, no matter how much he might have deserved it.

Before Jamie had time to fully process this, a shadow came over him. He looked up into the face of the large Clem warrior with red hair, who hovered over both him and Caldred.

"Little Galantra," the warrior noted, seeing the knife in Jamie's hand. "Guess we won't be cutting off your balls just yet."

The Falls

Phaedra emerged from the water, her feet sinking into the black sand a few hundred yards from where the Longfin had been freshly moored at the docks. She didn't like the process of arriving at port and walking to her home; Phaedra preferred to swim over to the private entrance of the royal palace herself.

Built centuries ago into the side of a huge cliff that faced the Great Sea, The Falls was Phaedra's family home on the island of Silvercliffe. Unlike some of the other castles she'd heard about, The Falls was more of a residence than a fortress (calling it a palace was generous), and it could barely hold the dozen or so members of the Skybane extended family who lived there. Named after the pair of bubbling waterfalls that sprung forth from its first floor and splashed onto the smooth rocks below, the limestone structure favored function over elegance. The view from the parapet surrounding the north and east walls was expansive enough to reveal ships that were still miles away, while the walls facing the island itself were angled slightly to protect against breaching. The truth was that nobody had ever dared or cared enough to attack the island and its royal dwelling. The Fins were loyal to a fault when it came to the Skybane dynasty, so defending

The Falls from internal threats was never really a concern. As for external dangers, the other realms had yet to find a good reason to face the Fins' fleet in open water just for the honor, if they somehow prevailed, of invading and conquering such a small island.

Not since the Flyers anyway.

Phaedra let the icy water douse her head and shoulders as she walked under the waterfall toward the stone steps. Tetria waited for Phaedra with a grave look on her freckled face.

Tetria was one of three servants who lived at The Falls with the Skybane family. She was older than Phaedra's mother, but her freckles somehow made her appear younger, childlike even. Her confounding appearance was complemented by her clever wit.

Tetria watched the webbing between Phaedra's toes retract back into her feet as her body dried. The webbing was a purely physical response to water. Fins like Phaedra had no control over their body's reaction to water—the webbing between the toes, the lung expansion, and the tightening of their skin. Phaedra stopped when she reached Tetria. The older woman handed her a fig.

"You return skinnier every time," she admonished.

"I doubt a fig will fix that," Phaedra said, popping the small delicacy into her mouth.

"My job is to please you," Tetria replied.

"If that's your job, you're not very good at it."

"That's only because my real concern is keeping you safe," Tetria said, looking at Phaedra with stern eyes. "And I always like to give you something sweet before I deliver bad news."

* * *

Queen Perrin's diminutive frame cast a small shadow on the stone balcony. Phaedra stepped onto it. "Mother," she said, "my heart leaps with joy to see you back in our homeland."

The queen turned to face her daughter. The old woman was aging poorly, Phaedra thought, and for that she was grateful. As the daughter of a king, Phaedra had led a mostly charmed life, a fact that seemed to fuel her mother's jealousy and scorn. Consequently, the queen did everything she could to remove all joy from Phaedra's life. Sure, her mother called it having a stern hand, but Phaedra saw the treatment for what it was: payback for becoming the king's favorite person.

"You still have your sardonic tongue," the queen said.

"Sorry to disappoint, Mother, but I'm sure you're used to it by now."

"Quite." The queen stepped forward and embraced her daughter. "There's no need for dramatics, my dear. I'm proud of you. I'm just sad you aren't even more the woman you could be."

Phaedra bit her tongue. There was an easy joke to be made about her mother's weight or age, but she resisted. Still, it was clear the queen had enjoyed plenty of food and wine on her travels. She had been gone nearly two years, spending most of that time on a diplomatic mission in Maldovar. Feasts. Plays. Boring conversations. It was no wonder her mother, a native of the Republic, as she fondly called it, enjoyed such things.

The timing of her return was suspect. She hadn't been due back for months. When the queen finally ended the embrace and looked at her with a forced smile, Phaedra knew her angle.

"You heard," Phaedra sighed. She stepped back and slumped into a nearby chair on the balcony. Her mother had ignored her much of the past few years, but that would soon be a forgotten luxury.

"My love, the world has heard," the queen practically sang.

"Artie says prophecies don't always come true," Phaedra said, trying to deflate her mother's interest. All that did was annoy her.

"The prince's name is Arthur, and while he is often wise beyond his years, in the matters of the gods, he is utterly clueless," the queen said. She sat in the chair next to Phaedra and touched her shoulder with an icy hand. "Soon, it will be just the three of us. We must prepare ourselves …"

Phaedra shot up from her chair and glared at her mother, who didn't even flinch. "It will never be us! You forget how long you've been gone, dear Mother. I'm not a child anymore."

Phaedra stalked inside the residence, leaving the queen to gaze out at the ocean. "It will always be us," the queen said to herself, touching her gold bracelet that bore the Three Gods on it.

Once Phaedra was out of sight, Kywin appeared on the balcony, stepping out of the shadows. In some ways, he was a handsome man, with his roguish locks and dark complexion. But his eyes glimmered with deceit and anger, a fact not lost on the queen, who appreciated Kywin's lack of compassion. It made him a more effective agent to do her bidding.

"She is as fiery as you promised," Kywin noted. "The princess will be a formidable and beautiful leader someday."

The queen tossed a hand in the air, not giving in to Kywin's attempt to goad her about her daughter's beauty. "Her father has all but ruined her with his unconditional affection. She loses the Sacred Trident, the symbol of his power, and he pretends it doesn't matter."

"Or he knows it was inevitable," Kywin countered.

"A fair point," the queen conceded. "The king may have a soft spot for Phaedra, but he's no fool."

Kywin leaned on the railing and took in the view. The queen watched him as his mind spun. The man was deadly with a blade and had come highly recommended from her contacts in Lockewell, but he was most dangerous with his schemes.

"What do you think?" the queen asked him.

"I prefer the North Sea," he said.

"You know what I mean."

"I think you need to work on gaining your daughter's trust," Kywin said. "I hate to tell you this, darling, but it seems you'll have to actually be nice to her."

* * *

She felt him plunge into the chilly water next to her. She knew it was him; they'd been swimming in this same spot for years.

Phaedra kicked her legs, accelerating through the sun-dappled sea, cruising around the vibrant reef that surrounded the island. Fish of silver and blue darted out of her way as the princess navigated the reef from memory. Lucian gave chase. He was a strong swimmer compared to most Fins. Compared to Phaedra, he was as slow as a turtle.

After a few minutes exploring the shallows together, the two popped up for air. Phaedra's temper had cooled since her encounter with her mother, yet there was still enough venom in her eyes for Lucian to recognize his friend was not in a good mood.

"I see you spoke to your mother," he said.

Phaedra ignored his attempt to get her to talk about the queen. He always wanted her to express her feelings. According to him, it was a way to release tension.

Nope, she thought.

Instead, she looked back at the cliffs jutting from the shoreline as she and Lucian bobbed in the sea. A strong sense of nostalgia washed over her.

"Do you remember the first time we swam here?"

"You tried to kiss me!" Lucian laughed.

"I was nine and confused," she replied. "I'm talking about what happened after that."

"The shark."

"The very large, very determined shark," Phaedra corrected. "It chased us for over twenty minutes until we finally made it back to land. You would think our first instinct would have been to never come back here."

Lucian nodded, remembering how they had climbed to the top of the cliff and looked down at the ocean below. "We spent three hours watching it prowl the shallows, up and down the shore."

"And then we kept coming back, watching from the cliffs until we spotted it," Phaedra said. "The same pattern. Up and down the shore. I always wondered if it had been doing that before it almost caught us that day, or because it wanted another shot at us, so this part of the island became the shark's new hunting ground. Finally, after a week, it stopped showing up."

"Do you think it's still out there?" Lucian asked.

"Maybe. But if not, all that means is something even more deadly killed it, and now hunts those same waters."

"Yet you still swim here," Lucian said.

"We, you mean."

"I only swim here when I happen to see you heading this

way. Not that I'm following you around. I am a member of the king's royal guard and as such, I'm very busy."

Phaedra shot him a glance. Lucian grinned. "Still want to kiss me?" he teased.

"Not right now," Phaedra said, although the thought had occurred to her.

"We've come out here dozens of times without worrying about that shark. Why is today different?"

"Because whenever I talk to my mom, I'm reminded that the world is full of danger. Most of it you don't see coming until it's too late. I got lucky with the shark. I'm not sure the queen will be so easy to escape."

Lucian tilted his head. "Would it be rude if I said she looked more like a seal to me? Those whiskers, you know."

Phaedra laughed, agreeing. "Rude, but appreciated."

"Don't you feel better now?" he asked as he continued to chuckle, proud of himself.

Phaedra looked back to the water, hoping to spot a glimpse of their nemesis. "I'll feel better when I see the shark again."

Snakebit

The place smelled like incense and sheep shit.

A small adobe structure with a thatch roof, Banner's Rim Cantina was packed with thieves and criminals. Roughly a dozen of them huddled around various tables, drinking whiskey, gambling on games of Scorpion Cards, and generally plotting ways to kill each other. A pair of companions leaned against the wall behind the bar, loosely covered in sheer scarves.

Gods, Acasta loved taverns.

He stepped up to the bar and scanned the bottles on offer. They would get the job done, he decided. Acasta swept his sandy hair out of his face and locked eyes with the scraggle-faced owner. Maybe it was Banner himself. *Who really gives a fuck?* Acasta thought. The man looked away before Acasta could peer into his thoughts. Apparently, he wasn't the first green-eyed mage to grace this tavern with his presence.

"Rum?" Acasta asked.

The owner grunted and pulled a dark bottle off the shelf. He poured a fair amount of the purple-black liquid into a cracked glass and slid it over to Acasta. "Closest you'll get to rum for a hundred miles anyway."

Acasta smiled. He liked this guy. After he took a swig of the not-rum, he liked the guy even more. His liquor wasn't entirely terrible. "Acasta," he said with a grin.

"That a name or your way of asking how much?" the owner replied. "Five bits."

"Name. And make it ten," Acasta said, draining the rest of the glass and placing a pure silver coin on the bar. That got the attention of more than a few people in the room.

"Portillo," the tavern owner said, introducing himself properly now that he'd seen Acasta's silver.

"I'm looking for a woman," Acasta said.

"Aren't we all?" Portillo lamented. "Just so happens I've got two for you to choose from."

He waved his hand to motion the companions over, but Acasta shook his head. Portillo shooed the women away.

"I'm looking for a very particular one. White hair. Gold teeth. Eyes like mine. You know the person I mean?"

Portillo laughed. It was a genuine belly laugh, and Acasta saw no sign of falseness in it. "You think she'd be caught dead in here?" Portillo roared.

"I don't," Acasta said. "But there's gonna be a lot of other dead people in here if I don't get some answers."

Acasta whirled around and shot a hand out at a table across the tavern. The table flew into the wall with enough force to shatter all four of its legs. The men sitting around it hadn't even had a chance to flinch. One still had his hand on the mug that had been resting on the table. It fell from his fingers and clanged onto the ground. The whole place fell silent. Acasta scanned the faces of the patrons and settled on a rotund sheepherder with an eye patch. "You know what I am?" Acasta asked.

The sheepherder nodded, avoiding too much direct eye contact. It was easy with just the one eye.

"Say it," Acasta demanded.

"A mage," the man sneered.

"And I look for another. Much older than me. You can tell by her white hair and less-than-sunny disposition. I was told she frequented this area," Acasta explained. "Judging by the looks on your faces, she may have given our kind a bad name, what with her murdering and thieving and such. Well, I'm here to rid you of that problem. So, if anyone knows where the mage who goes by Osprey is, now would be the time to speak up and rid yourselves of her."

Acasta sneaked a glance at Portillo, but the big man's blank look betrayed nothing. After waiting a few moments, Acasta grabbed the bottle of not-rum off the bar.

"Well, it was worth a shot," he said. Then he left a second piece of silver on top of the first and walked out, bottle in hand.

Once outside, Acasta surveyed the golden sand dunes in every direction. He knew Osprey wasn't east; that was the way he came from to arrive at this godsforsaken stretch of Tufthorn. He'd been searching for the white-haired mage for nearly six months, following the trail of death she left in her wake. Acasta himself was by no means pure of heart, but he was not a cold-blooded killer. The unwritten code of the mage forbade the use of powers on the defenseless outside of battle.

Osprey had flouted this code for decades, and had finally drawn the ire of Queen Amira, who dispatched Acasta to capture or kill the rogue witch. Even though his search had taken longer than he expected, Acasta knew finding Osprey would be the easy part of his mission. More than forty years his senior, Osprey would pose a serious challenge for Acasta in a fair fight, meaning he had to hope for the element of surprise. He'd already decided that killing her was the far simpler option. Trying to capture and transport her back to the capital seemed an impossible task.

Acasta's horse snorted at him as he approached with the bottle of liquor. "Sorry, Jester, not for you," Acasta said, instead offering the brown-haired, slope-shouldered animal some water from his canteen. Jester lapped up the water and snorted once more in mild satisfaction. Acasta climbed atop the saddle.

"How do I know I can trust you?" Portillo asked.

Acasta glanced at the large man standing in the entrance of his tavern. His face was even harsher to look at in broad daylight. However, he had a certain air about him that Acasta appreciated.

"Depends on what you're trusting me to do or not do," Acasta replied.

"I mean are you asking because you're gonna kill her?"

"And if I am?"

"Then I might know where one might go looking for that witch … er, mage."

Portillo flushed from embarrassment, knowing it was frowned upon to call a female mage a witch. Acasta wasn't bothered by Portillo's choice of words. He had called Osprey a witch himself just minutes earlier. And he'd call her worse to her face once he found her. Still, one mage calling another a derogatory term was one thing; if Portillo had let that phrase loose in front of pretty much any mage besides Acasta, who didn't give a shit about insults, the man would likely face swift and merciless punishment.

"Whatever I plan to do with this witch, as you say, you

can trust me not to divulge where my information on her whereabouts came from," Acasta promised.

Portillo nodded curtly, then approached, not wanting to speak too loudly in case anybody inside the tavern was eavesdropping. Acasta's face darkened as the man told him what Osprey had done to a local blacksmith and his family a few weeks earlier before heading north. If nothing else, she deserved to die as retribution for those horrific acts alone. Acasta thanked Portillo and told him he'd do his best to bring the old mage to justice. The sun was beginning to set as he rode north, but the evening breeze did nothing to cool his temper as he imagined the damage one person could do to the reputation of an entire race of people.

* * *

So much for the element of surprise.

As flames licked at his clothes, Acasta wondered if Portillo had known he was sending him into a trap or if the fat man had simply been an unwitting participant in Osprey's plot to ensnare him. He liked to think the tavern owner was merely trying to help. That was a ponderance for another day, Acasta decided, as he sent a gust of force toward the nearby barrels that were on fire, catapulting them twenty feet away, directly at the archer trying to line up another shot at him. Acasta cursed Osprey as one of the barrels hit the archer in the chest, killing him upon impact. The old mage had clearly bewitched the people in this small encampment and was using her power to control them.

They had no real reason to kill Acasta. In fact, they may have been perfectly nice and gentle people. They were just being compelled to do the witch's bidding. The Code clearly gave mages the right to defend themselves against all foes, even those under the spell of another mage, but hurting the innocent still didn't sit well with Acasta. He would have tried non lethal force if there were fewer attackers or they hadn't been lying in wait for him.

Playing nice was not a luxury Acasta could afford this evening.

He'd arrived at the small camp well after dark. There was a stillness in the air that he mistook to mean most of the inhabitants were asleep. The moment he dismounted Jester near the cluster of tents, he was greeted with an arrow in his leg. The damn thing hurt like the devil. Luck was on his side, as it missed anything too important. The next few minutes were a blur of awkward hobbling, close-range weapons, and fire. A lot of fire. He'd sent Jester off into the night while he battled no fewer than eight of the camp's residents. Acasta knew they'd been bewitched because he could see their enlarged pupils every time he struck one of them down with his powers or short sword. He was equally deadly with both.

After battling Osprey's army, as it were, he found himself pinned down behind a stack of rice barrels. He tore the arrow from his leg and cried out in pain.

"Acasta, is it?" Osprey called from across the camp.

Acasta knew damn well that she knew his name.

"What's up?" Acasta answered as nonchalantly as possible.

"I suppose you're currently questioning your decision to track me down," Osprey said.

"Not really, no."

"Well, nobody ever said being a mage guaranteed you

wisdom."

"I guess I did walk into that one," Acasta admitted.

"Just like you did my trap. I hope my men didn't hurt you too badly. I'd like to think there's enough left for me," she said. "Or perhaps you're thinking of surrendering?"

"No again."

"Last question: would you like to join me? I'm having great fun."

Acasta looked at the devastation around him. One of Osprey's fallen soldiers lay nearby, mouth agape, eyes frozen in death. This was not exactly Acasta's idea of great fun. He tied a piece of torn fabric around his leg wound. The damage was already done, unfortunately. He was fighting both the pain and the blood loss, which was making him slightly woozy. It also inhibited some of his powers. Not the way you wanted to go up against a vicious mage with infinitely more experience.

"Gonna have to kill me, I guess," he said.

"Excellent!" Osprey shrieked, sending a burst of raw energy that exploded the barrels Acasta was using for shelter. He covered his head as shards of wood rained down on him. All mages shared certain powers, such as the ability to manipulate objects and divine people's thoughts. Beyond that, they were a bit like snowflakes. Some mages were experts in handling fire. Some could exert force on people and objects up to a thousand feet away. Healing powers. Supernatural speed. Mind control. Acasta had even heard of one mage who could move the very earth under her feet. As for him, he was a jack of all trades, not necessarily exceptional in any one area, but crafty enough to have stayed alive with his wits and his powers. Osprey's ability to bewitch multiple individuals combined with her sheer brute strength meant Acasta was in for a rough ride.

He sent a whirlwind of sand into the air and used the cloud as cover to scurry to another spot behind a nearby tent. Osprey laughed and flung the tent away with a flick of her wrist. Expecting this, Acasta was already sending a barrel in her direction. She easily stopped it in midair a few feet from her face. She then nodded, sending it back toward Acasta at twice the speed. He rolled out of the way, narrowly avoiding the deadly barrel.

Acasta focused his will and sent every piece of wood or metal within a ten-foot radius back at Osprey. She raised her hand, palm out, and sent up a shield of air current, stopping almost every projectile. A length of sharp wood sneaked through and struck her in the leg, knocking her over. Even as she was falling, however, she laced a ring of pure fire at Acasta and singed his clothes as he tried to dive out of the way.

"You have skills, young warrior! Why sacrifice your life when we can wreak havoc together?" Osprey bellowed.

Acasta knew she was right. If he extended this fight much longer, she would surely destroy him.

"All right!" he yelled. He stood up and faced Osprey, who was twenty feet away from him. She rose as well. He'd heard rumors of her being one hundred years old, but she didn't look a day over forty. She was lean and muscular, wearing a simple white dress with a gold belt that matched her gold teeth. Her hair was stark white, and her skin was olive.

"You find me attractive?" she mused.

Acasta strengthened his mental defenses against the powerful witch.

"It's nothing to be ashamed of, my dear boy. I find you suitably sexy as well."

It had been a long time since someone had called Acasta,

thirty-five years old, a boy. He didn't enjoy it coming from the likes of this woman. "What's in it for me?" he asked.

"You don't die, for starters," she said. "Beyond that, whatever you like. That is how it should be, is it not? We are mageborn. We do not trifle with the lives of ordinary people. We take what we want, when we want."

"Sounds cruel."

"That is a matter of perspective. Is the tiger cruel to the boar? Or is it just the way of the jungle? The way of life? I think you've been worried about the righteous mage code too long."

"Even if I wanted to join you, I couldn't."

"Ah yes, that whore who wears the crown. She is not worth your obedience, or your life."

"Yeah, but I kinda like her is the problem."

Osprey's eyes narrowed and she bared her shimmery teeth in anger. "So be it! You are weak and have no skills I do not already possess. I will toy with you no longer!"

"No, you won't. Because I know something you don't."

"What is that?"

"I can bewitch beasts."

Suddenly, a snake slithering near Osprey's feet struck at her ankle, sinking its fangs into her calf. She screamed in pain and shot a finger at the snake, instantly snapping its neck. As she was distracted, Jester raced from the shadows toward Acasta, who grabbed the reins and jumped on the horse while it was in mid-gallop. With his free hand, Acasta whipped up more sand.

Still stunned from the snakebite, Osprey hurled a ten-foot-wide column of fire at the sand cloud, but when the sand dissipated, Acasta was gone. Osprey's anger was balanced by covetous admiration. She smirked.

"Well, that certainly is a new trick," she said, eyeing the dead snake at her feet. "I think I'd like to collect that young man."

Grayfork's Army

The limestone rocks were still smouldering when Grayfork approached what had been a five-foot-thick wall. The little that remained of the structure was scattered fifty feet in all directions. The rest had been pulverized into dust and ash.

Grayfork kicked a small piece of charred brick, satisfied.

"Impressive. Will it pierce ten feet?" he asked.

"With a big enough projectile, don't see why not. We have all the iron we need and those green-eyed bastards aren't messing around," General Bowles answered. He was a large man with squinty eyes and a heavy jaw. Every word that came out of his mouth was accompanied by the stench of rotten teeth and small sprays of spit. "The soldiers are ready. Just give the order."

"After years of training, the soldiers better be ready," Grayfork cautioned.

"They are. Trust me on that."

"We also shouldn't be too hasty to show the world our full strength."

"Of course," the general backpedaled. "Just saying the troops are spoiling for a fight and itching to get off this damn island. If we don't start killing enemies soon, they're likely to turn on each other. Could get ugly. Good problem to have, you ask me. Last thing we need is a bunch of weak-kneed cowards."

The two men looked across the field at an area of the training ground dedicated to light weapons. A few hundred soldiers were spread out across the large swath of land, sparring in groups of two and three. They were stout men and women. From a distance, they moved with a beauty Grayfork found intoxicating. He closed his eyes and enjoyed the distant clangs of metal as knives hit shields. Grayfork smiled, knowing similar sessions were taking place all over the secluded island. Unlike the king, who was reticent to spend the sums of treasure that true greatness required, Grayfork was happy to do so. As the richest man in Lockewell, he had gold to spare, and he wasn't afraid to put it to use, nor was he afraid to go behind the king's back to establish his own power base. The resources it took to gather this army and provide an entire island to secretly house it were immense, but as he saw the soldiers training, he was sure his investment would be paid back tenfold.

A tall man with green eyes approached, wearing a dirty gray tunic.

"This is Farrer," the general told Grayfork, motioning to the tall man. "He's recruited six mages to our cause."

"Are you the person I should thank for this new weapon?" Grayfork asked.

"It is an easy trick," Farrer said. He looked at the rubble at their feet. "One we are happy to replicate on the field of battle, assuming we are paid well enough."

"See general, I told you mages were just like the rest of us," Grayfork chuckled. "At the end of the day, it's all about being paid. Money breeds loyalty."

Grayfork produced a small satchel from under his coat and handed it to Farrer. "I trust this will keep you and your fellow sorcerers loyal?"

Farrer reached into the satchel and removed a few gold coins. There were plenty more still inside the bag. The mage nodded.

"There's more where that came from if you have any more friends from Tufthorn," Grayfork said.

"We stand apart from Tufthorn," the mage replied, then walked away.

"I like his attitude," Grayfork told Bowles.

"That's a lot of coin," the general said, jealous. He was being paid nothing near that. Nor were his soldiers.

"Perform impressive displays of savagery like this," Grayfork said, spreading his arms wide at the scorched earth and rocks surrounding them, "and you too would be paid as handsomely."

The general had no choice but to agree. The mages could very well be the difference in winning and losing the war to come. Still, it rankled him that the mages had an unfair advantage over even the toughest soldiers. "Magic is for the weak," Bowles said.

"Tell that to Farrer's face."

"Humph, I might," Bowles replied.

Grayfork was already moving, walking across the field, his eyes fixed on the horizon. Bowles saw that he was deep in thought.

"What is it?" Bowles asked.

"Perhaps you are right to be impatient about setting our plans in motion," Grayfork mused. "Every great war begins with an act of great showmanship, and I have just the target in mind. A kingdom that would never suspect us."

"Tell me where and when, and I'll have this entire island ready to mobilize. The ships can be prepped in a day," Bowles said, his voice tinged with bloodlust. Grayfork looked at the squat man with the oversized chin. There were finer war tacticians in the land, but Grayfork had chosen Bowles because he was the most ruthless; the man loved to lead fighters into battle, and he was not known for taking any prisoners.

"Relax, general," Grayfork said. "We will not show our full hand just yet, but merely give the realms a taste of what is to come. But we'll do it at a place nobody has dared to attack in living memory."

Bowles followed Grayfork toward the fieldhouse. "Have ten thousand of your soldiers ready within the week. I'll send your orders then," Grayfork commanded over his shoulder.

"Yes sir," Bowles replied. "Where are you going?"

"I have business in Maldovar to attend to," he said. "Of the diplomatic variety. Your services will not be needed on that front."

Maiden Voyage

According to Fiero, the gangly third mate tasked with keeping watch over Jamie and his fellow prisoners, the ship was as good as they came.

"You boys got lucky with this one," he told them. "The *Bitch's Roar* is the smoothest boat I been on. Oh yeah, I been on some real puke schooners. Couldn't keep one meal out of three down on those bastards. But not the *Bitch*! This boat is a pleasure cruise."

Jamie tried to imagine a choppier ride than the one he was currently experiencing. Yes, they were in a storm. And yes, it was his first time on anything bigger than the Tarlintown Ferry, which was basically a glorified raft, but he still couldn't believe there were worse-sailing vessels than this one. Fiero cackled as he looked at Jamie.

"Better give Little Galantra some room, boys! He's greener than a frog in heat!" Fiero yelled.

The other six prisoners backed up in the cell, not wanting to be in the splatter zone if Jamie threw up. It didn't help that the first meal they'd been served was a curdled rice porridge of some kind.

"Don't barf on me, okay?" Caldred half-joked. He was lying

on the floor near Jamie, somehow clinging to life. The beating he'd taken from the bandit would've killed most boys their age, but Caldred was a survivor.

"I won't," Jamie promised. It was the least he could do. If Caldred hadn't tripped the bandit on the dock, Jamie would probably be dead. Instead, he was a killer everyone insisted on calling Little Galantra. He guessed that's how nicknames happened. Truth be told, he hated it. A week ago, he would have been overjoyed if people were comparing him to the greatest swordsman that ever lived. Now, knowing the price he paid to earn the title, he wished people would call him anything else.

The ship continued to roll with the tide, testing Jamie's resolve. He did his best to ignore the sloshing in his belly. There were plenty of other things to worry about, after all. Fiero, for instance, was prone to mad mood swings. One moment he was joking with Jamie and the other boys; the next he was whipping one of them for looking at him wrong. A very tall man with crude tattoos of skulls all over his arms, Fiero was what Jamie had pictured Clem warriors looked like. His missing teeth made his smile comical, but Jamie saw the hardened eyes of a murderer, no matter what his crooked mouth was doing.

The Bitch was a three-deck ship. They were in the lowest deck, which had no windows, suggesting they were fully submerged under the sea at all times. Fiero made it clear if the boat took on water, they'd be the first to go. Depending on the tattooed man's mood, Jamie didn't expect he'd unlock their cell before fleeing up the stairs. Other than the cage holding the seven prisoners, the deck seemed to be full of junk and storage. Random bits of food, but mostly it looked like nets, broken weapons, and empty crates. The level above was lined with cannons on either side and had bunks for the crew. Jamie guessed there were about fifteen men aboard the ship, not counting him and his fellow captives.

"Chew the inside of your mouth," a boy told Jamie. His name was Peter. Or maybe Pod. Jamie couldn't remember. The boy was about ten.

"What?" Jamie asked.

"Whenever I get nervous or think I'm gonna be sick, I just chew my cheek. Forget all about the other stuff once I start tasting the blood," he said.

Jamie nodded and looked back to the corner of the room, where he was counting mice as they scurried between the crates. He sank his teeth into his cheek and bit down, trying to distract from the nausea. Heavy thuds on the stairs preceded a man even more menacing than Fiero. His head was shaved and featured a long scar from front to back. He touched it as he considered the kids in the cage. His gaze eventually settled on Jamie.

"That one with the mage eyes, let him out," the man said.

Shit. Jamie was worried it would come to this. All mages were born with green eyes, he'd heard. That didn't make life easy for regular people like him who also happened to have green eyes. Fiero unlatched the gate on the cell and motioned for Jamie to exit, one hand on the hilt of his axe.

"What's wrong with him?" the bigger Clem asked.

"He didn't like his dinner. A delicate stomach, this one," Fiero answered.

The other man looked over the prisoners once again, then grunted. "A shit lot. He's still the best of 'em. C'mere, boy, and be quick about it!"

Fiero winked as Jamie walked past him, worried he was on his way to be thrown overboard or maybe hanged from the ship's mast. Clem were rumored to hate mages of all kinds. Most people hated mages out of fear. Jamie followed the man through the cannon deck and up the next set of stairs topside, where he was surprised to see just how roughly the storm was battering the ship. Maybe Fiero had a point about the *Bitch* being one tough ship. The main deck was engulfed in chaos. Huge men pulled at the sails and swore at the sky as lightning illuminated the night. Waves crashed over the sides of the ship. Nearby a man stabbed something gangly and wriggly on the deck, then kicked it into the ocean.

"Take this," the Clem commanded Jamie, handing him a rusty sword. "Kill anything that washes up on the deck that ain't got a Bear tattoo on his arm."

Jamie looked at the man's arm and tattoo, then at the sword in his hands.

"What the hell you waiting for? Maybe I need to throw you over the side?" the Clem barked. "Get over there!"

He pointed to the aft of the ship. Jamie gripped the heavy old sword and staggered to the rear of the ship, his feet slipping on the watery boards of the deck. He scrambled in horror as the ship rose and crashed with each set of waves.

He felt a thunk on the deck near his feet. Jamie wiped away the wet hair matted over his eyes and saw the ugliest creature he'd ever come across. It had a large, spongelike body and long red tentacles that extended a few feet in every direction. Just as Jamie was wrapping his head around what he was looking at, the nasty thing started crawling toward him. He jumped back then instinctively stabbed at the creature. He would've struck it, but the boat rocked and he landed hard on his ass right next to the grotesque fish or whatever it was. He barely rolled out of the way in time to escape one of its tentacles, which he now realized was lined with sharp hooks. He hopped to his feet and jabbed again, this time burying his blade dead-center in the animal's body, popping it like a pig bladder. Clear gunk of some kind oozed out as the creature fought like mad to escape. It reminded him of squashing a spider back on the farm, only on a much scarier scale.

Before the thing could wriggle away, Jamie swung the sword toward the ocean and flung the creature back into the sea. Unfortunately, he lost his grip on the sword and sent that off into the water as well. Jamie frantically looked around to see if anyone else had noticed. Luckily the other men were all too busy with their own problems. Nearby, Jamie saw a long metal hook hanging from the mast, so he grabbed that. It would have to do. He assumed his next foe would be another of the slimy, tentacled creatures, but it was actually a small shark that he was able to kick off the boat in one swift push of his boot. The next ten minutes, or maybe twenty (he was really starting to lose track) produced more sponge monsters and fish that Jamie worked hard to clear from the deck.

Eventually he heard a man screaming from behind him. He turned to see a giant Clem on the deck, being mauled by a crab the size of a small goat. But it was unlike any crab Jamie had seen in books. This one had razor-sharp teeth and a blue shell that looked like it was made of iron. Jamie hurried over and tried to kick the crab, but it simply swatted him away with a clubbed paw and went back to chewing on the Clem's back.

"Argh!" the man cried in agony.

Jamie picked himself back up and launched toward the crab, raking his metal hook into the beast's mouth and catching it on the corner of the jaw. Jamie pulled with all his might, and the crab finally let loose of the Clem sailor. Both the crustacean and Jamie tumbled back to the deck and Jamie soon found himself holding off the crab with his hook, which was still stuck in the creature's maw. Those damn teeth were clattering away just a few inches from Jamie's face. The horrible thing was strong as hell. Jamie used all his might, but the crab kept inching closer and closer until Jamie could smell its breath and see the whites of its eyes as it prepared for the killer bite.

Then it was gone.

Jamie looked up to see the injured Clem sailor holding a war hammer. He'd just kicked the crab off him and then wasted no time in swinging down with his weapon and cracking the crab's shell in half with a satisfying crunch. It died instantly. The man then turned to Jamie, smiled an ugly smile, and offered him a hand up.

* * *

It felt weird eating at the same table as a dozen ravenous Clem sailors, and not just because they were all quite literally twice Jamie's size.

The other boys were all prisoners on the bottom deck, and here he was, breaking bread with some of the most feared men in the realm. Sure, the bread was stale, and the fish was turning his stomach again, but Jamie wasn't about to complain. In fact, he hadn't uttered a single word since the storm passed and the men all decided it was time to feast and drink to celebrate still being alive. They had even offered him some ale, which was so bitter he had trouble not coughing it back up. The sailor he saved from the crab, and who had in turn saved him, sat beside Jamie. His name was Bargoosh, and he loved to talk. Mostly about Clem women. The way they smelled. The way they fucked. Even the way they fought.

"The gods made no finer creature on land or sea than a Clem woman, Little Galantra. Don't you ever forget that," he said between swigs of the bitter ale. "Shit, maybe when we get to port, you'll get lucky with one of them! Though she'd probably break you in half faster than I cracked that crab!"

This gave all the men at the table much reason to laugh and yet another reason to raise their mugs. "To Little Galantra and his little pecker! May they both be cracked by a lady Clem!" one shouted.

They all drank and guffawed. Eventually, the captain of *The Bitch's Roar* stood up from the table. The men all settled into a quieter form of eating and drinking.

"They call you Little Galantra," the captain said, pointing his muscled finger at Jamie. The man's name was Aldrick, and he was the smallest man at the table. "That's a good name. Galantra is rumored to be deadly with a blade, though I'd wager this entire ship on Rawk in a fight over some gentleman from Maldovar. What's your name, boy?"

"Uh, Jamie, sir," he managed.

This made the entire table laugh once again. They were drunk, so it didn't take much.

"Sir? I like that. Maybe I'll be a knight someday!" Aldrick boomed, before turning serious. "We don't use shit titles like that in Clem. Best you get used to it. You call me Captain or Aldrick, nothing else."

"Yes, Captain."

"Good. Now you're still a prisoner, and I'm gonna fetch my price for you, but that don't mean you didn't prove yourself," the captain said. "You saved ugly ol' Bargoosh here from a sea crab with nothing but a net hook. And before that, you killed your captor. That's how a boy becomes a man round here. To Jamie!"

The men echoed the cheer and drank.

"To Little Galantra!" the captain said next.

Once again, the men echoed and cheered.

"Enjoy your dinner, boy, you earned it," the captain told Jamie before sitting down. "Then it's back to the cell for you until next time we need some crabs dealt with."

More laughs and guffaws. Jamie wasn't sure if he was joking or serious, but he had an inkling he'd be sleeping among the other prisoners that night. And that suited him just fine.

The Hunt

The smell of roasted boar tantalized Anke as she walked toward the great fire at the heart of the Clem camp. She had chosen two clans to hunt with her, the Halfmoons and the Red Bears. They were the most talented fighting men and women in all of Clem—and fierce rivals. There had already been multiple skirmishes between them. Normally, Anke would not have approved. But on this particular hunt, she wanted the two clans at odds with each other.

"I know I've said negative things about Clem wine and food, but roasted game is definitely one area where the brutes of the west have no equal," Laroche said, also enjoying the aroma of sweet meat in the air. He was a good fuck, Anke had discovered, and not altogether unpleasant to be around, but he did love to hear his own voice. "Not that I'm calling you a brute, my lady."

"Call me a brute if you want, but call me *my lady* again and you'll be on the spit with the hogs," Anke replied without a trace of humor.

Laroche nodded obediently and watched as a Halfmoon woman and a Red Bear man engaged in a spirited arm-wrestling match that involved punching each other in the face with their free hands.

"While I do agree with your reasoning for selecting rival clans to accompany us on this … hunt … I wonder what the eventual rate of attrition will be," Laroche noted.

"Attrition? Speak plainly, man," Anke said.

"I was trying to decide how many of them will kill each other before we need their services," he clarified.

"Wait until I tell them where we're really going," Anke said, glancing at Laroche before stepping away from him, toward a group of men standing near the beer kegs.

"Skullcrusher," one of them said in deference, offering her a mug of ale. She accepted and drained it in one gulp, then eyed Rawk, who was with the men.

"Need to talk with Rawk if you boys wanna go gnaw on some boar for a while," she said.

The men dispersed, leaving just Anke and Rawk. Unlike the other members of the hunt, he wasn't drinking from a mug. He had a jug three times the size in his hand. He took a long draw of beer and waited for Anke to start the conversation.

"Glad you came," she began.

"Boss says come on hunt, I come on hunt."

"If you were the boss, you could do whatever you wanted."

"Nah. Bosses do what other people want. You learn that soon. If you don't know already."

Anke nodded in agreement. Rawk wasn't wrong. In fact, he was wiser than she imagined he'd be, which only made her more sure of her decision. "I want you to be my second," she told the big man.

Rawk looked down at her over his huge beer jug. He continued to swig for a few seconds as he looked at Anke. He couldn't have been surprised by the question. Finally, he lowered his drink.

"Every boss man ask me that, and I say no," he said. "Now a boss woman ask me."

"And?"

Rawk sighed. "This time I say yes. But I don't kill any children."

"I would never ask you to."

"You say so now. We will see."

"Okay then," Anke said.

She couldn't believe it, but she tried her best to play it cool. Anke nodded and placed a hand on his shoulder. He lifted his steel ax in a sign of agreement.

"Rawk of Clem, Tribe Darden, Son of Hanar, I name you my second, until the day one of us no longer walks this land," Anke said.

"I start tomorrow," Rawk said, lifting his jug to his lips and emptying it. He nodded at Anke and headed over to the keg to refill.

The Clem warriors lingering around understood the moment and raised their mugs in salute. Anke wanted badly to ask why Rawk had said yes to her instead of all the previous Clem rulers who had tried to convince Rawk to be their second. She fought the urge and walked away, satisfied with her triumph. With Rawk watching her back, her list of enemies would grow thinner. But that was a consideration for tomorrow. Tonight was for celebration.

"Laroche! My tent. Now," she commanded.

"Yes, my … what shall I call you if not a lady?" he asked.

* * *

Morning arrived with a blood-red sun and a searing headache for Anke as she relieved herself on the small hill overlooking the tents below. The rest of the camp was beginning to stir, just about as slowly as she. Apparently, everyone had a late night.

Good. They would be in no mood to argue with her when she told them her plan. As she pulled up her trousers, she heard heavy footsteps approaching. Anke grabbed her war hammer and whirled, then relaxed with a smile.

"Better get used to pissing and shitting in front of me," Rawk said, watching impassively as she finished tucking her shirt into her pants before tying her leather vest together.

"Just don't stand downwind, and we'll have no problems," she replied.

Rawk let out a high-pitched grunt. Anke realized it was the first time she'd ever seen the great man smile, let alone heard his oddly feminine laugh.

"You bed with the skinny spy every night?" Rawk asked, referring to Laroche, who was stretching as he exited Anke's tent.

"And if I do?"

"Do not care. Just want to know if he is always there or just when you want."

"Ah. Right. I guess it's both. I'll let you know if the situation changes," Anke said. "Also, he's no spy."

"If not Clem, they are all spies."

Anke nodded, not wanting to debate with her second at the moment. Already she felt safer, though, as Rawk followed her down the hill toward the camp, which was quickly bustling to life. They walked past the slaves and servants, who were the first to rise and were preparing breakfast. Anke snatched a piece of bread off a shelf and chewed on it. She offered Rawk some.

"Ate much boar before sunrise," he said. "Downwind from me is bad too."

Anke smiled and looked at the large man with his ridiculous shoulders and thick neck. He was built for killing by the gods, she thought. But nobody had ever told her he liked to make jokes.

"Don't be in such a good mood," she warned him. "I have news that will make some men very angry this morning."

Rawk shrugged. "Men always angry."

Anke made her way to the center of camp, drinking fresh water and eating some eggs her servant Lukas had brought her. When the thin teen was introduced to Rawk, he didn't shy away at all. He actually shook the warrior's hand. Afterward, Rawk had told Anke that he would train the boy to fight if she liked. She accepted.

Once she was convinced enough of the hunting party was awake and present, Anke climbed atop a table and whistled loudly. The crowd quieted down. Rawk took position next to the table, his jaw set, his ax ready. *Nobody is going to fuck with him*, Anke thought.

"I can tell by the way the whores waddled around this morning you all had a good night!" Anke yelled, prompting fits of laughter and cheers. "I almost broke my lover last night too!"

More laughs. Laroche played along, embarrassed.

"By now I'm sure you all know that I have made Rawk the Fearsome, Son of Hanar, my second," she said. "From this day forward, if you have a problem with me, you have a problem with him. Though I hope it does not come to that. All I want is glory. For Clem. I want more land. For Clem. I want every Clem man, woman, child, servant, whore, and dog to know that we are the most feared people of all the realms!"

"She does play them well," Laroche whispered to Lukas, who simply took a step away, not wanting to be too closely associated with the foreigner. "But can she reel them in?"

"Sadly, that is not what the world thinks of us!" Anke bellowed. "They think we used to be strong and feared. Back when our fathers' fathers walked the earth. Today, they think it's okay to give us shitty goods and even shittier prices for them!"

She really had the mob going now. It didn't matter if they were Halfmoons or Redbears, they were righteously pissed off.

"Well, I have an idea to change all that," she said. "And it starts right now. This is no ordinary hunt, my Clem brethren! We are not just here for boars and antelope! This ... is a *raiding* party!"

About one quarter of the gathered Clem cheered and roared, but the majority grew uneasy, wondering what she had in mind. Even Rawk flinched. Clem had not been at war with any other realm for decades. Was she now, in this moment, about to start one? Sensing their apprehension but also knowing their true nature, Anke pressed on.

"I, Skullcrusher, will restore dignity to the Clem nation. With the clans Halfmoon and Redbear, I will go east to the land of Lockewell. I will sail to Maldovar. Cut my way through the forests of Fidora. We will go wherever is required to find the boy who will unite the realm. You know of whom I speak! Only the gods had it wrong. We will not bow our knee to this Flyer—we will make him Clem! And then, we will rule all the realms, as our ancestors many moons ago before us once did!"

Anke waited as silence fell over the camp. She had laid it all on the line. She had even spat in the faces of the gods. Just as she wondered if she'd gone too far, the men and women around her erupted with shouts of "Skullcrusher! Skullcrusher! Skullcrusher!" Anke raised her war hammer high and saluted them all. They continued to chant her name as she and Rawk walked among them back toward her tent.

Laroche eventually slid beside her. "I think you convinced them," he said. "The only question now is how you plan to find this chosen one."

Anke laughed and slapped Laroche on the shoulder roughly.

"Oh, did I not mention?" she asked. "That will be your job."

Laroche stopped dead in his tracks as Anke walked on, trailed by Lukas and Rawk. If he didn't know any better, he would've sworn he heard the huge warrior squeal out a laugh.

"Fuck," Laroche said.

Legacy

As soon as Henry Martin's carriage passed through the front gate of his estate, he knew something was wrong. Before he could react, his longtime coachman, Charles, jumped from the seat out front and ran off.

"Charles!" Henry shouted in bewilderment.

Henry turned just in time to see the gate close behind him. He tried to open the carriage door and figure out what was going on, but it wouldn't budge. A rough-looking, bearded man appeared in the carriage window and grinned. He unlatched the door and stepped aside in mock formality.

"Mr. Martin, if you'd please come with me," he said with a thick western accent.

"Who the bloody hell are you?" Henry scoffed. "Get off my property!"

"Walk," the man said, brandishing a knife.

Henry grumbled and trudged alongside the bearded man toward his own home. Along the way, Henry saw another carriage next to his residence. It was black and had a crest on it he'd never seen before. The horses looked weary from a long trip. A large coachman reclined in the front seat, sunning himself. He smiled at Henry and tipped his cap.

"I demand to know what is going on," Henry said.

He received no answer. The bearded man simply shoved him through the open door of his house. Henry was greeted by another person he didn't know, a handsome gentleman with a finely trimmed mustache. He wore traditional Lockewell attire.

"First Minister, a pleasure to meet you," he said, extending a hand.

Henry refused to give him the courtesy of a handshake.

"This is trespassing," Henry seethed. "I will have you imprisoned for this."

"I told you he wouldn't appreciate the cloak and dagger." Henry turned to see Lower Minister Black enter the room. She nodded at him.

"Henry, this is Sir Alan Grayfork of Lockewell," Black said, motioning to the mustached gentleman. "He's here with a proposal."

"Philipa, I trusted you," Henry said.

"You never did have sound judgment," she replied. "But let's not trouble ourselves by looking at the past. This is a chance for us to move forward. For *you* to move forward and chart a new course for your family."

For the first time, it dawned on Henry that his wife and two children were nowhere to be seen. He'd been so startled by the strange people in his house, he'd barely had time to think of his family. Sir Grayfork held up a hand.

"They're fine," he said. "Your lovely wife Gwendolyn and darling little James and Elizabeth are safe and sound. For now."

"This is intolerable!" Henry yelled.

"Sit down!" Black countered, with a measure of anger and

strength in her voice Henry didn't recognize.

He did as he was told, crumbling into a nearby chair. His heart was pounding so hard, he pulled his hand to his chest.

"The poor man looks like he's going to pop," Grayfork joked. "Henry, Henry, Henry. You are worried when you should be excited. This is a rare opportunity for a fading man like yourself to salvage some semblance of victory."

"What are you talking about? And where is my family? You can't hurt them!"

"I certainly *can* hurt them. One snap of my fingers and you'd become a bachelor again. But I don't want to do that. Instead, I'm here, along with your trusted friend, the lower minister, to give you a way out."

"A way out of what?" Henry spat.

"The capital is moving," Black interjected. "It's only a matter of time. You can fight the votes and the political momentum, but eventually you'll be defeated. So why not get ahead of it? The more you resist, the more likely it is you'll be ruined. Join with us now, however, and be part of writing your part of the story."

"How long, Philipa?" Henry asked.

Grayfork slammed his hand into the side of Henry's face, knocking the soft, chubby man onto the floor. Grayfork stood over him, annoyed.

"You've lost. We're giving you a chance to lose well, but you're too much of a sniveling shit to take it," he said. "You will reconvene the Senate and vote again, or you will die on your own floor right now, and your wife and kids will die moments later."

* * *

Henry stood on the dais, facing the empty Senate chamber. They had just voted to make Ravinia, the merchant city on the western edge of the realm, located in the province of Hillhome, the new capital. Henry had presided over the session and, once the vote had been ratified, announced he would be resigning from office two years before the end of his term to help with the transition.

The truth was that he would be receiving a large sum of money and new lands near Ravinia to stay close to the seat of power. His family was also not brutally murdered, which was another benefit of his deal with Grayfork. As Senate rules dictated, Philipa Black was elevated to the position of acting first minister, until such time as a new realm-wide election could be organized. But, given the complications of changing capital cities, that wouldn't be anytime soon.

Henry knew Black's first act as the highest-ranking official of Maldovar would be to open new negotiations with Lockewell for a more expansive trade partnership. He also suspected her true goal was to unite Lockewell and Maldovar into one realm, presumably under Lockewell majority control. Her grandfather had been from Lockewell, after all.

"That was most unexpected," Modano said.

Henry jumped, startled. He had thought the chamber was empty. Modano leaned on the balcony and overlooked the seats below.

"I would have made a terrible first minister myself," he said. "You, on the other hand, were above average."

"That's high praise coming from you," Henry noted.

"Which makes it all the more peculiar that you'd step down now and cede the capital to the west while also handing over control to your longtime rival."

"Philipa has been my longtime supporter," Henry said.

"Ah yes, just as Viceroy Renner has been my bosom mate," Modano snarked.

Henry looked at Modano with tired eyes. "I could no longer fight against the current, Asper. You said it yourself after the previous vote. This was going to happen. I decided I didn't want to be part of it when it did."

"Fair and even a bit noble," Modano replied. "If it were true. But I've heard about your new property outside Ravinia, dear friend. If one cared to dig deeper, one might find more motivation for your sudden change of heart. Might be wise to watch your back."

Modano turned to walk away.

"It's worse than you think," Henry admitted.

"If you're looking to unburden yourself, a man with better discretion you won't find."

"This is more than a power grab by the West Maldovarians. Lockewell is behind it. Just because I've resigned doesn't mean I'm done fighting for the future of the Republic. Because if we don't do something, there may not be a Republic or a Maldovar by this time next year."

"Odd words for someone who just traded the power to do anything about it for a new plantation."

"The only way to stop this is to do things your way: with money," Henry said.

"I don't believe money will get it done, dear Henry."

Henry acknowledged the comment with a resigned look at his old friend. "Whatever it takes. Will you help me?"

"That depends. Will I also be getting new property out of this?" Modano asked with a grin.

Unbalanced

Phaedra never understood what her father saw in her mother. Now, as she watched them sit together at the head table, exchanging pleasantries, she was reminded of how much she enjoyed being on fishing or warring trips. The king was there. The queen was not.

But here they were, together. And for the first time that she could remember, it seemed he was on the wane. It almost appeared like he had aged a few decades overnight, ever since … well, ever since she lost the trident. Prince Arthur sat next to the king. Reading. The kid was reading at a feast.

"Who is that slippery prick?" Lucian asked, referring to Kywin, who was also sitting at the raised table, a few seats from Phaedra's mother.

It bucked tradition for the princess to sit among the non-noble members of the feast, but that was how she liked it, and her father had allowed it for years. So, she was at one of the military tables. To celebrate the entire royal family being home at the same time, this feast was being held on the beach of Diamond Bay. Nearly two hundred people had been invited, and all of them showed up for free food and drink. The familiar scent of the ocean mingled with the aroma of the roasted meats and sweet fruits.

"I don't know," Phaedra said, eyeing Kywin. The man was handsome in a boring sort of way, Phaedra noted. It was clear he was some kind of advisor to the queen, obviously preying on her insecurities to get close to her. But to what end?

"Your mother doesn't seem to mind his attention," said Lucian.

"You could be executed for that suggestion," Phaedra said. She always teased him about being executed. Harsh, maybe. But she'd been doing it for years, and it worked for the two of them. "Is it me, or did she grow even shorter on her trip?"

"Not you. The woman is shrinking like an old dog," Lucian whispered.

Phaedra jabbed him in the ribs with a sharp elbow. They were sitting among other members of the royal guard. If someone overheard his jokes about the queen, they might not find them as humorous as she did. Lucian wheezed in pain.

"Whatever he's up to, it can't be good," Phaedra said, watching Kywin as he laughed and enjoyed a cup of wine.

The dinner crowd grew quiet as the king stood to address them.

"Friends!" he bellowed. "It has been many moons since we were graced with both the presence of our queen *and* our prince and princess, and for that I am thankful!"

The guests raised their glasses to the royal women and child. Phaedra smiled and nodded, doing her best impression of a princess who gave a shit about such gestures from her people. She would rather be one of them, toasting some other prissy girl. Artie looked up from his book to hollowly acknowledge the crowd, then he turned his attention to Phaedra with a foreboding look.

"My dear wife, Perrin," her father said, beaming as he took her mother's hand. "For two years, you have traveled the realms to strengthen our alliances. While the Fins are grateful for your service, I am more grateful you have returned. And I can see our people are happy too; they walk with an extra bounce in their step, knowing their queen is home safe."

Phaedra wanted to puke. The only thing that made her father's fawning okay was that she knew it was mostly for show. Yes, he loved the woman, but he was not a doting romantic. He did it for the people. They needed to see their leaders happy, he often told her, usually before asking her to consider smiling once in a while, if only for appearances.

"And our princess! A lady of the people!" he exclaimed, pointing to her.

More cheers and toasts.

The king grew serious, then looked at the queen, who nodded and stood at his side. They clasped hands. Phaedra had a bad feeling about what was coming next.

"They say nothing is forever," he began. "At three centuries old, I never quite believed them. But it seems age has caught up with me at last."

There were murmurs among the people as they grew restless.

"You are not rid of me yet," the king clarified. "For the good of the realm, however, I have decided that I shall do as my father once did and cede the throne to my queen, so that she may rule until it is time for Princess Phaedra to ascend to the throne."

Her father continued to talk, but his words faded as the scene before Phaedra blurred. She felt light-headed and sick to her stomach all at the same time. Not only had her fears about her father's health been confirmed, her mother had been given ultimate power over the kingdom and everyone in it, including her. Suddenly, she felt a rising sensation, as if she were being lifted off the ground. She looked to her right and saw Lucian's eyes pleading with her to snap out of it, while he subtly pushed her up out of her chair.

"Phaedra," he hissed in warning.

The princess blinked a few times and realized everyone else was already standing, and most of their eyes were on her.

"… uh, and we stand united as a family …" her father was saying, looking right at Phaedra. She did her best to stand and smile, as was expected of her. The king was satisfied and continued his horrifying speech about what a momentous occasion it was. All the while, the queen smiled icily in Phaedra's direction, holding poor Artie's hand so tight, Phaedra could see the pain in his face.

After he was done speaking, the king kissed the queen on the lips and placed his crown upon Queen Perrin's head. There would be a more formal ceremony in the coming days with much more pomp and circumstance, but the damage was done. The queen was now the leader of the realm.

* * *

Tetria was waiting in the woods for her.

"This is not the way, child," she said, a stern warning in her voice.

"She cares only for herself," Phaedra snapped. "My father knows this. And if he does not, he's a fool. Either way, I cannot live here under her reign."

"I do not disagree."

"Yet here you stand."

Tetria sighed deeply, the kind of sigh that held years of exhaustion and frustration in it. After all, she had been tasked with looking after Phaedra ever since the princess was a baby. It could not have been easy, given Phaedra's stubborn nature and wild ways. The old woman put a hand on Phaedra's shoulder. It would be a stretch to say Tetria was like a mother to her, but she was a trusted ally and mentor nonetheless. Phaedra steeled herself to prepare for the inevitable lecture.

"I say this is not the way because your mother's guards will be expecting you to flee aboard your own boat, the *Mantis*. Instead, you will take a much smaller vessel on the other side of the island," Tetria said.

"I don't understand ..." Phaedra stammered, stunned. "You're helping me escape?"

"If you do not understand why I would do that, then I am more disappointed than you could even know."

Phaedra rushed forward and hugged the woman. Tears fell down Phaedra's cheeks. She hated crying, but there was no stopping it that night.

"Your father will miss you," Tetria warned. "He may not be alive should you stay away too long."

"He will not die before I see him again," Phaedra tried to convince herself.

Tetria nodded, unsure. "I will take care of Artie the best I can."

Phaedra told herself the prince would be fine. As the second-born, he was no threat to their mother, the queen. Second-borns did not ascend to the throne under any circumstance in their kingdom. That burden fell to the firstborn.

Tetria handed Phaedra a satchel. "Food for a week and whatever spare clothes I could gather without arousing suspicion. Now go, child, along the beach until you reach the Crescent Cove. There you will find a small boat that belonged to your father long ago. He will be very upset you left, but in time, he will find comfort in the fact you set sail on that vessel."

"But why?"

"Because he once had to flee this island like you did, and that was the boat he did it on."

"Meaning that boat is three hundred years old?"

"No. It's much older than that. As are many things—and people—around you."

Phaedra looked at Tetria and realized she was talking about herself.

"I never knew," Phaedra said.

"When we're young, the hardest truths to see are those which lie right in front of us. Often, we don't even know the truth inside ourselves. You are much stronger than you realize, Phaedra. When your true power reveals itself to you, you must learn to control it. It has driven many a Skybane mad," Tetria warned, before smiling at her princess. "I do not think that will be your fate."

Tetria then kissed Phaedra on the forehead and stepped back into the darkness, disappearing from sight before Phaedra could even say goodbye. She heard footsteps behind her and turned to find Lucian there. He was also holding a satchel of his own.

Phaedra frowned. "Not a chance."

"Tetria told me we were going on a voyage," he said with a wry smile.

"This one really could get you executed," Phaedra warned.

"You do keep saying that."

Together, Phaedra and Lucian stuck to the tree line at the edge of the beach and followed it around the island. It was late and the feast was still going on, so if they were lucky, the queen would simply think Phaedra was upset and decided to leave the party early. Surely she knew how angry Phaedra would be at her elevation to the throne. But angry enough to run off?

That's when the words of her brother struck her. He had told her to disappear even before her father handed the crown to the queen. Did he already know this was going to happen?

"Shhhh," Lucian warned, tugging gently at Phaedra's arm to pull her into the bushes.

"What is it?" she asked.

"I heard someone …"

They waited in silence, crouched behind the dense foliage. Thirty seconds passed before Lucian turned to her and shrugged. Phaedra rolled her eyes and began heading toward the cove. Lucian followed. After a few steps, he stopped. Phaedra turned to see a figure behind her friend, a glint of steel in the man's hand. Lucian tried to say something, but all that came out was a hoarse gasp. He dropped to a knee, shocked. Now Phaedra saw the man's face. It was Kywin. He smirked.

"Out for a walk, I presume?" he asked, eyeing her satchel of supplies.

Phaedra rushed over to Lucian, ignoring Kywin. He stepped back a few feet to give her space.

"I'll have you drowned for this!" she told Kywin.

"I doubt the queen would drown me for stopping her daughter from abandoning the realm in this important time of transition. This soldier knew what he was getting into when he agreed to escort you."

"My father—"

"Your father now answers to your mother."

Phaedra wanted to tear him apart, but she turned her focus to Lucian. He'd been stabbed in the lower back. She didn't know if it was a fatal wound; she just knew Lucian was fading quickly.

"Stay with me," she told him, grasping his cold hand. His eyes were glassy. Still, he found the strength to smile at her.

"You were right," he joked. "It was bound to happen."

Phaedra lifted her eyes in rage toward Kywin, who held up his hands to calm her. It might have been more effective if he still didn't have a bloody blade in one of them.

"I would suggest you don't act on what I see in those eyes, young lady. If you come back now, we might even be able to salvage your friend's life."

Phaedra didn't trust this man, simply because her mother *did*. Phaedra looked down at Lucian and lowered him to the sand gently. "Don't you dare," she warned him.

"I'll do my best," he muttered weakly, before turning to Kywin. "You're … in trouble now …"

Phaedra stood and pulled two curved blades from pockets on the sides of her pants. They had the same general shape as oversized fishing hooks, and she'd been training with them since she was four.

Kywin again tried to calm her. "I don't wish to hurt you."

"The feeling is not mutual."

Phaedra circled around Kywin. He sighed and resigned himself to a fight with the princess. Before that, he whistled loudly. "I have found her!" he yelled.

Phaedra lunged at him with both weapons but only sliced

through air as he dodged the attack easily. She whirled, undeterred, and made another pass. Another miss.

Kywin smiled confidently. "You are running out of time. Though I admit I'm impressed with your speed. Against most foes, that would likely be enough."

"But not you."

"I'm afraid not—" Kywin was interrupted rudely by a blast of sand in his face. Phaedra followed through on the cheap shot with a foot to his jaw.

"Guess I'll have to fight dirty," she said, spinning into a crouch and sweeping Kywin's legs out from under him. He landed hard. Phaedra was on top of him a moment later, swinging down with one of her blades. He blocked it with his own, but her second blade struck deep into his shoulder. She yanked it back and used the curved hook end to rip his flesh, like she'd done to fish and even the odd shark.

Kywin pushed her off him and rolled to his knees in a fluid motion. He was injured but still confident. He whistled again; this time it was cut short as Phaedra whipped one of her blades at him, striking him in the neck. It was a glancing blow but had done the trick. Kywin crumpled to the ground, holding his neck to stem the blood flow. Phaedra was about to attack again when she heard the voices in the distance. They were coming for her. Satisfied that Kywin was incapacitated for the moment, she hurried to Lucian and willed him to get to his feet.

It was no use.

He was almost gone.

"Go," he urged her.

"I can't …"

It took all his remaining strength to find her hand and hold it in his. "You can … and you will. You know this …"

Phaedra wanted to stay with him. She leaned down and kissed him sweetly on the lips, then grabbed her satchel and ran away into the darkness.

Promised Knight

Acasta was nervous, and he wasn't afraid to admit it. To himself, anyway.

Outwardly, he tried to project serenity as the queen and her entourage approached. The royal chariot was flanked by two columns of lightly armored riders on horses, six rows deep. The majority of them were mages, and a few might even have powers that rivaled his own, aside from his ability to control animals. That was unique.

Acasta stood next to Jester, his arm draped over the horse's shoulders. "Should I be worried?" he asked.

Jester snorted.

"Right as usual."

The queen's chariot rolled to a stop twenty feet from Acasta. The riders continued forward, eventually surrounding Acasta and Jester in a semicircle. Acasta looked at the other mages, who were all wearing the standard Tuftthorn royal garb—golden battle mesh covered by light-brown pants and shirts. Acasta waved and smiled. They didn't respond in kind.

Queen Amira stepped out of her chariot and walked toward him. They had planned to meet at this spot on the Dune Road on her return trip from The Assembly. Acasta was not supposed to be without a prisoner, however. He bowed his head and waited for the queen to speak. She walked past him and stroked Jester's mane. The horse whinnied in delight.

Traitor, Acasta thought.

"A truly mesmerizing animal. What is his name, again?"

"Jester."

"I sense some projection, dear Acasta. Do you ever bewitch him?" Amira asked.

"Occasionally. He has a stronger mind than most, so it requires a lot of effort."

"Not your strong suit?" Amira joked.

Acasta furrowed his brow, not happy with the direction this conversation was headed. "I assure you I did everything I could to capture Osprey. Unfortunately, her reputation as a powerful and bloodthirsty witch was not earned without merit."

The queen stared at him. She was, objectively, an attractive woman. Acasta had been enamored with her ever since they were young mages together at the Institute. They had been friends during those days, often getting into trouble together thanks to their shared interest in breaking just about every rule their instructors gave them. But now she was the leader of the realm, and he was merely her hired hand. And he had failed her.

"You can tell me the details later. Presently, I have another mission for you." The queen looked at her entourage and motioned for them to back away. This required more privacy. Acasta tossed them a gloating glance. It did not go unnoticed by the queen.

"And you wonder why you are not more well liked among your peers," Amira said.

"I never said I wondered. And I don't recall saying they were my peers either."

"I remember when you were eighteen and that attitude was cute," she sighed. "The charm has worn off somewhat."

"So, you don't want me to find Osprey?" Acasta asked, changing the subject.

"I wish you *had* found her. Since you did not, I'm forced to delay that particular hunt and put you on a different path, one that's far more important to the realm."

"Forgive me, Your Highness, but I failed, and now I get an even more important task?" Acasta asked.

"Trust makes up for inadequacy," the queen said. "I need this handled by an old friend."

"I'm touched, Amira."

"Don't push it," she scolded.

Acasta bowed his head once more. The queen flashed a grin he was too slow to catch. She liked Acasta and had even once considered sleeping with him, but that was years ago.

"What would you have me do, Your Highness?" Acasta asked, doubling down on the snarky formality.

"Find the Knight of War and Dawn, and bring him to me."

"Oh, is that all?" Acasta joked.

The queen did not crack a smile.

"You're serious?"

"I hope Jester is okay on boats. Good luck."

* * *

Acasta felt like he'd been chasing a ghost for months. Now that he was finally getting close to catching her, the queen commanded him to find a boy shrouded in myth and legend.

It was an even more intolerable task than tracking Osprey. At least he knew where to start with her. Hell, he knew she was real!

The Knight of War and Dawn, also known as the Promised Knight, was a harbinger. With him came the return of the Flyer. Or so the prophecy went. Acasta was a skeptic when it came to prophecies; he had observed and possessed many strange powers in his life, but the idea that people could see the future was too much for him to believe. The queen did not share that view. She had always been a true believer in the gift of foresight. Acasta knew she went to The Assembly to give news of the Flyer's return. He thought it was a mistake and would harm Tufthorn's standing in the world. Now, he had been roped into her foolish fantasy.

Even if he did think this knight roamed the earth, he still wouldn't know where to start looking for him. Amira had told him she thought the boy, who would likely be a teenager, would reveal himself through his deeds. Whatever that meant. Her suggestion was to head west and search for young men with extraordinary fighting talent. She said she would send him a message when she had more information.

Acasta shook his head at the ridiculousness of the request as he and Jester approached the port city of Barandria. From there, they could secure passage across the sea to either Clem or Lockewell. He wasn't sure which way to go yet. Not that it mattered. Perhaps he would choose based on cuisine, which meant the destination would be Lockewell.

Barandria was Tufthorn's main trade hub, insofar as Tufthorn traded with other kingdoms. For the most part, the desert realm had kept to itself for nearly a century, a practice that Queen Amira was trying to change amid dwindling resources and a belief among the Tufthorn elite that they needed to reengage with the rest of the world. The fact she was heralding the beginning of a new era under the fabled Flyer, his Fin bride, and the Promised Knight while also trying to establish Tufthorn's place in the kingdom pecking order was curious to Acasta. If all would soon be subjugated by this new boy-ruler, he thought, then why the attempts to mend long-broken ties with the other realms?

Acasta considered the boats in the harbor, eventually settling on a midsized schooner with a Republic flag on it. He was no great fan of Maldovar, but they were known for decent accommodations and actually stuck to a price once it was negotiated. Acasta rode Jester down the main thoroughfare of the port town. Shanties gave way to produce carts and shops, and eventually the dirt road was replaced by cobblestone streets. The last time Acasta was in Barandria, he had been tracking horse thieves. They were taking horses from settlements in the desert and transporting them across the sea to Lockewell. Acasta wondered if any of the local pub owners would recognize him. Seven years had passed, but he'd caused quite a ruckus during that visit.

"Need to relax, green eyes?" a young man asked. He was hanging out near a brothel, his shirt open, blowing in the breeze. Acasta merely smiled as Jester moseyed on by. He was used to being targeted by both men and women of the trade, though he rarely took them up on the offer. He had no issues with it from a moral standpoint. He just didn't like to waste his money.

Acasta hopped off Jester outside a small tavern near the edge of the pier. It was an old brick building with no sign. Acasta watched as two dockworkers stumbled out and headed back to work for the evening shift.

"If I'm not back in an hour, I'm probably just getting drunk," Acasta told Jester as he tied the horse's reins to the hitching rail outside the tavern. Upon entering the establishment, he immediately drew the attention of the barkeep. Acasta waited a beat to see if the swarthy man recognized him. Apparently, he did not. *Good*, Acasta thought. Or maybe he was just getting old. Acasta walked to the bar and ordered a rum. The barkeep told him it was whiskey or beer.

"Whiskey is fine," Acasta sighed, looking at the patrons.

When the man delivered his drink, Acasta asked him who crewed the Maldovarian schooner. The barkeep pointed to a table of two men and a woman in the corner. They were playing Scorpion Cards. Acasta sipped the whiskey, which he suspected was actually some mixture of whiskey, water, and barley, and made his way over to the ship's crew.

"This seat open?" he asked, referring to the empty chair near their table.

The two men looked at the woman. She nodded, intrigued.

"Thank you kindly," Acasta said, sitting down. "I should warn you I'm something of an expert at this particular game."

"Got a name?" the woman asked.

"Acasta."

"The fat one over here is Keelo, and the pretty boy is Robin," the woman said, pointing at her crewmates.

"I'm not as fat as I used to be," Keelo clarified.

"Good to know," Acasta noted. He guessed the man was well over three hundred pounds at present.

"And I'm Drenna," the woman said.

"Captain Drenna, I presume?"

"One and the same," Drenna said. "So, first things first—how are you liking that piss-poor excuse for whiskey?"

"Sadly, I've had worse."

"So, you've been to Clem!" Keelo roared, laughing at his own joke.

Robin laughed too, but Drenna kept eye contact with Acasta. An unspoken moment confirmed they were the two adults at the table.

"New player. Your deal." Drenna handed over the thick paper cards. They were a cheap, well-used set. Probably belonged to the tavern. Acasta could feel the stick on them as he shuffled the set of forty cards. Half of them had scorpions on them, the other half numbers. The point of the game was to accumulate as many scorpion cards as possible while using the number cards to match your opponents' number cards when they showed them. Acasta was unnaturally good at the game, having gambled for food growing up in the slums of Paito. If he lost, he went hungry, so he quickly learned to win.

Acasta won the first few hands. Despite the fact he was taking their money, the crew quickly grew to enjoy his company and were soon sharing their pitcher of beer with him.

"So, tell me, could you blast a hole in this wall right now if you wanted?" Robin asked.

"Give me some more of that beer, and I'll try."

"Hot damn! I'd love to be able to do shit like that," Robin said.

"It's cheating," Keelo grumbled.

"You calling me a cheater?" Acasta growled, shooting eye daggers at the big man.

"No, I just meant … I mean …"

"Gods, Keelo, he's just fucking with you," Drenna said,

prompting Acasta to break the act. All four people at the table laughed heartily, including Keelo.

"Scorpions over tens," Acasta said, laying down another winning hand. Robin shook his head and tossed his cards in the middle of the table.

"I'm done, can't beat this mage today," he said.

"I didn't use any of my powers to win," Acasta said. "Just my gods-given ability to bluff and do math."

"Think I've lost enough pieces to you too," Drenna said. "We have to be off anyway, got a shipment of wheat to deliver to Lockewell."

"Maldovarian wheat, best in the world," Acasta said.

"Tufthorn wheat," Drenna corrected. "Such are the times. Everything is upside down."

"It just so happens I need passage to Lockewell," Acasta said, grinning. "We could finish this game aboard your schooner, if there's room for a cheating mage and a stubborn horse."

Pity Sword

Jamie stood tall with his shoulders straight and his knees locked.

Anke looked him over, unimpressed. "You call this boy Galantra?" she asked.

"*Little* Galantra," Captain Aldrick corrected. "You want new soldiers? He's the best of the lot. Saved one of my men from a sea crab and killed his captor with a poke in the eye before we took him aboard."

Anke once again looked Jamie over. His arms and legs were wiry and covered in bruises from daily chores on the *Bitch*. He looked soft, she thought, but she also didn't want to embarrass Aldrick or his judgment in front of the others.

"Fine, we'll take him," Anke said. "You have a name?"

"Jamie."

"Little Galantra is better. Maybe if we call you it enough, some of his famed skills will rub off on you."

"If you say so, ma'am," Jamie answered.

The Clem warriors all laughed, including Anke.

"I'm no Lady, so don't go calling me ma'am unless you want to live a very short life, boy. You can call me Skullcrusher or boss. Got it?"

"Yes, boss."

"Good."

Anke walked over to finish her business with Aldrick. Meanwhile, Jamie found himself staring at Rawk. He'd seen carriages smaller than the man.

"Best not to stare," Laroche said, stepping close to him. "Rawk no like that. Also, don't mock his way of speaking when he's in earshot. Name's Laroche."

Laroche stuck out his hand in a very western gesture. Jamie shook it.

"Where are you from?" Laroche asked.

"Maldovar. Uh, near Tarlintown."

"Never heard of Tarlintown. I'm from the capital, though I suppose that's changing soon."

Jamie had no idea what he was talking about.

"Let's go, Little G," Laroche said, trying out a new nickname before shaking his head. He didn't like it after all. "Little Galantra it will have to be."

"What about the others?" Jamie asked, pointing to the other prisoners from the ship. Caldred was sitting among them. He was on the mend but still didn't have the strength to stand for long periods of time.

"Sold as slaves, most likely," Laroche said.

"Can't they be of use?" Jamie asked.

Laroche tugged him along, not wanting to fall behind Anke and the group as they disembarked the ship. "No."

"Wait, boss!" Jamie exclaimed, causing Anke to stop and turn.

She looked at him with surprise. "When I said speak to me, I meant almost never and definitely not on your first day."

"You should take him," Jamie replied, pointing at Caldred,

who was still seated on a crate next to the other boys.

"The cripple?"

"He's not a cripple. He's just hurt, but he's getting better."

"Good for him. Don't tell me my business again."

"But …"

Anke looked at Jamie, then Caldred. She settled her gaze back on Jamie, her newest pain in the ass. Rawk took a step forward and glanced at Anke with his axe ready. She shook her head.

"Why?" she asked. "And this better be good."

"I owe him a debt," Jamie said. "He saved my life and is the only reason I was able to kill my captor. If I go with you, I won't be able to repay the debt to him."

Jamie had thought it was a shot in the dark, but the request seemed to resonate with the warriors. Anke thought for a moment. "You can help him for one day. If he's not walking by tomorrow, we cut him loose. Then your debt shall have been repaid. Don't open your mouth again."

Jamie nodded. He hurried over to Caldred and helped him off the crate. Caldred wrapped an arm around his shoulder and limped along with him.

"Why are you doing this?" Caldred asked.

"You heard me. I owe you a debt," Jamie said. "I also didn't want to be alone with all of them."

Caldred wheezed out a laugh while he struggled to keep pace. "That big one doesn't seem to like you much," Caldred said. "I'll have to tell him we aren't friends."

Rawk continued to eye the boys as the dozen or so Clem that had boarded the *Bitch* rejoined the larger group back on the dock. Their main reason for meeting up with the ship was to resupply. Jamie and Caldred were simply throw-ins. All told, there were forty or so of the men and women, Jamie noted. They weren't all Rawk-sized, but they all dwarfed the people back in Tarlintown. Just thinking about home made Jamie feel pangs in his chest. He'd done his best to get word to Aunt Berta, though he doubted the hasty note he'd shoved into the hands of a total stranger would ever make its way back to her. He'd been gone for weeks now. She probably assumed he was dead. In reality, she might have thought his new fate—being trained by Clem to fight for them—was worse.

Anke led the group up a hill and back into the dense forest. Jamie watched the way others regarded her. Of all the Clem stories, nobody spoke of the women being warriors, and here they were, following one as their leader.

"I wonder how she got the name Skullcrusher," Jamie said.

"I don't," Caldred quipped, looking at her war hammer. "Gods, why did it have to be uphill!"

He was right. They'd only walked a few hundred feet, and already Jamie was worried about their ability to keep up with the group if Caldred's health didn't improve rapidly. The terrain wasn't helping them. He looked at the sun, which was well past its high point in the sky, and hoped they would be camping for the night once dusk arrived in a few hours.

Caldred pulled something from his pocket and offered it to Jamie. It was a bag of herbs for chewing.

"Where'd you get that?" Jamie asked in disbelief.

"Nicked it from Fiero, that son of a bitch," Caldred said, sticking a small wad in the corner of his mouth. "Helps with the pain. Want some?"

Jamie shook his head and focused on the path. One misstep and they'd both be in for a tumble.

"You like Fiero or something?" Caldred asked.

"Shit no."

"Then what?"

"You're asking for another beating," Jamie said.

"Way I figure it, I'm gonna take a beatin' eventually either way. Might as well make it worth it in the meantime."

Jamie smiled. Caldred had a point. The world was a much harsher place than he thought it was a few weeks earlier. They were both in for trouble, regardless of what they did. Still, Jamie worried Caldred's thieving might land them in the kind of trouble they couldn't get out of.

* * *

The gods looked kindly on Jamie that day, as the hunting party did in fact stop to make camp as the sun dipped toward the horizon. What kind of hunting party this was, Jamie still wasn't sure. He had heard a mix of excited chatter and grumbles during their hike through the hills of Clem. The latter of which seemed to suggest Skullcrusher's plan was a bit crazy. Jamie left a weary Caldred to rest beneath a large tree, then walked over to Laroche, who was drinking from a flask.

"If you've come to ask for a sip, I regret to inform you I just emptied the last of the Maldovarian rum into my eager belly," Laroche said. "Not that I would have shared it anyway."

"No, I was wondering what we're doing out here," Jamie said.

Laroche looked around, his eyes somewhat softened from the booze. "I suppose you could say we're making camp." He tried to walk away, but Jamie persisted, sidling up next to him as the fancy man headed toward Anke and Rawk.

"I just want to know what's going on," Jamie pleaded.

Laroche turned and looked at him with a degree of sympathy. "As you wish, Little Galantra. What's going on is that you've been spared a life of slavery because a captain on a boat named *The Bitch* thinks you are tough due to the fact, in his words, you killed a man by poking him in the eye. I assume with a blade of some kind or at least a sharp stick. I do not pretend to care which one. Perhaps it was your finger, though I highly doubt that. Instead of said slavery, you and your pitiful friend over there are now being given the chance to become true Clem warriors, a status you can achieve over time, if you kill and hunt and pillage enough. While you are men, or boys, without this status, you will be given information only on a need-to-know basis. I can assure you that nobody here currently thinks you need to know anything, other than how to find your own spot to piss, how to not slow us down and perhaps how to kill a small animal or two once in a while to help feed the group. They are a hungry lot, I assure you. As a fellow native of Maldovar, it could be fairly said I have sympathy for your plight, but it is a very small amount, almost immeasurable, especially when I'm out of rum. So, unless you or your friend know how to fucking fly, I suggest you do your best to stay out of everyone's way. Including mine at the moment, as my way is that way, to the boss woman's tent. She likes to fuck before dinner. That, my young friend, is what is going on."

Laroche then nodded courteously and went on his way, leaving a stunned Jamie in his wake.

Over the next few days, Jamie and Caldred slowly gathered more pieces of the puzzle. They learned about the Flyer. The Fin princess. One morning while serving a pair of Red Bear warriors their breakfast, Jamie overheard the men talking about how Skullcrusher was begging to be challenged in the circle for this stunt. Jamie didn't dare repeat that to anyone. All the while, Caldred continued to regain his strength. He still looked a mess but was able to walk on his own as the group made the trek to the Maldovar border.

Jamie was also proving himself useful. On the second night, he was tasked with helping keep watch while the rest of the party slept, in case any wild animals happened along. Just before dawn, as Jamie began to doze, he was awakened by a rustling in the bushes. He watched, half-frozen, as a pair of orange eyes peered at the camp from a dark spot in the foliage. He'd never been in such dense and remote forest before, so he could only guess what predator those eyes belonged to; though he didn't have to guess for long, as he could soon make out the stripes and coloring of a tiger, a creature he'd only heard stories about and, until that moment, wasn't even convinced was real. Behind Jamie, a Clem warrior stirred in his sleep and snored loudly, which was enough to set off the large cat. It bolted for the man.

Before Jamie knew what was happening, he had reacted. Armed with nothing but his trusty knife, which he'd reacquired when Captain Aldrick forced the angry Fiero to give it back to him, Jamie leapt toward the beast from the side, letting out a wild scream as he blindly stabbed toward where he thought the tiger was going to be; he'd never seen an animal that large move that fast.

His blade struck thick flesh and muscle, and the tiger let out a pained growl, then recoiled and spun. It was a true hit, but not nearly enough to stop the five-hundred-pound cat. It stared Jamie down and let out an evil noise Jamie wouldn't soon forget. He stood his ground but was sure this would be his end. The tiger wasted no more time, launching himself toward Jamie. Then, suddenly, he was struck down midflight.

A lightning-quick axe had slammed into the tiger's back, swatting it out of the air like a bird and forcing its broken body to the ground. It died on impact, a huge axe buried in its spine. Jamie looked up to see Rawk holding the weapon, his shoulder muscles bulging from exertion. The big man grunted as he yanked his axe from the animal's corpse.

"Thanks," Jamie managed to whimper.

Rawk nodded. It was not a nod to acknowledge Jamie's gratitude, but rather one of respect. Rawk turned to the Clem warrior who had been the tiger's initial target.

"You owe boy your life," Rawk told the warrior, using his shirt to wipe the crimson blood off his axe. He walked away, leaving a dozen men and women to look at the tiger, then Jamie.

Caldred arrived and put a hand on Jamie's shoulder. "You got the shine of the gods on ya, I'll give ya that."

By the time breakfast rolled around, the whole camp had heard the story of how Little Galantra and Rawk had slayed the beast. Even Skullcrusher had come by to congratulate Jamie on his courage and skills, while marveling at his simple nine-inch blade. She offered to furnish him with a better weapon but said if she were him, she'd keep the knife. The weapon had chosen him for a reason, she said. He dutifully agreed.

"One more thing," she told him. "From now on, you'll rise every day an hour early to learn how to fight. I would not disappoint your new teacher."

With that, she motioned to Rawk and laughed heartily.

Relic

The moon's reflection rippled in the dark water.

On any other night, the gentle sea breeze would have put Phaedra in a perfect state of mind. She loved being on the ocean. As a Fin, that was to be expected. Her people were descended from dolphins, according to legend. But even among her kin, Phaedra had a special affinity for the water, whether she was sailing across its waves or diving into its depths to swim among her ancestors.

That night, she took no comfort in the vast beauty below. That night, she was too busy thinking of the chaos she had left behind. Lucian, her closest friend, was likely dead. Her father had abdicated the throne. Her mother had already shown her desire to control Phaedra. The world was broken, and even the one place she could always rely on for refuge—the sea—could not console her.

She looked at the meager fifteen-foot boat Tetria had said once belonged to her father. Sturdy enough, but nothing to distinguish itself aside from a few ancient markings carved into the wood here and there. They were symbols she didn't understand in a language she'd never seen before. The sloop's structure was ancient as well, weathered by centuries, if Tetria was to be believed. Given the boat's age, it was actually an impressive feat of craftsmanship. The sails had been replaced recently, meaning someone was keeping an eye on the boat. Perhaps Tetria herself.

Phaedra had barely found the sailboat. Tetria told her it was in the Crescent Cove, but she'd neglected to mention the vessel was behind a set of large rocks in a black corner of the cove. If she hadn't been told to look for a boat in the area, she never would have found one. Luckily, Phaedra hadn't given up after searching the rest of the rocky enclosure. Once she unmoored the boat and navigated to the edge of the inlet, she saw torches a few hundred feet away. They were looking for her, and they were many. Phaedra waited for more than a half hour until she found just the right moment to set off into the night. The queen's guard didn't spot her, or if they did, they weren't able to give chase before she crossed beyond the reef.

Now, alone in the ocean, she needed a destination. If she continued northwest, she'd eventually hit Maldovar. The ocean was not too treacherous this time of year, so she would have an easy three-day trip there. But what she would do once she arrived, she had no idea. It seemed her best bet was to blend in with the local people. Her mother had spies in Maldovar, no doubt, but nobody knew her face in the Republic. Then what? She had never been particularly enamored with her role as Skybane's heir apparent, but now that her claim was more tenuous, she realized how much being the princess had loomed over her, influencing every decision she made.

Phaedra grabbed a piece of bread from the bag Tetria packed for her, hoping to settle her stomach while she figured out what the hell to do next. As she was eating, she explored the sloop a bit more. There wasn't much to it other than the basics: a seat, mast, headsail and mainsail, and oars. She felt something near her feet she hadn't noticed before—a wooden chest. It was unlocked, so she opened it with a satisfying creak and saw a few items inside. One was a compass. Handy. There was also a piece of very old and delicate parchment. Whatever had been inked on it was mostly gone. It could have been a map or even a letter at some point. She set it aside and saw a glint of metal at the bottom of the chest. Reaching in, she was surprised by the touch of cold steel on her fingers. She removed a finely crafted, mini-trident. Not unlike the one that used to belong to her father. Just a much smaller version. It was in perfect condition, with no rust or patina from age. Phaedra marveled at it. She saw the same ancient markings on it that had been carved into the boat's mast. Holding the trident, she felt connected to Skybane again, almost as if the weapon had some innate link to the realm. It seemed to ring with energy.

The trident was light and small enough to fit under a belt loop. It would make a nice companion for her lone curved blade she had left; the other was somewhere back on the beach of Silvercliffe, or perhaps in her mother's possession already.

Phaedra wondered what her father was thinking now. Was he disappointed in her for abandoning the realm? Proud she had struck out on her own, defying her mother? She also worried she may never see him alive again. The idea seemed ridiculous, but he looked to be aging rapidly after being in stasis for basically her entire life. At that moment, she remembered something her father told her once: "If ever you want to make me proud, don't do it by listening to me." That made Phaedra smile. She adjusted the mainsail to catch more of the night breeze, checked the stars to be sure of her bearing, and hoped she didn't run across any ships on her way to the Republic.

Worktown

Acasta lay in Drenna's bed, fully spent, his heart thumping in his chest. It had been far too long since he'd had a proper fuck.

The same was true for the captain of the *Widow's Crow*, so she and Acasta had wasted no time once the ship set sail. They were practically finished before Barandria disappeared on the horizon behind them. There would be opportunity for foreplay and romance later, Acasta knew. The first time was quick and to the very satisfying point for both of them. Drenna handed him a sweet-smelling pipe, and he took a long drag of the cava leaf. It tickled the back of his throat as he exhaled.

"Well, I've had longer," Drenna teased.

"I haven't," Acasta replied.

Drenna laughed, delighted. Acasta looked at her short, wavy brown hair. He normally preferred longer locks on women, but she was a ship captain after all, and braids or ponytails weren't practical and didn't seem to suit her, besides. She was a lean woman with the best legs he'd seen on land or sea. He might even tell her so next time, if he could find a way to make it sound unrehearsed.

"I do like a man who can make fun of himself," Drenna said

before taking back the pipe. "Not too much smoke for you. We're gonna go another round soon."

She reached down to check if he was ready.

"I might need a couple minutes, if the lady doesn't mind," Acasta said, closing his eyes and letting the effects of the cava leaf wash over him. "A glass of rum wouldn't hurt, either."

"Feel free to get yourself one. It's on the table over there," Drenna said. "Grab me one while you're up."

She pushed Acasta playfully off the bed and he tumbled onto the hard deck, barely avoiding the sharp edge of a chair. "Yes, a splendid idea," he said.

Drenna's cabin was just big enough for a bed and a small sitting area with a table and chairs. A makeshift office. The schooner wasn't huge, but the cabin had the right feel to it. There were about ten crew aboard the *Widow's Crow*, and they all seemed to respect Drenna, as far as Acasta could tell when she was giving him the tour. At first, he wasn't sure if sleeping with her would be a problem for her crew, but that notion was quickly dispelled when Keelo announced to everyone that Acasta and Drenna were going to be busy for a while, before looking Acasta up and down, and adding, "so nobody bother them for at least five or six minutes!"

Acasta smiled at Keelo's accurate assessment. It didn't bother him in the least. Acasta poured a healthy glass of rum and returned to the bed, sitting on the edge of it, still naked. Drenna took a sip and enjoyed watching him wait for her to finish before she handed the glass back.

"Never rolled with a mage before," Drenna said, resigning herself to the fact that they probably wouldn't be having sex again until later that evening. She had too much to do, and Acasta seemed too content for another tussle anytime soon.

"Was it magical?" he asked with a serious furrow of his brow.

"I bet you ask that of all the women," she said.

"Not really, no. Just the captains," he said, leaving her an opening to tell her tale. It wasn't every day a woman chose a life on the high seas surrounded by gruff men.

Drenna shrugged. "No big story here. I've always been drawn to the water. So like my father and his father, and … you see where this is going. I come from a long line of people with salt in their veins and very little coin in their pockets. But I'm free, and in that regard, I've got everything I need. Assuming we don't run out of rum or cava leaf."

"Naturally," Acasta agreed.

Drenna heard a ruckus followed by thumping on deck. She sighed and started to pull her clothes on.

"Won't they sort it out?" Acasta wondered aloud, pulling on his own shirt.

"They are children in constant need of care and guidance," Drenna explained. "In other words, they are men. Feel free to finish your drink before you head back up."

"Don't you worry about leaving me alone with your possessions?"

"If you can find something worth possessing, more power to you," she said, then hustled out the door. After a moment, Acasta heard her reprimanding her crew for the fight that was taking place. It promptly ceased.

Acasta looked about the cabin. There was nothing he would steal, even if he were so inclined. So, he tilted his head back and closed his eyes for a while.

* * *

The trip to Lockewell took nearly a week. During that time, Acasta spent most of his nights in Drenna's cabin and most of his days either playing Scorpion Cards with the crew or attending to Jester, who was sharing stables aboard the ship with three horses on their way to auction. Acasta pitied the animals. In Tufthorn, a mage and his horse were linked since the animal's birth. These horses would need to adapt to new owners in a strange land. One afternoon, while still high on the cava leaf, Acasta tried to convince Jester how good he had it compared to most of his kind. Jester rewarded him with a firm nip on the shoulder. Meanwhile, during his card matches with Keelo, Robin, and a rotating cast of sailors Acasta easily fleeced, the mage was annoyed to learn how many people in the realm were putting stock in the prophecy.

"Way I see it, we was due for a Flyer," Robin said one afternoon while losing yet another hand.

"We *were* due," Acasta said, correcting him. He'd been trying to instill better grammar in Robin ever since the young crewman told him his dream of someday running for a minor position in Maldovar's Broad Council, the lower house of the Republic. He had good looks and a certain charm about him, but his poor verbal and written skills would not aid his cause among the senators, who selected the members of the lower house from a pool of candidates every four years. When Robin asked Acasta to help him improve his speech, Acasta had thought he was joking. But the young man was earnest, and Acasta figured it was a way to kill time on the trip. He'd found Robin to possess solid intellect, even if his words often failed him.

"Why do you think we're due?" Acasta asked.

"Flyers had been around for thousands of years, then they

disappeared for a couple hundred. Seems more likely they was … or *were* … skipping a few generations and bound to come back. You see it in horses," Robin said.

Acasta thought about it. Robin was right. Certain traits skipped many generations in horse lines, then suddenly reappeared stronger than ever.

"How do you explain only one Flyer returning, though?" Acasta challenged.

"You don't see it, do you?" Robin asked. He eyed Acasta to gauge how the mage responded.

"I give up. What don't I see?"

"Everybody is so worried about the one Flyer the prophecy promised, but I didn't hear nothing about him coming back alone."

"Meaning you think he's just the most important Flyer, the one who rules the world. For all we know, a hundred could reveal themselves," Acasta reasoned.

Robin touched his nose and winked. Acasta considered it. Who's to say the entire race wasn't about to reemerge and not just one lonely boy who could fly?

"I think you done popped his wizard brain!" Keelo bellowed, laughing at the look on Acasta's face.

Later that night in Drenna's bed, Acasta brought up the subject after a lengthy session of rum and sex.

"If there's one thing I've learned about Robin, other than the fact he's a terrible lay for someone with a body like that, the boy has some bright ideas," Drenna said.

Acasta tried to appear unsurprised that Drenna had slept with another on the ship, but he failed miserably, much to Drenna's delight. "Aw, are you jealous?" she mocked. "I daresay you yourself would roll in the hay with him if given the chance. He's prettier than near every woman I've met. Maybe in addition to words, you can teach him some other skills. That way when you're gone, I can still enjoy my nights."

"No, I don't think I'll do that," Acasta said. "Getting back to the other subject we were talking about, what's your opinion?"

Drenna rolled her eyes, then rolled off the bed to hover over her chamber pot and relieve herself. "I'm a sailor, Acasta. I don't give a rat's ass about some silly words or some promised boy."

"That's exactly why I want to know your thoughts."

"Oh, because I'm a commoner."

"In many ways, you are singularly *uncommon*, but in this instance, yes, your opinion as an average person."

"Fine. I think it's horseshit. Yes, I know people like you have magic, so I'm not gonna discount the possibility of gods and such. But the idea of one boy coming to rule us all? Just because he can fly? Nope."

"I tend to agree," Acasta admitted.

Drenna furrowed her brow.

"What's wrong?" Acasta asked.

"Just trying to figure you out, mage," she said. She called him mage because she knew it bothered him. Not to be identified as what he was, but because the way she said it made him sound sly or wrong somehow.

"I am an open book, woman," he countered.

* * *

The next day, Acasta rode Jester through Worktown, one of Lockewell's two ports in Trader's Bay. Historically, the port had been named Shark Haven, due to the icy, shark-infested

115

waters, but more recently, people had begun calling the port Worktown, as the majority of goods that came through this city were of the human variety. Aside from the Republic, slavery was practiced in all the realms. But only in Lockewell was it ingrained in the culture as a key feature. Nearly half of the souls in Lockewell were either current or former slaves. They were brought here from all over the world—against their will, of course—and forced into fifteen years of slavery. The men became indentured tradesmen or soldiers. The women, household servants, seamstresses, or in some cases, prostitutes. After a decade and a half, if the slave was still alive and of sound mind, they were given the chance to be free. About half chose to remain in slavery, as the prospects of being a former slave were dim at best. The ones who did choose freedom mostly fled or died trying, for yet again, there were just some people in Lockewell who didn't abide "free" slaves.

As he and Jester made their way through the mud-slick streets, harassed by traders trying to sell fabrics, pelts, and cheap weapons, Acasta set his mind back on his task. He was to locate a boy and bring him back to the queen. How different was he than a slaver, he wondered? While it was true that Amira was an honorable woman, she was also royalty, which meant her morals were flexible enough to accommodate decrees that were, in her mind, in the best interest of the realm. Such a rationale had been used by kings and queens to justify horrific actions since the dawn of time.

In Acasta's experience, every city had a unique smell that reflected its trade or geography. He had once visited the city of Thistlecrown in Fidora and was amazed by the ever-present lush aroma of trees and lilacs. White Hawk, a Tufthorn stronghold, smelled of bread, thanks to the large bakery in its plaza. Worktown's scent was acrid. The pungent sea breeze combined with burnt coal and urine to perfectly encapsulate the dreary city in Acasta's nose and mind. Jester too seemed bothered by the smell, if his constant snorts were any indication.

Eventually, Acasta came upon his destination. He secured Jester to a post outside the unmarked brothel and stepped inside. His nose was immediately battered by a new array of scents. They were meant to be delightful, but the incense was too strong. The proprietor was clearly hoping to mask other smells in this establishment.

"A handsome traveler with green eyes," said Madame Red, the plump, fashionably dressed woman near the entrance. "My day is looking brighter already."

"I'm not here seeking entertainment," Acasta explained, averting his gaze from the three companions who had appeared in the decadent parlor. *Companion* was just a nice term for a slave, he mused.

"We also provide punishment, should that be what you seek, *mage*," Madame Red offered.

Acasta looked at the crest on the wall above the woman's head. The letters *VR* were emblazoned in yellow gold on the dark wood. Madame Red followed his eyes to the crest, then excused the companions from the room with a glance. She took a step closer to Acasta.

"I need to send a message to your boss," Acasta said.

Madame Red sighed.

"My *boss*, as you say, is a busy man. It can be difficult to contact him. Difficult and expensive."

Acasta removed a wooden coin from his pocket and offered it to her. She narrowed her eyes at the coin, seeing the familiar crest on its face.

"I've not seen one of these in five years. How do I know it's real?" she asked.

"The more important question is how do you know it's not? Refusing one of Viceroy Renner's personal markers is a serious offense. For all you know, I could be his dearest friend in all the realms."

Madame Red stiffened slightly before slipping the coin into a hidden pocket and easing back into a placating demeanor. "Yes, he's always been quite fond of magic folk."

"Indeed," Acasta replied.

"I'll find you a scroll."

"There's no need for pretense," Acasta said, knowing full well she would read any message he wrote the moment he left the brothel.

"Very well. What message would you like to convey?"

Acasta thought for a moment, then grinned. "Tell him I'm looking for a boy."

Gang of Five

"My first order of business was to see how deep the rot went," Modano said, before taking a foreboding sip of his tea. "I'm afraid it runs to the very core."

"How many?" Henry asked.

"It's not a question of numbers, dear Henry. It's a matter of influence and fear. Even those who might oppose Black and her Lockewell cronies in theory would never do so in practice, for fear of severe repercussions."

Henry knew the kind of repercussions he meant. At that very moment, his family was hidden away in the countryside, staying with a rather simple second cousin they barely even acknowledged as a member of the Martin clan. Henry's wife was none too happy about that. The former first minister looked at the other people at the table. Along with him and Modano, there were two longtime senators—Edward Deguerrin and Loak Farnosh—and a fifth man Modano had not yet introduced. He was a short, round fellow with an affable look about him. They had all gathered in the back room of a small tavern on the outskirts of Genora proper. The only people who might overhear their conversation here were drunk shepherds or the local blacksmith's apprentice.

119

Still, Henry was uneasy.

"I don't think we should be having this discussion with a stranger," he said, referring to the round man.

"Poor, principled Henry," Modano lamented. "Of the many sadnesses this situation has wrought, seeing you corrupted will be high on my personal list, I fear. This man is no stranger to the rest of us at this table. He is Marco Belor."

Henry's eyes went wide. "The Butcher of the East?" He had lost all sense of discretion, his voice carrying across the tavern.

"It would be best if the entire borough didn't know he was here, with us, having a *clandestine* meeting," Senator Farnosh sneered, dismayed. He had never liked Henry, mostly because of his high-minded morals. "It is long past time you got your hands dirty, Henry."

Henry tried to collect himself. "I am sorry for the outburst, and I mean no disrespect to you, Mr. Belor, but are we now at a point where we consider enlisting the help of … of …"

"A businessman?" Belor offered with an easy smile. "Or perhaps you were going to say *killer*. Or *slayer*? Either would be inaccurate. I've never spilled another man's blood, you see. They call me butcher because that is what I am, just as my father was before me. Why, the average pig has far more to fear from me than you do. That said, from time to time, I have been known to connect individuals with certain other individuals who do happen to be in the business of killing. I am not so blind that I don't see the pall that fact may cast over my reputation, but I assure you I am quite the ordinary gentleman."

Belor leaned back in his chair and enjoyed another gulp of his mead. Modano was amused at Belor's characterization of himself, Henry noticed. He didn't share in the humor. He turned to the others, careful to keep his voice barely above a whisper. "What exactly are you proposing?"

A knot formed in the pit of Henry's stomach as Modano laid out the plan. Blood would have to be spilled, he argued. If they chose just the right targets at just the right time, they might even be able to avert a civil war while achieving their goal of keeping Maldovar an independent republic. Henry thought back to what his father used to say about their realm's politics. It was a dirty business, he had told a teenage Henry, but it was preferable to more violent forms of governance. *More* violent, Henry thought. His father apparently accepted violence as a feature of politics.

"What of this Sir Grayfork character?" Deguerrin asked.

"We're still gathering intelligence on him," Modano said.

Deguerrin snorted. "Just say you don't know shit about the man. We have no need for pretense or obfuscation here."

"He would be more accurately called Baron Grayfork, as he purchased his title," Belor noted. "But in Lockewell, they did away with baronets last century to simplify matters."

Modano eyed Henry, the hint of a grin curling his lip. "This is why we need a businessman such as Belor on our side. Go on."

Belor nodded, finishing his mug of mead before continuing. According to his sources, Grayfork was the patriarch of a large merchant family. They were diversified, dealing in everything from dry goods to slaves. A few years earlier, hoping for an audience with King Edward Harwick, Grayfork had bought the honorific. When the king refused to grant him a meeting, Grayfork fomented a small rebellion in the eastern parts of the realm. He did it covertly, but the king knew he and his merchant allies were behind the trouble. So, in exchange for tamping down the gentry, Grayfork got his audience and convinced the monarchy to name his family Merchant Royal, making him one of the wealthiest men in Lockewell.

"So, he's not afraid to kill people to get what he wants," Henry grumbled.

"Most people aren't in this world. Honestly, stop being a child, Henry!" Deguerrin sniped.

Henry opened his mouth to respond, then thought better of it. The other men at the table were right. Politics was a dirty business. If saving Maldovar meant killing a few rogue actors, so be it.

"We're agreed, then," Modano said, picking up on Henry's silent assent. "Here is the list so far. If these heads roll, so to speak, then we might just be able to convince the Senate that an independent Maldovar is better than one subjugated to Lockewell's rule. And make no mistake, gentlemen, that is what Lockewell wants. They are a land of slavers, and they seek to enslave our entire system."

Modano produced a list of names and laid it on the table. Henry scanned it, surprised at its length. Having never been in the killing business before, he had guessed there might be half a dozen people who needed to be eliminated. But there were twenty, many of whom he'd once called colleagues. A few he had even considered friends.

Trials

Jamie had been tracking the boar since before sunup. It was now well past noon, if his rumbling stomach was any indication. He inspected the hoofprint in the mud and tried to discern which way the animal had gone. Finally, he pointed south.

"This way," Jamie said with confidence.

Rawk stood nearby. He leaned on his mighty axe and exhaled between his teeth. "Yeah."

Just as Jamie started to head south through the forest, Rawk tripped him with the handle of his weapon. Jamie fell to the ground face-first, then looked back, furious.

"Deer go south," Rawk said. "Boar go west."

Jamie looked at the tracks again. He realized there were two sets of prints. They were similar, but boar tracks were slightly rounded, while deer hooves came to a point. Jamie wanted to scream in frustration. Lukas, who was also training alongside Jamie, remained silent. Rawk had told them early on that they would split the sessions, and when it was not their turn to participate in the training, they should observe and keep their mouths shut. It didn't stop Lukas from smirking at Jamie's mistake. Annoyed, Jamie began to walk west. He made it a few steps before Rawk halted.

"What is it now?" Jamie asked, nervous the big man had sensed a looming threat.

"Done for day. No more tracking. Little Galantra not good at it," Rawk said. Then he turned back toward camp. Jamie and Lukas followed.

A week had passed since he and Caldred joined Skull-crusher's hunting party. Jamie was now training each day with Rawk and Lukas, and it seemed the majority of that time was dedicated to finding things Jamie had no talent for. He wasn't adept at hunting or tracking. He was shit at crafting bows from raw wood. Just about the only thing he seemed good at was fighting—in the moment. If you told him ahead of time he was going to be in a fight, he had no skills at planning a proper strategy. To Jamie, it seemed his success could be attributed as much to luck as to any natural talent. Still, Rawk and others told him he was uncommonly quick and had a certain knack for putting his weapon in just the right spot at the right time. He wondered if the precision came from years of writing and drawing, but that seemed like a bit of a stretch. Regardless, Rawk had proven surprisingly patient with him, compared to the horror stories he'd heard of Clem warriors training their slaves and soldiers to the brink of death. Lukas, by contrast, had proven himself to be a smart tactician, always thinking ahead and rarely making the same mistake twice. Rawk had yet to pit the two boys against each other in a sparring match, but Jamie was pretty sure he could outmuscle Lukas, even if he couldn't out-finesse him.

Jamie was so lost in thought, he barely heard the rustle behind him. By the time he turned around and got his knife up, one of the boar's tusks had already pierced his leg. He was knocked four feet off the path, his back slamming into a tree as he fell. The boar was about to charge him again when it shook and squealed. One of its front paws was leaking blood and the heavy animal was having trouble putting weight on it. Jamie had caught the boar with another of his signature quick strikes. Before the angry animal could do anything, it was thrown to the ground by the force of Rawk's airborne axe that thumped into its chest.

Rawk walked to the boar and retrieved his weapon, then he looked at Jamie and chuckled. "Beast track *you*."

Jamie held his leg. The pain was immense, but given the small amount of blood, it seemed the animal's tusks had caught mostly skin, missing the fleshy part of his leg. Lucky again. Lukas sighed and shook his head; he didn't think much of Jamie as a fighter.

A few hours later, Jamie watched the animal roasting on the spit, fat dripping and sizzling in the flame. Caldred arrived and tossed a few logs next to the fire pit, then sat down, winded. Jamie raised an eyebrow.

"Nine," Caldred said. "Ain't even lunch yet. I could go for the record today." His body fully healed, Caldred was taking shape to be a fairly robust kid. Combined with the rigorous labor involved in being the group's designated firewood gatherer, Caldred's steady diet of meat and mead had done wonders for the boy's body. In another week, Jamie guessed Caldred might actually outweigh him.

"You seem in good spirits," Jamie said.

"Beats slavin' on a farm," Caldred replied.

Jamie nodded. "So, you don't miss being a petty thief?"

Caldred snorted and gnawed on a big hunk of meat. Jamie was the one being groomed for battle, yet it was Caldred who seemed more at ease among the Clem warriors. They joked with him and listened to his tales of thieving and general hijinks, probably seeing some of themselves in the kid with the rough edges. Unlike Jamie, he didn't annoy them with his ability to read and write. Sure, most of the Clem had a certain respect for "Little Galantra." They just liked Caldred more. Still, there was a bond growing between the boys, partly out of necessity and partly because each owed the other his life. They understood their best chance of survival was to stick together.

"Happened there?" Caldred asked, pointing to Jamie's torn pant leg. The fabric was coated with dried blood, and a bandage was visible through the sliced wool. "Rawk hack at ya?"

"The leg would be gone if that was the case," Jamie said before motioning to the boar on the spit. "This bastard surprised me."

"Well, I guess we got him back!" Caldred exclaimed, before taking another big bite of boar meat.

Jamie smiled, finding at least a bit of humor in Caldred's words.

"You gonna die or something? Seems like a scratch," Caldred prodded.

"Huh? No, it's fine. I mean it hurts like hell, but it'll be all right," he said. "I just don't think I'm good at this."

"At what?"

"Any of it. Rawk's training me to be … what … a warrior?" Jamie wondered aloud, though not so loud anybody but Caldred could hear. "A few weeks ago, I thought I was going to be a scribe or an artist."

Caldred gave him a solemn look. "Want my advice? Forget

a few weeks ago. Don't be tellin' these folk about the artist stuff, either."

"You're probably right," Jamie moped. He couldn't but help but let his mind drift back to his farm and his aunt, the only mother he'd ever known.

"No *probably* about it," Caldred said. "You might not be good at all this stuff, but you're a killer, whether you like it or not. Maybe not cold-blooded like this lot here, but you're good at it, Jamie. Damn good. Get used to it."

"Kindling, jackass!" a Red Bear warrior yelled from another fire pit. The hunting party was so large, they had three pits going anytime they set camp. Caldred sprang to his feet and flashed Jamie a grin before darting off into the woods, faster than a spooked deer. Jamie was left mulling over Caldred's characterization of him when the scent of cologne wafted his way.

"Good afternoon, Laroche," Jamie said without looking. The handsome man was the only one in the entire hunting party who didn't smell like sweat. He sat down near Jamie.

"Don't be vapid," Laroche sneered.

"Uh, okay."

"Do you know what vapid means?"

"As in … a drink that has no flavor?" Jamie asked.

Laroche looked over at Jamie, then shook his head. "You're too smart for your own good, boy. That will get you in trouble. I know from experience."

"How was I being vapid?"

"The afternoon is not good. We are on an aimless quest that will ultimately prove to be Skullcrusher's undoing. This entire camp reeks of shit. And those are rainclouds on the horizon. So, you greeting me with 'good afternoon' is, simply put, you lacking any substance whatsoever. It was just a thing for you to say. And as the one person in camp beside me who seems to possess the ability to form complex thoughts, I expect more from you."

Jamie took a bite of his lunch and motioned to the sky. "At least I didn't talk about the weather. *That* would've been vapid."

Laroche couldn't help but laugh. "Too clever by half and then some. But no, I did not sit down to discuss the weather. I came to grumble."

Over the past few days, Laroche had been seeking Jamie out more and more. At first, Jamie found it annoying, but he'd learned to talk as little as possible and just let Laroche ramble. It was a great way to learn the gossip of the camp as well as news from the outside world. While he didn't exactly like the businessman, Jamie did appreciate Laroche's wit.

"Not to belabor the point, but it's fitting that rain is coming our way," Laroche groused. "It will help wash away the blood of another caved-in head."

Jamie reacted, unclear of what Laroche meant.

"Josef has challenged our leader in the circle," Laroche said, pointing out a hairy beast of a man who was busy sharpening his sword and singing to himself in some ancient Clem dialect. He was a Red Bear. "She will defeat him, I'm sure."

"I didn't know she could be challenged outside of Kragon's Lair," Jamie said.

"There are many things you don't understand."

"True. Here's one more. If you have no doubt she'll beat him, why are you upset? I thought you … favored her."

"I favor her every chance I get," Laroche replied. "The problem is not with the challenge but what comes after."

Laroche gave Jamie a meaningful look as a horn sounded three times. Everybody around Jamie stirred. Jamie and Laroche followed the crowd to the center of camp, where Skullcrusher's servant Lukas was dragging a spear in the dirt to create a circle roughly twenty feet wide. Skullcrusher stood nearby, her mouth a flat line. If she was nervous, she did not show it. Rawk stood by her side. He was also not nervous, but he did look upset, though Jamie knew he often looked that way. Jamie was expecting a speech or some type of lengthy ceremony before the fight. Instead, Josef the Red Bear simply walked to the edge of the circle, removed his shirt, and spat on the ground.

"Challenge," he said.

All eyes were on Skullcrusher as she nodded at Josef, then slung her war hammer over her shoulder and stepped inside the circle. Josef ran toward her with a loud grunt, thrusting his longsword at her midsection. The great woman sidestepped the attack with surprising speed. She whirled and swung her hammer round, nearly clipping Josef as he passed by.

This was not his first battle, either. He rolled with the grace of a man half his size and popped up in time to swipe at Skullcrusher's legs. He grazed leather but was unable to break the tough hide of her pants as she darted out of danger. With the first engagement out of the way, both warriors began to circle and appraise their opponent a bit more.

Jamie glanced at Laroche and saw some of his prefight confidence had waned a bit. He suddenly didn't seem so sure of the outcome.

"I think I'd like the name Ladyslicer," Josef taunted.

"Should you be lucky enough to slice me, it would be the first time you split a bitch, from what I've heard," Skullcrusher retorted.

Enraged and embarrassed, Josef made another lunge toward her. This time, he tried to lop her head off her shoulders. He missed. He was in too close for Skullcrusher to bring her hammer fully to bear, so instead she kicked him hard in the stomach with a steel-tipped boot, sending him onto his ass. The crowd cheered and hissed, depending on who they were rooting for. It was more of an even split than Jamie figured it would be.

The next minute or two featured both fighters testing the other's defenses, with Josef landing a shivering elbow to Skullcrusher's side and receiving an equally brutal blow from the hilt of her hammer. Just as it seemed the battle might go on for quite a while, Josef made a fatal error. He got in close again and tried to stab at Skullcrusher's gut, but she was ready for it. She stepped to the side and let the blade slip between her hip and her arm, then she clamped down hard on it and whirled around, breaking it free of Josef's grasp. He barely had time to be stunned before the heavy head of Skullcrusher's hammer swung into his temple so hard that it didn't even clang against the metal of his helmet. It produced a sickening thud as Josef was swept off his feet and spun in midair, a mess of blood and brain matter spitting out his mouth and ear.

The crowd fell silent as Skullcrusher walked over to Josef's twitching body. She raised her weapon and smashed it down upon him, ending his challenge. And his misery. Skullcrusher took no joy in it, nor did she gloat. She simply sighed, exhausted, and walked between the parted sea of Clem warriors back toward her tent.

Rawk stepped forward and slammed his axe on the ground. Once. Twice. Then he picked up the rhythm as other men and women joined. Only a dozen or so, though. A good number of both Halfmoon and Red Bear clans seemed less than enthused with the outcome.

"That could have gone better," Laroche said to him.

"How? She won," Jamie replied.

"She defeated the challenger, but I would say the damage was already done before either of them stepped in the circle," Laroche noted. "That anyone felt the need to challenge her is the real problem."

* * *

Laroche was right. Later that evening, the Red Bear leader announced he and his clan would be heading back to their lands instead of continuing what he called "this stupid hunt."

Rawk growled and protested, threatening to punish anyone who dared leave with treason.

Skullcrusher calmed the angry giant and spoke clearly to the assembled warriors. "You invoke Clanright, then?" she asked.

The Red Bear leader paused for a moment, suddenly unsure of himself, but steeled himself and finally nodded his assent.

"So be it," Skullcrusher decreed, raising her voice. "You and all who follow you may go in peace, but from this day forth, the Red Bears stand apart from Clem Nation, until there is another on the throne. You will not be subject to our laws, nor will you be granted our protection. Go your way, Clan Red Bear."

And so they did. Every last Red Bear left camp. That would have been trouble enough for Skullcrusher's rule, but then one fewer than half of the Halfmoons left. According to Laroche, the Halfmoons could avoid the punishments of invoking Clanright by keeping half their force with Skullcrusher. Of the sixteen Halfmoons, nine stayed to complete the journey with Skullcrusher. It was a meager victory for her, however, as the mere act of sending their people home spoke nearly as loudly as the Red Bears invoking Clanright.

"This will prove the end of her reign. Perhaps not tomorrow or the next day, but soon," Laroche told Jamie between glugs of ale. "No faction has invoked Clanright in a hundred years."

"What will she do?" Jamie asked.

"How should I know?"

"You're her advisor."

Laroche cast his eyes to the darkening sky.

"It's possible this was all destined to happen," he said.

"You of all people believe in the gods and the fates?" Jamie asked, hiding none of the surprise in his voice.

"The gods, no. I am not a simpleton, dear boy. But I do believe in the inextricable nature of ambition and destiny. They find each other and cross paths like a vast spiderweb across all the realms of our world. Enough people whisper of a prophecy on one hand, and enough people strive to make it so on the other …" Laroche trailed off. He could tell he was losing Jamie. He decided to try another tack. "Are you familiar with the Bailor's Hill?"

"The children's game?" Jamie asked.

"Yes, though I would argue it's more than that. But the rules are clear. Both players have a set of pieces, and they try their best to avoid certain areas of the game board. But because the board is slanted toward the middle and all moves eventually lead to the center, the pieces inevitably converge in battle."

"I never liked that game. It felt pointless," Jamie said.

132

"I agree! If your goal is to avoid the inevitable, because simply by playing, you will be drawn into battle. Into the end of the game. So it is with life, in my experience. We can try to avoid our destiny all we like, but eventually, we must face it. And all of us here? I sense we are headed toward a great convergence. One that will not end well for some of us," Laroche said before grinning. "Except for you, he who cannot be killed."

Jamie shook his head and poked the campfire embers with a stick, sending a trail of ashes and gray smoke into the air. "I do not think I have a part to play in the game you're talking about. All I want is to get home."

"To this aunt of yours. Yes, you've mentioned. With all due respect, I do not believe that for one second. You may miss this kind woman, but you are not as out of place here as you once thought you were. The same may not be true for me, as luck would have it."

"How do you mean?"

Laroche returned to something Jamie had said a few minutes earlier. "You called me an advisor. Is that what you think I am?" he asked, forcing a laugh. "Hardly. I am but a spy in their eyes."

Jamie looked at the camp around them. They were now down to fourteen people, he and Caldred included. The two boys, of course, had nowhere else to go and had sworn allegiance to Skullcrusher. Jamie was about to say something, but then he thought better of it. Laroche caught the hesitation and offered him a mug of ale.

"Go ahead," he chided. "I always like to hear what's on the mind of Little Galantra."

Jamie wasn't sure if he should proceed, but he guessed it

was now or never. He decided it was best to be direct.

"Not only in their eyes, though," Jamie said, making sure nobody else could hear.

"I'm sure I don't know what you mean," Laroche replied.

Jamie didn't flinch and pushed forward with his assertion. "You said you are but a spy in their eyes, making light of it, as if the very idea was ridiculous. Yet not two days ago, I saw you in the woods, placing a small scroll on the foot of a pigeon. Not any pigeon native to these parts. One that must have come from far away."

Laroche turned to Jamie, giving the boy his full attention. Laroche was going to make him actually say it, Jamie realized. He took another swig of ale and continued, already having committed anyway.

"I think you do spy, but not to the detriment of Skullcrusher or her people. Your ... heart seems too true in that regard. But you do serve a hidden purpose here. I don't have any desire to share that purpose, but in return for keeping your secret, I would simply ask for the same discretion."

"While I admit nothing and have a good mind to cut your tongue out right now, I will indulge you, *boy*," Laroche hissed. "What type of discretion could you possibly require?"

"I don't know yet," Jamie said. "I just want you to know you're in my debt should I, like you, someday have my own motives that don't directly harm this hunt or the boss herself."

A new realization dawned on Laroche. Jamie was more cunning than he'd ever imagined. Laroche slowly nodded his agreement.

"I'm beginning to see why you have survived thus far," Laroche said.

"So, we understand each other?"

"In this matter, I believe we do." Laroche stood up as Caldred returned with more firewood, startling the boy, who dropped a log on Laroche's foot. He shook off the pain, annoyed. "You two are either lucky charms or harbingers of my demise. Gods!"

Laroche stormed off. Caldred turned to Jamie.

"What was that all about?" Caldred asked.

"Secrets. The kind you don't want to know."

Caldred looked for a sign that Jamie was joking. When none came, he shrugged. "So do you think we get promoted now?"

Freedom

Stealing was surprisingly easy.

Phaedra crouched in the alley, eating the hard cheese and half-loaf of bread she had swiped from the belligerent man's cart, and it dawned on her that she had never stolen anything before.

Princesses had no need to steal.

Perhaps this meant she was no longer a princess. She turned that thought over in her head a few times and decided no, she was still her father's daughter, heir to the throne of Skybane. To the people of Corcoran, she was just another street urchin to be ignored or, in the right circumstances, taken advantage of. She'd been in the Maldovarian town a few days and had slept in a different dark corner each night. Her clothes were tattered, and she was a grubby mess, so she couldn't blame anyone who looked at her and saw nothing more than a runaway or an orphan. The city was full of both. For a land that prided itself on being known as the only "free" realm in the world, there sure were a lot of poor people about.

They certainly didn't *look* free.

Phaedra didn't know what the rest of Maldovar was like, but these citizens of the Republic had hollow, desperate eyes. Phaedra couldn't tell who seemed more hopeless—the vagrants or the ones who actually worked for their meager living. She had encountered a mix of apathy and venom from both groups since the moment she arrived, having fought off two attempted muggings and a rape. She did not feel bad for the state in which she left those attackers.

Despite the physical dangers, her bedraggled appearance did provide a fair amount of protection. Nobody would mistake her for a princess or a noble of any sort.

The trip here had been a smooth one; the ocean never gave her a moment of worry. She had even had the good fortune of arriving at night, so it was easier to sneak her boat into the slumbering harbor. There, she met a port guard who agreed to hold her boat in exchange for her silver necklace. It was hard parting with the necklace, but much easier than parting with her father's sailboat. She had also negotiated a satchel in the bargain, into which she deposited all her worldly possessions, including the items from the boat's chest.

And so, she blended in with the homeless of Corcoran, partly out of convenience and partly out of necessity. Upon finishing her stolen bread and cheese, it occurred to her she might consider trying her luck farther up the coast. She could sail by night in search of a more hospitable port where she could settle for a while. She was an excellent fisherwoman, so perhaps she could find honest work at the docks. She could meet a man, raise a family, become a normal person. No. That wasn't her. She actually laughed aloud at the idea of becoming some fat Maldovarian's wife and bearing his chubby, pale children. The thought of it brought her mind back to Lucian; there was no time for that pain now, she decided. She hid it away and promised herself she would have her vengeance someday.

"That's my crate!" a man yelled at Phaedra, jostling her leg with his boot. Phaedra looked up to see a dirty, wild-eyed drunk leering down at her. He smelled of urine and rancid fish. Apparently, he was partial to the broken crate Phaedra was using as her chair. Judging by the way he swayed back and forth, he had spent most of the morning drinking a bottle of some poor excuse for liquor.

"You can have your crate, but touch me again and you'll have half of it up your ass," Phaedra replied.

This jolted the man. He wasn't expecting that kind of language or fight from her. A smile formed on his cracked lips, and he bared a medley of gray and brown teeth. Phaedra could smell his laugh more than she heard it. At the same time, something in her resolve put the man on notice; he wasn't looking for a fight at the moment. He took a step back and mocked a bit of propriety.

"As the lady wishes," he said with a slight bow. In that moment, Phaedra thought she saw a flash of who the man might've been before, in another life. A shopkeeper perhaps. Maybe even a father or husband. She sighed as she stood up. As she passed him, she flashed a hint of a smile and nodded a minor bow back to him.

"Don't that beat all," the man said to himself, watching her walk away down the alley. When he saw the small hunk of cheese Phaedra had left for him, he laughed again. It was probably the greatest kindness he'd seen in years.

It was a cool afternoon in the port town. Phaedra held the straps of her satchel tight against her shoulders as she wound her way through the thoroughfare, negotiating past fruit carts and loud street merchants. It felt odd to be so alone.

Everywhere she went, she was the outsider. The unimportant one. It was the exact opposite of her entire life up until that point. Nobody was there to coddle her or expect anything of her, but nor was anyone there to watch her back. She was truly on her own. In an attempt to form some sort of structure around her time in Maldovar, she had decided to give herself one main task each day.

That day she hoped to wash herself.

It was not a lofty goal. Given the fact she hadn't found the time or opportunity to bathe in over a week, it might prove challenging. Having already bartered her necklace, she was left with little to trade. That meant a hot bath was probably out, as she had nothing of value to an innkeeper. Phaedra had been walking for a half hour when she came upon a row of small cottages at the edge of town. There were fewer people milling about here, and the homes looked quiet. Rentals for traveling merchants, perhaps. She made her way to the last cottage of the group and glanced in the window as she passed by. It was empty. Not wanting to be too obvious, she continued walking toward the woods past the small house, then slipped in among the trees and doubled back. Hiding behind a wide tree trunk, she watched the cottage for a few minutes. All was still.

The door creaked loudly as Phaedra entered the two-room structure. She winced and was ready to run, but there was no need. Nobody was home. She closed the door behind her and stayed low, in case anybody happened to be looking through the window. Phaedra scanned the cottage. No tub. No fresh water. But there was a bucket. A bucket meant water nearby, she figured. Taking a peek out the window, she spotted a well about one hundred feet away. Phaedra took the bucket and found some lye soap on the table. It would have to do. Before heading back outside, she chanced another sweep of the cottage and was rewarded with a pair of men's work shoes. They were far too big for her, so she found a pair of socks and stuffed them into the nose of the shoe. Even with the ill fit, they were much better than the soft leather slippers she'd been wearing.

* * *

Her bathing had been surprisingly uneventful. Nobody spotted her at the well getting water. Or in the woods cleaning herself and her clothes. Phaedra's luck faltered when she stepped out of the woods to head back to town.

"Much better," the man said. He was a short, thick man with greasy hair and a devilish smile on his face. "You clean up nice."

Phaedra's first instinct was to bolt back into the woods, but she knew the man would give chase, and unlike the other would-be attackers she'd easily fended off in Corcoran thus far, this guy looked like he knew how to fight. He saw her eyeing the short sword hanging from his belt. He tapped the hilt.

"Name's Jenner, but you can call me Jenny. Everyone else does," he said. "And you are?"

"Not interested. Move along."

Jenny nodded as if he'd expected Phaedra's reply. The two stood there for a few seconds, each considering their next move. When the moment stretched long enough, Jenny held his hands wide, urging Phaedra to go for it. And that she did, producing her remaining curved blade in a sudden flash and hurling it toward Jenny's head. The short man was ready for it and ducked out of the way. The blade nipped his ear on the way by and planted itself into a tree.

"You're as fast as they said you'd be, Your Highness," Jenny joked, touching the tip of his ear.

Phaedra froze. She had assumed the man was just a local deviant of some kind, but the fact he knew who she was startled her. Before she could stop herself, the question was spilling from her mouth.

"But … how did you find me?"

"The real question is how did I find you so fast?" Jenny replied, taking a few steps toward her. "Simply put, I'm the best at what I do, and ten gold coins will motivate any man of my trade. I also found this."

He produced the necklace she had traded to the port guard in exchange for hiding her boat. Did that mean her boat had been discovered now too?

"First rule of being on the run: never pawn or trade items that are this fucking unique. Frankly, I'm disappointed in you, and I don't even know you," Jenny teased. Then he produced a pair of cuffs attached to a chain in his satchel. "Now if you play nice, I won't have to hurt you."

Phaedra's head swirled. She was disappointed in herself; how could she have been tracked down so easily? Phaedra watched Jenny take another step closer, gauging whether she planned to run or fight. Phaedra answered the unspoken question with a quick hop forward, combined with a roundhouse kick to the man's head.

Or where his head had been a second earlier. Once again, he proved his quickness and evaded the attack. Before she could reposition to defend herself, he smacked her in the side of the head with an open palm. It wasn't the hardest strike ever, but it had struck true, right above her ear. Dizzied and staggering, Phaedra swung wildly, trying to keep Jenny at bay until she recovered. He simply moved aside and regarded the stumbling princess with a sigh.

"I suppose it is because of your long journey and many travails," he said.

"What?"

"The reason for your poor showing," Jenny explained. "I was told to be wary of your blades and cunning."

Phaedra straightened up, trying to focus her eyes. "Kywin," she spat.

Jenny nodded. "Though I suppose he's better at stabbing people behind their backs than he is in a fair fight. Now, time to go home, little girl."

Phaedra stared at the man, furious. She could feel the anger welling up within her. She would rather die fighting than be taken back by this bounty hunter, she decided. Jenny saw the glint in her eyes and paused for a moment, wondering if there was more to this princess than he had seen thus far.

"Have it your way," he said, brandishing his short sword.

"No!" Phaedra howled. Jenny was struck not just by the sound of her voice, but a wall of wind that came with it. As if hit by a sledgehammer in the chest, he was lifted off his feet and blasted backward into the air. He slammed into the side of a nearby cottage with a sickening sound and dropped to the ground.

All was quiet as Phaedra tried to process what had just happened. She was breathing heavily and suddenly felt weak. She dropped to a knee and nearly fainted. Forcing herself to look up, she saw the devastation around her. Not only had

Jenny been flung backward like he was shot out of a cannon, but a few of the trees behind him were bent backward and broken. The cottage's windows were shattered. Phaedra's eyes fell to the bounty hunter. His body sagged at the base of the cottage, blood trickling from his mouth. Dead. Very, very dead. She walked over and removed her silver necklace from his front pocket.

Phaedra heard a gasp and looked toward the road back to town. A young boy and his mother were standing, awestruck, gaping at her. The woman pulled her son closer to her body.

"I didn't … I don't know what happened," Phaedra said.

The mother didn't wait around to hear or see any more. She grabbed the boy's collar and hurried him away.

Phaedra looked down at her own hands. They trembled. She held one of them to her chest and could feel the quick thumping of her heart. If she had been able to see her own eyes at that moment, she would've been surprised to learn they had shifted from sea blue to a deep purple color.

Harbinger

Renner was not a man of conscience. It was part of what made him a successful businessman. Unlike most people, he was not bound by the constraints of morality; he was perfectly content to act in self-interest, a habit that had served him well over the years.

The bastard son of a prostitute and a senator, Renner had followed in both his parents' footsteps in his dual role as the proprietor of dozens of brothels across three realms and the chief economic advisor of Maldovar. In the current political climate, he was aligned with those who backed Lockewell's shocking gambit to absorb Maldovar. He could see great profit in a Lockewell at twice its current size. So, from a business standpoint, he was inclined to ignore the mage's request for information.

If only it were that simple, he thought, as his boots sank into the bog that surrounded the witch's cabin. Renner stepped out of the muck and climbed up the weathered steps of the small dwelling, swiping at the mosquitoes that bit at his neck and ears. They were relentless, and they were the least of his worries in this place. The bog was home to any number of creatures that could end a man. And if a slithering, crawling, or stomping predator didn't get you, the stench just might. Renner had been breathing through his mouth ever since he entered the foul swamp. Before he could knock on the front door of the cabin, it creaked open, as if it was expecting him.

Renner moved inside to see Vinerva at her table. The old seer was blind, but only in the physical sense. She had the gift of foresight and had led Renner on the path to good fortune more than once. Now he came to ask the pale, wrinkled woman for a different kind of advice. The smells of the bog mingled with Vinerva's incense to assault Renner's nose and test his stomach.

"Son of Lualla," she said, not bothering to turn her head in Renner's direction. "You were right to come." Renner sat down in the chair opposite Vinerva at her small table, where she continued making a necklace out of bone charms. Renner placed a gold coin on the table between them. Vinerva nodded, knowing Renner would not dare cheat her with anything less than gold.

Renner had first met the woman nearly two decades earlier. At the time, he was looking for a very specific kind of poison to eliminate one of his rivals in the brothel industry; she had told him the poison was not needed, as the other man would die within the month of other causes. When he turned up dead on the road two weeks later, robbed and disemboweled by bandits, Renner decided Vinerva possessed a particular kind of wisdom he valued.

"Give me your hand," she said.

He always hated this part. It wasn't just the woman's smell. Her touch was cold, and yet somehow it sent hot tendrils of sensation through his body as she spoke. Not quite pain. Not quite pleasure. Still, he reached out and gave her his hand.

"You stand at the crossroads, much like the rest of the world," she began, clasping his hand. "Tell me why you think you have come, boy. And I shall tell you why you are really here."

Boy. He was in his late forties. But for all he knew, the woman was over one hundred years old. "The mage I told you about years ago … he has asked for my help," he said.

"And?"

"And I want to know if I should help him."

Vinerva threw her head back and cackled, causing the various crows in her home to mimic the sound. "You are right to fear the Beasted One."

"Beasted One?" Renner asked, eyeing the black birds flapping about Vinerva's small home.

"He has a magic few others possess. A dark, old magic that allows him to control the birds of the sky and the snakes in the ground," she said. "Does that frighten you?"

"You know it does," Renner uttered, trying to contain his composure.

"But not as much as what he did to you," Vinerva said.

Renner was normally immune to fear. Growing up, he'd been beaten and abused in every way a person, especially the son of a whore, could be. By the time he reached adulthood, he'd taken all the world had to offer and was ready to deal it back tenfold. But Acasta had shown him something. A new kind of pain he'd never experienced, before or since. It was almost a decade ago, but Renner still felt his heart tense as he remembered that night in Worktown. He had met Acasta at a feast at the mayor's estate on the edge of the city. Renner was there to grease the proverbial palms of local officials, while Acasta seemed bent on causing trouble. According to the mage, he was serving as an emissary of Tufthorn, but all he did at the gathering was insult the other guests, scolding them for their slaving ways. Renner had found it tedious and decided to send two of his men to remove Acasta from the grounds. They failed miserably, and Acasta turned his unnatural rage on Renner, using his powers to seize Renner's heart in his chest. Other guests scrambled to help him as he lay dying on the floor, while Acasta watched with an evil grin, sucking the life out of Renner with a satisfied gleam in his green eyes. Time seemed to stop for Renner; the seconds passed like hours as he experienced the surreal touch of magic clenching his body. Finally, the mage walked over and feigned helping Renner, releasing him from his magic's grasp. Later that evening, Acasta had demanded a marker from Renner.

Ten years later, Renner had nearly forgotten his debt. Then the bird arrived.

"He is looking for the Knight of War and Dawn," Renner spat.

"Interesting," Vinerva replied. If the news surprised her, she didn't let it show.

"It's a wild goose chase. He looks for a boy of legend, and the fool thinks I know where he's at?"

"The Beasted One is no fool. And he does not ask you where the harbinger is; he asks me through you," she said. "Acasta is aware of my gift, though he pretends not to value it. The woman he serves does."

"So, you know where the Knight is?" Renner asked. If the boy really did exist, knowing how to find him could be extremely profitable.

"You would be wise not to seek fortune in this endeavor," Vinerva cautioned. The old woman tilted her head, attuning her ears to the sound of her birds. "My pretties grow restless.

They know I am not long for this world, and they wonder who will take care of them. What they don't realize is that they only depend on me because I am here. When I'm gone, they will find their own strength once again."

"If there's a lesson in that, it's lost on me," Renner said.

"I do not doubt that," Vinerva chuckled. "I will say this: Do not confuse your wealth with your station in the grander scheme of things. You are but a man with money."

It was hard for Renner to swallow that truth, but he gritted his teeth and asked Vinerva what he should relay back to Acasta.

"The truth," she said. "That he shall find what he seeks at the border of Clem and Lockewell. But he may also find his ruin there."

Crossroads

Jamie spent years examining the lines on maps that carved up realms and provinces. On parchment, they were clear and definitive. The reality was far different. He didn't even know he'd crossed the Lockewell border until one of the warriors in the hunting party pissed on a tree stump and claimed it for Clem.

"Urination is indeed nine-tenths of the law," Laroche quipped. He winked at Jamie and Caldred, then walked ahead, chomping merrily on an apple.

"Who did he get fresh fruit from?" Caldred asked.

"I'm not sure who, but I can guarantee how," Jamie said, implying it was stolen. "He doesn't seem to be very liked among the Clem."

"Or anyone else, for that matter," Caldred offered.

Jamie nodded. They reached the top of a rocky hill and looked down at the valley below. More rocks. The trees of Clem had given way to a charred and gray terrain littered with giant boulders and razor-sharp slivers of hard gravel.

"I wasn't born with the feet for this," Caldred complained.

"Nobody was," Jamie agreed.

They'd been walking for weeks now. There were only

four horses left in the caravan, and they carried Skullcrusher and her inner circle of warriors. Except Rawk. He was too burdensome for the horses and had to trudge alongside with the rest of the hunting party. Since the majority of the warriors had departed a few days earlier, the pace of the march had quickened. They were headed to Shadowstone, a small town on the western edge of Lockewell. According to Laroche, the people there were much more welcoming to foreigners than those who lived in central Lockewell. It was another day's walk to Shadowstone. Jamie was wondering how many new blisters had opened on his feet that day when the first arrow struck. Jamie watched the man in front of him stagger and fall forward, rolling down the hill.

"Cover!" Skullcrusher yelled.

Jamie dropped to the ground and crawled to the safety of a nearby boulder. An arrow skittered off the face of the boulder, narrowly missing his head.

"Other side!" Rawk roared at him. *Ah.* Jamie realized he was hiding on the near side of the rock, where he would be an easy target. Everyone else was hiding on the other side of the boulders and outcroppings.

"Much better," Caldred teased Jamie when he scurried around the rock to join him. Laroche was also sharing the boulder for cover.

"Where are they?" Jamie asked.

Caldred pointed to a nearby ridge. Jamie popped his head out to get a look. He saw a smattering of gold-and-green uniforms before Laroche yanked him back to the safety of their hiding spot.

"It's generally not a good idea to stick your head out with archers around," Laroche said. "Even I know that much."

"Right," Jamie replied, embarrassed. "Whose colors are green and gold?"

"Mercenaries," Laroche said. He was nervous, his eyes darting about as he looked for a chance to escape.

"What do we do?" Caldred asked Jamie.

"How the hell should I know?"

"You're the one who's been training with Rawk every morning," Caldred said.

"And if a deer wanders across our path, there's one chance in three I might be able to kill it," Jamie replied.

The arrows continued to rain down upon the Clem group. Jamie watched Rawk and Skullcrusher bark orders at the other warriors, who began the dangerous task of working their way down into the valley, a few feet at a time, their shields up to counter the barrage from the mercenaries' bows. Jamie was thinking he might just wait for the battle to be over when Rawk growled for him.

"Little Galantra, to me!" the big man roared.

"I'm going with you," Caldred decided.

Jamie took a deep breath to steel himself, then bolted into the open toward Rawk's position behind a supply cart and the last few trees that were the vestiges of Clem as the landscaped transitioned from forest to stony pastures. By the time Jamie arrived, the speedy Caldred was already there and waiting. Jamie awkwardly dove behind the trees, forcing a sneer from Rawk. A few seconds later, Laroche also arrived.

"Nobody ask you," Rawk said.

"And so I freely volunteer myself to help our dear leader in any way I can," Laroche said, motioning to Skullcrusher, who was about ten feet away, still yelling commands to the warriors advancing on the archers below. Jamie could see

Laroche was more scared than any of them and simply didn't want to be left alone in their previous spot.

"You and skinny one will run around side to come up behind them," Rawk said, pointing at Jamie and Caldred. "Like hunting boar, only this time be good at it."

"Uh … yeah, we can do that," Jamie said, surveying the valley below. It was not the easiest task, but going the long way meant staying out of the middle of the battle. Already three of the Clem warriors had fallen. Looking down at the uniformed mercenaries, he saw two splayed out on the ground as well, arrows in their backs. Jamie scanned the area and saw two Clem women at the edge of a clearing, launching arrow after arrow into the air.

"What will you do?" Jamie asked Rawk reflexively. The brute looked at him, surprised Jamie had asked.

"Charge them," Skullcrusher answered. She had moved next to them and was strapping a knife to her thigh. "Go now before I change my mind and have you charge with us."

Jamie didn't need to be told twice. He and Caldred ran along the tree line, disappearing from sight.

"What should I do?" Laroche croaked.

"Nothing," Skullcrusher replied, eliciting a grunt from Rawk.

"I can do that," Laroche replied lightly, trying to maintain some semblance of dignity.

* * *

"Slow down," Jamie told Caldred, breathing hard as he tried to keep up with his friend. "It's not a race."

"If it was, you'd have no chance," Caldred said.

They reached a large depression in the ground and hunkered down to get a look at the opposing force.

"How many are there?" Caldred asked.

"Two for every one of ours. Maybe three."

"Ours …" Caldred repeated, letting the word float in the air between them. Jamie saw the look in Caldred's eyes and had the same thought. They could run if they wanted. Skullcrusher might not make it out of the battle alive. And even if she did, they'd have a head start, and would she really take the time to go after them?

"You think we could make it on our own?" Jamie wondered aloud.

Caldred thought about it for a moment, then his shoulders sagged. "We'd probably end up as slaves. At least with Clem, we have a shot at freedom, or something like it."

Jamie noticed movement nearby and froze. He lifted a finger to quiet Caldred. Jamie slunk down to his stomach and peered around a pile of rocks. A lone mercenary had the same idea they did; she was trying to sneak around the edges of the battle to outflank the Clem forces. She hadn't spotted Jamie or Caldred yet, meaning they could probably stay hidden and let her pass by them without incident. Jamie considered that option, then quietly removed his knife from his belt. Caldred agreed. They had to act.

"I'll cut her off, and then you surprise her," Jamie whispered.

"Brave," Caldred snarked.

"You have a better idea?"

"I do not," Caldred admitted, gripping his short sword. He didn't look entirely comfortable with it, but he swallowed his nerves.

Without any further delay, Jamie jumped up and moved

right into the path of the green-and-gold-cloaked fighter. The woman was tall and thick, with a grimy smile that flashed wide when she saw a teenage boy opposite her, brandishing nothing more than a knife.

"Must be my lucky day," the woman joked, removing a sword from its sheath. She advanced quickly on Jamie, thrusting her blade at him; he parried well enough, avoiding the attack and managing a swipe of his knife. It didn't connect. His meager training kicked in, and he evaded another jab of the longsword, this time stepping aside and connecting with a quick poke of his knife. He had drawn blood in the woman's shoulder, enraging her. Her amused demeanor faded and was replaced by an angry scowl. She feigned another thrust of her sword, got Jamie off balance, and knocked him on his ass with her shield. She raised her sword for a strike, then paused in motion. Jamie looked up at her and saw blood trickling from her throat. The blood mixed with air and bubbled forth from her mouth and neck as Caldred removed his blade from behind. The woman clutched her throat as she sank to her knees. The next few seconds were filled with awful gurgles and gasps until she finally fell flat on her face in the mud. Caldred breathed heavily as he stood over her, feeling the weight of his first kill.

"Didn't feel like I thought it would," he said.

"I know. But it was me or her," Jamie replied. "C'mon, let's get out of the open field."

Jamie stood up and pulled Caldred back to the safety of the tree line at the valley's edge. A few hundred yards away, the Clem warriors began their charge down the sloped ground toward the larger force. Jamie swore he could feel the earth shake with each of Rawk's footfalls. The big man was outpacing all but a few of his fellow Clem in a surprising display of speed and agility. As Rawk reached the mercenaries, he swatted away an arrow with his shield and simply ran over the archer who had let loose the volley. It was like seeing a horse run down a child. More impacts followed as the two opposing units clashed into combat.

Jamie and Caldred quickened their pace and were eventually behind the mercenaries. The momentum was definitely going against the contingent from Clem. Other than Rawk and Skullcrusher, the Clem were being overpowered by the sheer numbers of the mercenaries.

The boys were about to engage when Jamie saw a pair of horses tied to a tree off to the side of the battle, near a still-smoldering campfire. "Can you ride a horse?" he asked Caldred.

Caldred smiled.

The log was hot in Jamie's hand, but the spectacle of two riders surprising the mercenaries from behind—while holding flaming torches and screaming bloody murder—was enough to shock the mercenaries crowded around Skullcrusher and Rawk. Jamie launched the flaming wood at one of their heads, then ran down another with his horse. Seizing on the confusion, Rawk unleashed his axe in a wide arc, taking out two foes with one mighty swing. For just a moment, Jamie felt like he and Caldred had turned the tide of the battle.

They hadn't, of course. Jamie was quickly pulled from his horse by a swarthy man in a gold uniform and tossed down into the blood and muck. It would take more than a little fire and a couple of horses to take the day, Jamie realized. He rolled out of the way just in time to avoid the swipe of a sword from the mercenary that had knocked him off the horse.

Jamie kicked at the man's legs but was not in a position to defend himself. The man heaved his sword for another strike, but it was stymied by a flash of iron. Lukas. Skullcrusher's manservant and Jamie's fellow apprentice had stepped in to block the attack. Before the mercenary could react, Lukas slashed him across the face with his shield.

"Get up!" he barked at Jamie, who gathered his wits and stood next to Lukas. They went back to back and began awkwardly defending themselves against the more experienced fighters. Seconds passed like hours as the opposing warriors enveloped them. The only things keeping them alive were the chaos of the battle and the fact that Skullcrusher and Rawk were nearby, leaving mayhem and carnage in their wake. Out of the corner of his eye, Jamie saw Caldred darting around and holding his own. Maybe his friend could escape, he thought.

Eventually, the mercenaries were too much. They pushed the few Clem left into a killing box, and it was only a matter of time before they all fell, even Rawk. Jamie was grabbed by the arm and swung down to the ground by a large, fearsome woman with spiked steel gloves on her hands. She caught him on the leg with a strike, and the pain was so great, it radiated up his body and into his chest. He nearly lost consciousness but was able to wriggle back a few feet to avoid another hit. He flailed at her with his knife, with no real hope or chance of inflicting damage. Drained of strength, Jamie tried one last jab. He wasn't surprised that he missed. He *was* surprised *why* he missed.

Without warning, the woman was launched ten feet in the air and hurled out of sight. Jamie looked around him and saw other things he couldn't believe. Men set ablaze by fast-moving balls of fire. Trees uprooted and catapulted across the battlefield like spears. At one point, Jamie watched a giant boulder crush three mercenaries in a horrific mess of blood and bone. Through the chaos, Jamie saw a man with brilliant green eyes and wild hair wreaking havoc.

A mage.

A mage with a smirk on his face, like he was enjoying himself.

And he seemed to be on their side; he was inflicting the damage only on the mercenaries. In the span of a minute, he truly had turned the tide of the battle. The Clem fighters didn't question it. They killed and maimed ruthlessly until all the green-and-gold cloaks were face down on the mud, soaked in crimson.

Skullcrusher, spattered in the blood and viscera of those she'd slain, looked across the now-silent battlefield at the mage who had helped tilt the day in her favor.

"Hi there!" Acasta said cheerfully. He was winded from his exertion but seemed nowhere near as tired as the Clem combatants. "I'm hoping you're the good guys. And ladies."

Skullcrusher was caught off guard by the comment. Rawk grunted and gripped his axe, ready to attack.

"It's okay, Rawk, this one seems to be a friend," Skullcrusher said.

"What she said, big guy," Acasta agreed. "Today, at any rate. Watch your back."

Before Acasta could finish his sentence, Rawk had kicked out with his giant boot and slammed a dying mercenary in the face. The man had been trying to get one last slice in, to avenge his own inevitable death. Instead, he got a caved-in skull.

"Would anyone care for a drink?" Acasta asked, holding up a skin of ale he'd pillaged from the mercenary camp.

Soldiers

They'd moved a few hundred feet from the battlefield, but Jamie could still smell the blood and death around him. Or perhaps it was in his mind. Or stuck to his clothes. He helped Caldred bring more wood to keep the fire going. The mercenaries had apparently been camped here for a few days, lying in wait for them. The benefit of that was plenty of food and supplies. Jamie was already feeling a bit lightheaded from the ale he'd drunk to calm his nerves after the melee. He'd been in scrapes before, but that was his first proper battle. And he hoped it would be his last, though he knew better than to share that feeling aloud.

What was left of the Clem group sat around the campfire. Along with Jamie and Caldred, there was Skullcrusher, Rawk, Lukas, and two Halfmoon warriors. Laroche, who was wearing a predictably clean set of clothes, had also survived. He admitted to not engaging in the "festivities," as it wasn't his field of expertise.

A coward, Jamie thought.

At the edge of the campfire's glow, Acasta gave his horse an apple and ambled over to sit near Skullcrusher. Rawk shifted uneasily, moving his hand closer to his weapon, just in case.

The gesture was not lost on Acasta, who nodded.

"You are an interesting group," Acasta said, scanning the range of faces and sizes of those who sat before him. His gaze lingered on Jamie, Lukas, and Caldred. He watched Caldred go back to the woods for more kindling.

Skullcrusher sighed. "We have lost many of our people, but we owe you our lives. What is your name, mage?"

"Acasta," he said. "I am sorry for your losses. If I'd been here sooner, perhaps I could have helped more. I have no love for the mercenaries of Lockewell."

Laroche perked up at the mention of Acasta's name. The mage noticed and flashed a grin. "I see you've heard of me. I suppose one out of nine isn't bad," Acasta joked.

"He has name?" Rawk asked Laroche.

"He has name, yes," Laroche teased, mimicking the warrior's speech pattern. "Acasta is quite famous indeed. Though I have heard him called something else, a moniker I will not utter for risk of offending our dear savior."

"Who is he?" Jamie asked before he could stop himself. He thought he would receive a swift rebuke from Skullcrusher, but she merely raised an eyebrow at him. Apparently, his part in the battle had earned him some favor, or at the very least, credibility. Acasta spoke up before Laroche could answer.

"He is just an interested party, following a hunch and a prophecy," Acasta said, looking at Skullcrusher. "It appears I am not alone in that regard."

For a moment, the only sound was that of the crackling fire. Skullcrusher studied the mage and wondered how much to divulge of her quest to find the Flyer. Before she could answer, Caldred interrupted. He was dragging an injured mercenary with him.

"Found this one trying to sneak off toward the south," Caldred said, a short sword poking at the man's back.

"Please, I am just a servant!" the man yelped.

"A servant with a fighter's boots and chainmail under his cloak? I think not," Skullcrusher observed, motioning for one of the Halfmoons to take him from Caldred.

"I took this off one of our dead!" he whined and was thumped hard for his lie by the Halfmoon. Skullcrusher walked closer, towering over the man. She looked at her war hammer, then at the trembling mercenary.

"No more lies now," she said. "I will ask this once, and if I don't like your answer, you will meet your end in the worst way I can think of. Understand?"

"Yes," the mercenary managed.

"Kill him before he spouts any more lies," Laroche said. "The mercenaries of Lockewell are not to be trusted."

"Do not interrupt me again," Skullcrusher admonished Laroche.

"Sorry, Skullcrusher, but it is well known—"

She quieted him with a withering glare. He stepped back, bowing his head. Skullcrusher stared at him for a few moments, wondering why he had chosen that moment to defy her. Then she turned back to the captured fighter. "How did you know we were coming?" she asked.

"We did not …" the man began, stopping himself before he lied. He recomposed himself, and a realization dawned on him. He looked at Laroche. "Is he the Maldovarian?"

All eyes turned to Laroche.

"Why?" Skullcrusher asked.

"We came for him," the man said.

"Lies!" Laroche yelled. He tried to take another step back

but hit Rawk's chest with a thud. The big man placed a vise grip on his shoulder.

"Speak the truth," Skullcrusher told the mercenary.

"He is a spy," he said. "We were told to kill your party and retrieve him alive if we could."

"This *is* an interesting situation," Acasta quipped.

Skullcrusher ignored the mage. "A spy for who?" she asked.

The mercenary blinked, before answering. "Lockewell."

A lot of things happened at once. Laroche tried to break free and run, but Rawk shoved him to the ground and raised his axe to finish the job. Skullcrusher yelled for Rawk to wait, but it was of no importance, as Rawk was suddenly unable to swing down his axe on the frightened Laroche. He grimaced and tried to move his arms, but they were stuck midair.

Acasta stood nearby, his hand poised, a bead of sweat on his brow. "You are strong, big guy. And I mean no disrespect by using my power to keep you from dispatching justice, but we must hear him out first."

"I will kill him, then you. Witch!" Rawk snarled, still frozen, his muscles bulging as he tried to free himself.

"Stop!" Skullcrusher commanded. "He will release you, Rawk, and you will not strike the spy. Yet."

Rawk and Acasta regarded each other, and an uneasy nod passed between them. Acasta lowered his hand. Rawk lowered his weapon soon after, but his rage for Acasta now mirrored his feelings toward Laroche. Skullcrusher grabbed Laroche by the arm and lifted him roughly.

"I'll give you the same warning I gave him," she said, gripping her hammer. "Speak, spy."

Jamie thought Laroche might try to deceive his way out of danger, but instead he sighed and resigned himself to the truth.

"I was a spy," he said. "At first."

Rawk barely restrained himself. "He admits it. Death!"

"Sir Alan Grayfork of Lockewell hired me over a year ago," Laroche explained. "He is a man of great means with plans for many realms, most of all Maldovar."

"I've never heard of him," Skullcrusher said.

"He fancies himself a new kind of ruler," Acasta offered. "Commerce above the old ways of royalty or strength. What was his purpose for hiring you?"

"Like you said, he's a businessman, so he wanted me to spend time in Clem and learn how best to trade with them. *Spy* is a strong word for it. I was more of a liaison or a merchant, really," Laroche claimed, turning to Skullcrusher. "And it was over a year ago, so he sent me to learn about your predecessor. When you took power, I ceased sending him messages almost immediately."

Skullcrusher wasn't impressed. "Almost immediately?"

"I may have kept him updated for a short time, but I did stop, which is probably why they came for me."

Jamie watched Skullcrusher mull Laroche's words. Was she considering letting him go? Eventually she pulled a knife from her belt.

"I believe you," she said. "So, I will give you the choice of the knife or the hammer."

"No, please! I would never betray you! Anke!"

Rawk propped up Laroche as he tried to recoil from Skullcrusher's advance. Rawk looked on in satisfaction.

"If I may," Acasta interjected.

"This isn't your fight, mage," she warned.

Acasta pressed on, trying for his most diplomatic tone.

"While I would dispute that, I have a more important question."

Skullcrusher gritted her teeth. "I will have my justice, and he will have his punishment."

"I have no desire to stand in the way of that, but I don't believe he's told us the full truth yet."

Skullcrusher examined Laroche's fearful face and realized Acasta was right. "Go ahead," she agreed.

"I guess I'm just wondering why Sir Grayfork would send three dozen warriors to dispatch one spy who was no longer even feeding him information. And that information, if we are to believe Laroche here, was simply inside info on how to best fleece Clem on trade deals. That seems like a stretch to me. I don't suppose our mercenary friend would shed any light on it?"

The captured mercenary, who had been content to be the forgotten man, if only for a few minutes, shook his head.

"I figured not," Acasta said. "They don't tell the soldiers anything. Which means we'll need to hear it from the horse's mouth."

All eyes once again turned to Laroche. "If I tell this secret, I am as good as dead."

"No worse off than you might be already," Acasta pointed out.

"Talk or die," Rawk threatened, squeezing Laroche's shoulder so hard it was in danger of separating from the socket.

Laroche squirmed in agony. "Okay! Okay, there's an island!"

"There are many islands," Acasta said, unimpressed.

"A secret island in the South Sea, where soldiers train."

"What soldiers?" Skullcrusher asked.

"Former slaves, criminals, boys like Jamie and Caldred that have been taken from other realms, prisoners of war. It is an army paid for by Sir Grayfork's shadow empire and created for a single purpose: to conquer all the realms," Laroche said. "They call it the Fifth Legion."

Skullcrusher laughed. "You are a crafty and entertaining liar, spy, I will give you that. But any Lockewell army that hopes to conquer all the other realms would have to be thirty thousand strong at least."

"I have heard it to be fifty thousand strong," Laroche said. Acasta examined Laroche's eyes and found no trace of deceit in them. "Even the king doesn't know about them. It is Sir Grayfork's legion to control … and the prince. They scheme together."

"I kill him now?" Rawk asked.

"No. He's coming with us," Skullcrusher declared. "He may prove useful as a hostage."

"Hostage?" Laroche gasped.

"You'd rather I let Rawk dole out your punishment right now?" she spat back.

For once in his life, Laroche bit his tongue and accepted his good fortune without any smart-ass comments.

The mercenary from Lockewell was stripped and sent on his way. He no longer served any purpose as a captive, and Clem tradition frowned upon killing enemy combatants off the battlefield or outside the circle. They could have forced him to fight under Skullcrusher's banner, but he was deemed too cowardly. As for Laroche, his feet and hands were chained, and there was little chance he'd be visiting Skullcrusher's tent anytime soon.

* * *

"It's not wise to sneak up on a mage," Acasta said, not bothering to turn around.

"I didn't mean to sneak," Jamie replied. He watched Acasta brush his horse's mane. The animal looked directly at Jamie and snorted twice.

"He likes you," Acasta said, finally turning to face Jamie.

"He's a beautiful horse. What's his name?"

"Jester."

"Does he have a sense of humor?"

Acasta tilted his head. "I like to think so." He appraised Jamie in the morning sun and focused on his green eyes. They were the same color as Acasta's. Jamie looked down, unnerved.

"How old are you, boy?" he asked.

"I'll be sixteen in a few months."

"Based on your accent, would I be right to assume you were captured in Maldovar and forced into the lady's service, as it were?" He motioned to Skullcrusher.

Jamie nodded. "Wouldn't call her a lady if I were you."

Acasta nodded, knowing just the kind of response he'd get from Skullcrusher if he showed her too much chivalry. "I'm going to ask you something," Acasta said. "It would really help me achieve my objective if you could fly. Or, it would be equally helpful if one of the other boys here could fly. So, yes?"

"No, I'm afraid not."

"You're sure?"

"I think I'd know if I could fly, sir," Jamie said.

"First, don't call me sir. It sounds ridiculous. I prefer Acasta or handsome guy," Acasta snarked. "Second, that's too bad about the flying."

"I was wondering …" Jamie trailed off, unsure of how to

phrase the question. "I don't want to be rude, but I was wondering about our eyes."

"I had a feeling that's why you snuck over here. I'll say this. Green eyes such as ours don't always mean we have inherent abilities. Sometimes they're just eyes. Especially when they're on the face of someone born in Maldovar."

"It's just that my whole life, I've been treated differently because of them," Jamie said. "Almost as if I couldn't be trusted."

"Ah, so you know what it's like to be a mage after all," Acasta grinned.

Jamie smiled back and started to walk away.

"Boy. You never told me your name."

"Jamie," he replied. "But everyone calls me Little Galantra. Kind of a long story."

That got Acasta's attention. He watched Jamie walk away, the knife strapped to his belt, suddenly thinking there might be more to this teenager than just his green eyes and proper grammar.

From the Depths

"He made me tell him," the port guard claimed.

Phaedra pressed the tip of her hook against his neck, trying to read the skinny man's eyes. He wasn't lying.

"I didn't want to say anything about you, but I couldn't resist him … it was like he forced the words to come out of my mouth, I swear!" the guard explained.

So. The bounty hunter had possessed magical abilities. Like she did. Phaedra pulled the hook away from the man's throat. He relaxed and then brightened a bit.

"Your boat is still here, though! He never came back. And I see you have your necklace back."

Phaedra tucked her necklace under her shirt and was about to put her hook back into a makeshift holster on her belt when it suddenly vibrated. Phaedra looked at the miniature trident, surprised. Was she imagining things? It had certainly been a confusing few hours.

"Go," she told the guard.

He didn't waste any time disappearing into the night. Phaedra looked at the hook in her hand and waited. Nothing. She needed sleep. But first she needed to get back on the water. Her dad's boat was right where she'd left it, hidden in plain sight among the other sloops its size in the harbor. She untied the boat and paddled away from Corcoran, less than a week after she arrived, looking for a place to regroup and lay low. Instead, her life was even more complicated than ever. She'd killed a bounty hunter sent by her mother and had discovered she was a witch. Or mage. Or whatever someone like her was called. She knew her father had powers of his own, but he'd been the first in his line to have an extended life; all others died at a normal age, if battle or disease didn't take them sooner. Aside from his near-immortality, however, he had no other magelike talents she knew of.

The hook vibrated again, this time for two straight seconds. It was no illusion. Phaedra stopped adjusting the sails and let the boat glide as she waited for the hook to do something else. She hoped she wasn't losing her mind. A moment later, the metal weapon jiggled in her hand again. It didn't show any signs of stopping, so she lifted it to her face for a closer look. The vibration waned a bit when she did that, so she lowered it again, and the reaction was stronger. She continued moving it around and learned that the closer it was to the water, the more strongly it vibrated. She tried different directions too and started to think the hook might be guiding her somewhere. Or perhaps it was being pulled toward something. The boat cut through the dark water, drifting on a light breeze. The vibration in the hook became weaker, almost as if she was moving away from the source of its reaction.

Phaedra turned the rudder and quickly dropped anchor. She wasn't too far off the coast yet, so the boat stopped in a reasonable amount of time. She pointed the small trident back toward the area the boat just passed through, and the vibration picked up in intensity again. She removed her outer layers of clothing and dived into the frigid waters.

Once she was under the surface, the hook sprang to life. She swam through the murk, trying to follow the strength of the metal's pulsing. Ahead of her, she spotted a glint of silver. Maybe a small shark or other fish cruising about. She continued in the same direction and soon was able to make out the shape of something vaguely triangular. Wait, no, it was spiked. Definitely metal.

Phaedra's heart leapt in her throat as she approached a glistening weapon floating in the ocean. Her father's trident. She almost turned around to swim back to her boat, for fear it was a dangerous illusion, a trap of some kind meant to lure her in. But she couldn't turn away. She reached out her fingers and grasped the long wooden handle, immediately feeling the carved runes in the ancient walnut. She'd held the trident many times before, but when she gripped the weapon tight this time, she felt a strange and powerful current coursing through her body. It was as if she had bonded to the trident. The feeling was like none other she'd experienced. At first, she was excited. Then, she wondered if it meant her father was dead. Why she thought that, she didn't know; it was just a gut reaction. She was brimming with questions and yearned for her dad, his trusted advisor Dall, or even her little brother Artie, but there was nobody here.

* * *

Witch. That would take some getting used to. As she held the Sacred Trident, Phaedra could feel the power of it in a way that made her uneasy about her own body and the weapon itself.

It had never felt that way before.

A few times, when her father had let her swim and hunt with it, the trident seemed to give her confidence, but she always attributed that to her own feelings about the weapon. Now, as she stood on the sloop with the long handle of the family heirloom in her hand, she was more than a princess. She was an instrument of power. They were one, Phaedra and the trident. Why had it abandoned her a few weeks earlier, only to follow her across the ocean?

As she pondered that question, she saw a ripple in the ocean ahead of her. Originally, her plan was to stay close to shore and travel north along the coast, hoping to find a more hospitable place to hide in Maldovar. But the wind and ocean currents had conspired to push her further from land than she intended. The ripples dissipated, then another set appeared less than one hundred feet from her boat.

The trident thrummed with energy, as if it were cautioning Phaedra. Though she needed no warning. She looked more closely at the dark mass under the water and knew something very large was headed right toward her. Bigger than a shark or whale. The distressing part was that she saw no fin sticking out of the water. Combined with its size, that meant it could only be one thing: a leviathan.

Phaedra cursed herself for letting the current take her this far from the shallows in unfamiliar water. She moved to the back of the small boat and set her feet, poised to jump in any direction. She waited for what felt like an eternity for the monster to emerge from the water, but the attack didn't come. Had she misjudged the movement of the waves? Imagined it? Or maybe the creature was simply passing by and hadn't noticed her boat at all.

Phaedra peered down at the water on either side of the boat and saw no signs of the creature, so she turned to check the sloop's wake. Phaedra lurched backward in shock when she saw the sea serpent's massive head above the stern of the boat, its silver eyes fixed on her. Phaedra's breath caught in her throat as she stared at the huge water snake. She'd never seen one in person but had heard the tales of sailors being sliced in half by a leviathan's powerful jaws; each fang was as long as a sword and twice as hard as steel. Even if a fang somehow failed to make a kill with sheer force, the leviathan's venom was deadly enough to kill a whale, let alone a human.

Phaedra considered trying to stab at it with the trident but recognized the futility of such a move. If the snake wanted, it could use its body to overturn her boat, and no matter how good a swimmer Phaedra was, she would be no match for the beast underwater. Besides, it was likely so fast, it could strike her before she moved her weapon.

And so, they regarded each other for a few moments. Easily the scariest seconds of Phaedra's life. Finally, the leviathan tilted its head and seemed to push against Phaedra's mind with its own thoughts. Phaedra felt a coldness in her body as something slithered into her consciousness.

"Daughter of Waves," a voice hissed.

Phaedra looked at the serpent before her. It hadn't moved its mouth. This was all happening either in Phaedra's mind or on a telepathic level.

"Yes," the snake's voice affirmed.

"How is this possible?" Phaedra asked. Only she didn't use her voice. She simply thought the words. They must have found their way into the leviathan's mind, for it nodded its prodigious head.

"Our minds are bonded, young one," the snake communicated.

Great. The only thing more distressing than battling a snake the size of a ship was being bonded with one.

"You are right to be scared," it said.

The serpent's head and body were covered in dark scales that shimmered in the moonlight, reflecting the moon at some angles and turning black as the void the next moment. It was a beautiful creature. Terrifying, but beautiful. Phaedra wondered how many people had seen a leviathan up close long enough to admire it.

"What do you want?" Phaedra asked, this time aloud.

"It is not what I want, Daughter of Waves, it is what we are meant to do together," the snake communicated.

"Together?"

"Humans are not alone in their fates and destinies. Even the lowliest fish of the sea has a purpose, and as you can see, I am no lowly fish. I am Princess Elok. Oh yes, like you, I too am a princess. Only I have been one for nearly two hundred years."

"And you seek me?"

"I seek peace for humanity. Your father understood this."

"You know my father?"

"Ha! He is the king of the ocean and as much a father to me as he was to you, in different ways."

Phaedra reeled at the information being revealed to her. It was too much all at once, and she felt her knees going weak. She sagged to the edge of the boat and sat down.

Elok suddenly snapped her head to the side and narrowed her great silver eyes. "I can feel a ship approaching. We must not linger here. You will follow me northeast to the home of my kin."

Phaedra was hesitant. "I … do not understand."

"There is no time, Princess. You will follow me, or you will die. Many people on many ships have set out to find you. It is only a matter of time. The choice is yours."

Elok slipped beneath the surface, leaving nary a ripple this time. Phaedra remained frozen, awed by her encounter and all the snake had told her. In the distance, to the south, she saw a faint light cutting through the night fog. A ship's lantern. And it was growing in intensity.

Phaedra grabbed the rigging and had a decision to make—follow the leviathan or continue up the coast in search of a new place to hide. She took a deep breath and realized it was no decision at all. Phaedra set sail for open water, feeling like the princess she imagined her father would want her to be.

The Silver Castle

The messenger sheepishly backed out of the room, having delivered his report. Sir Grayfork waited until the meek boy shut the door to the chamber, then sighed heavily.

"Things must be going well if news of that nature warrants little more than an annoyed sigh," Philipa Black said.

Sir Grayfork raised an eyebrow and turned to the third person in the room, Prince Cecil Harwick, son of the king. He was an ambitious young man of twenty, like his father in many respects, save one: he was far more vicious. This was no small feat given the iron-fisted manner in which the king ruled Lockewell. The prince's dashing looks and charm only made him even more dangerous. He and Sir Grayfork understood each other perfectly.

"One spy escapes, while a dozen others stay in place," the prince said. "Even an old political hack like you should understand that. Honestly, Roy, why do we bother with people like her?"

Black bowed her head, not so much admitting she was wrong as not wanting to challenge the prince and get on his bad side.

"We have more important matters to discuss," Sir Grayfork

said, changing the subject. "An attempt on my life will be made tonight."

"I can't say I blame them," Prince Cecil said. "Who did you piss off this time?"

"It seems our plan to subjugate Maldovar has earned us a few enemies. While I don't find that surprising, the fact that Henry Martin is part of the cabal trying to kill me does trouble me. Mostly in my choice of allies," Sir Grayfork said. He turned to Black.

"I'm almost proud of him, to be honest," Black said. "I didn't know the limp prick had it in him."

"Are you speaking from personal experience? Because I could imagine many men having that problem with you," Prince Cecil sniped.

Black obliged him with a smile before she spoke to Sir Grayfork. "You knowing about the plot does speak more to the kind of slaying planning I'd expect from him, though. Well-intentioned but amateurish."

"Our source says Martin and Viceroy Renner, among others, have enlisted the services of the Butcher of the East for the job," Sir Grayfork explained.

"That fat bastard," the prince spat.

"In an attempt at subterfuge, the Butcher enlisted the help of a poisoner, as opposed to employing his usual methods of stabbings, faked suicides, and the like," Sir Grayfork said. "Fortune has smiled upon us, my friends."

"How so?" Prince Cecil asked.

"I think we should let this slayer do his work," Sir Grayfork replied. He gave the prince and Black a few moments to mull over that comment. When neither figured out his plan, Sir Grayfork smirked. "Only instead of killing me, we trick him into killing the king."

* * *

The dark castle rose up from the rocks and shale, nearly indistinguishable from the night sky, save for the torches and tower lamps illuminating its outline. Called the Silver Castle, it was decidedly black. The structure was designed by King Stracken, a builder turned king nearly two centuries earlier, and his attention to detail was still serving the rulers of Lockewell to this day. The castle he created was surrounded by three separate walls. The outer wall was the tallest and thickest and was set on the edge of a murky moat, famed for its foul smell and the many eels and venomous fish that were dumped into it each year. The drawbridge over the moat was fifty feet long when lowered, and once you crossed it, you had to get through two gates to reach the second wall. Beyond that, a series of guard towers were connected by an iron fence with thick bars every eight inches.

No army had ever breached the outer wall, let alone crossed the moat.

No army had tried in over a hundred years.

Dormond smiled to himself as he strolled across the drawbridge. He was not an army, after all. He was just one man, and he knew that sometimes where thousands of men failed, one could succeed. The handsome slayer ran a hand through his thick, curly hair and then produced a letter from his finely embroidered silk tunic. He paused a respectable distance behind a small group of socialites as they spoke with the guards at the gate who were receiving the guests.

"They weren't exaggerating the smell," a man said.

Dormond turned to acknowledge the people behind him with a slight bow. "My lord. My lady. First time here, I presume?"

The couple nodded, crinkling their noses. Dormond returned a serious look. "The price you pay for security," he said. "Though I'm told you can hardly smell it once you're inside the eighth wall."

"Eight? I was told there were only three!" the lord exclaimed. His wife rolled her eyes.

"He's having a little fun with you, Arthur," she said.

"I meant no offense, my lord," Dormond apologized with another bow. "In my line of work, I've developed the habit of letting my imagination run away with itself."

"And what line of work is that?" the lady asked.

"Forgive me, my lady. My name is Daren Haverford. I sell ships."

"Ah, a shipbuilder," the lord said, intrigued.

"Wish that I were, but I've never been any good with an ax or a saw," Dormond said. "I merely sell the ships. Not to be too gauche and speak of business at a social affair, but I plan to sell a few tonight to the crown."

Dormond winked conspiratorially, and his new friends nodded again, entertained by their new acquaintance and his schemes. They reached the gate together, as Dormond planned, and were quickly let into the castle upon presenting their letters of invitation. It was much easier to be inconspicuous when laughing and chatting with nobility than it was to be an unknown merchant trying to enter the king's gala alone. Once they were inside, Dormond begged off joining them for a drink, instead disappearing into the crowd of nobles, wealthy merchants, ladies of the court, and a surprising number of the king's men. Dormond slipped into an alcove of the great hall, and from there made his way down a corridor leading to the kitchens. Before he emerged from the corridor, he'd shed the fashionable silk tunic and was now wearing the nondescript shirt and leggings of a servant. He produced a hat from his pocket and tucked his hair under it.

King Edward was notoriously cheap, preferring to keep a barebones castle staff unless he was forced to hire extra help for social events. The celebration of Lockewell's quincentenary qualified as such an occasion, so it was easy for Dormond to blend in with the scores of temporary hired help. Most of them were unknown to the head cook. Dormond navigated his way past the food-prep area where pheasants and ducks were being butchered by the dozen, and searched out the select wines for the head table.

A burly guard stood watch alongside the king's personal taster. Dormond had no interest in the king's special cask. He had his eyes on the various drinks set aside for the rest of the nobles who would flank the king at his table that evening. Stopping to stir a bowl of mashed potatoes, he scanned the drinks table and found the specific wine he was looking for: a red flagon with the crest of House Roy on it. Dormond waited until a portly server walked by, then promptly tripped the man, causing him to drop an entire pot of porridge onto the floor. The thick white soup splattered at the guard's feet, soiling his boots and trousers.

"You clumsy fool!" the guard howled, stepping forward to rap the server on the head with an open palm. The poor staffer went tumbling to the stone floor, getting a face full of porridge. By the time the guard was done berating the server, Dormond had slipped the foxglove extract into the wine flagon and disappeared from sight.

A few minutes later, content his job was completed, Dormond emerged from the alcove, once again dressed the part of a ship salesman. He acquired a mug of ale from a serving wench and mingled with the lords and ladies, keeping tabs on the comings and goings of the high table. King Edward and his queen dined and received court members. The prince and a few nobles Dormond didn't know were there as well, drinking and cavorting. Sir Grayfork's seat was empty.

"Ah, here he is. Daren!" Lord Arthur called.

Dormond turned to see the lord escorting a tall, handsome man toward him. Sir Grayfork.

"This is the shipman I was telling you about," Arthur said, before turning to Dormond. "May I present Sir Alan Grayfork of the Merchant Royal."

Sir Grayfork offered a wolfish grin in Dormond's direction, meeting the slayer's eyes. Dormond concealed his surprise and smiled back.

"Daren Haverford, at your service," Dormond said with a slight bow.

"Indeed, so Lord Arthur tells me. As a man always in need of ships, I was interested to make your acquaintance," Sir Grayfork said. "I must apologize, as I've not heard your name before. And I have to further beg your pardon, as I don't recall seeing your name on the guest list."

"The need for a pardon is entirely mine, I assure you," Dormond responded smoothly. "My name is only known to my customers, of which I would like to consider you someday. The Merchant Royal could certainly benefit from the fastest and finest schooners on the sea."

"I do like the finest things," Sir Grayfork said, snapping

his fingers. A server appeared with the very flagon of wine Dormond recently poisoned. He poured three cups for Sir Grayfork, Dormond and Lord Arthur. Sir Grayfork picked up the cup for Dormond and handed it to him. Dormond accepted the wine, his face betraying no trace of concern.

"What shall we drink to, I wonder?" Sir Grayfork pondered.

"New and lasting relationships?" Dormond offered.

Lord Arthur smiled cheerily and raised his wine. "To new friends and associates!" Then he clinked his cup against those of Sir Grayfork and Dormond, and drained it. Sir Grayfork glared at Dormond as he too drank from the poisoned wine. Dormond followed suit, calculating how long he had before he needed to take the antidote stashed inside his sleeve. Twenty, maybe thirty seconds.

"That certainly is a fine Maldovarian red. Wouldn't you say?" Sir Grayfork beamed.

"Splendid," Dormond replied, readying himself to make a quick exit.

"The king!" someone shrieked.

Dormond looked to the high table, where King Edward was convulsing in his chair, a trail of pink foam oozing from the corner of his mouth. Just as he fell face-first into his food, the queen also began to spasm.

"The wine is poisoned!" a man yelled, and all mayhem broke out. Dormond tried to step away, but a firm hand gripped his shoulder. Sir Grayfork stared daggers at him.

"Stay to watch what you've done," Sir Grayfork growled.

Dormond saw the scene unfolding at the high table. The king was dead, the queen was well on her way, and two other people were also in the throes of the foxglove powder.

How is this possible? he thought.

Sir Grayfork barely restrained his glee as he watched the guests scurrying around. "The Butcher isn't as secretive as he once was, I suppose."

"You knew?" Dormond asked. Then it dawned on him. "And you switched the wine … but why?"

"Why would I want to live? Or why would I want my king to die?"

Dormond watched as the prince rushed to his father's side.

"He's on our side," Sir Grayfork said, motioning to the prince, the only person at the high table who wasn't retching or dead.

"Our?" Dormond said, confused.

"I can always use another spy, especially one with talent," Sir Grayfork said, relaxing his grip on Dormond's shoulder. "I should probably go assist my king. The new one."

Sir Grayfork patted Dormond on the back and hurried to the high table, feigning concern for all to see. Dormond regarded the scene, finally unclenching his hand that had been gripping the antidote for the last minute. He exhaled and took a sip of the nonpoisoned wine in his hand. Good. He was tired of being on the losing side anyway.

Advance Warning

The Halfmoon nocked another arrow and took aim, this time more carefully than before. He spat a few words in ancient Clem and released the metal-tipped arrow, missing the carrier pigeon. Again.

This time the bird was smart enough to turn back the way it came, flapping its wings in a burst of speed, trying to escape the threat from below. Rawk roared at the Halfmoon in disgust. Caldred took off after the bird, hoping to keep pace with it on the ground. He disappeared into the woods.

"That one is fast," Acasta said, watching the branches sway in Caldred's wake. "But not fast enough."

Acasta closed his eyes and began to focus his mind. Jamie raised an eyebrow at Skullcrusher and Rawk, then watched Acasta take a deep, purposeful breath. His muscles tensed.

A caw from above. Jamie looked up to see the pigeon returning to the camp, but it was flying oddly, as if fighting its own wings. Rawk tracked from the bird to Acasta, the realization dawning on the big warrior that Acasta was controlling the animal with his mind.

"Not natural," Rawk muttered. He took a small step away from the mage.

Without breaking his concentration, Acasta grimaced. "And not easy. This bird has a stronger will than many people I know. Think your half-blind archer can hit him this time?"

Not wanting to take any chances, Skullcrusher grabbed the bow from the Halfmoon and took the shot herself. It lanced one of the bird's wings and brought it down in a flurry of flapping and squawking. Acasta relaxed his body and rolled his neck. The others looked at him with a newfound mix of respect and wariness.

Skullcrusher came back from the brush with the now-dead bird in her hands. She removed the small scroll that was strung to its leg and tossed the carcass aside. Using the tip of her dagger, she ripped the seal of the note and unrolled it.

"Code," she snarled.

"Surely someone here can decipher it?" Acasta wondered aloud, looking at Laroche, who was sitting on the ground leaned against a tree, his hands and feet bound by chains. Rawk thudded over and lifted Laroche up with one hand, dragging him to Skullcrusher and discarding him at the Clem leader's feet.

"I would've walked if given the chance," Laroche said, though nobody cared.

"Tell us what it says," Skullcrusher demanded.

Laroche took the note from her and studied it for a few moments. His expression darkened.

"Well?" Acasta asked.

"I should clarify that it was meant for the mercenaries of this camp, not me," Laroche answered. He raised his nervous eyes to look at Skullcrusher. "Were it sent to me directly, I would have warned you."

She responded by hefting her war hammer. "The message.

Now."

Laroche sighed, not wanting to relay the contents of the scroll. "The Fifth Legion is on the march. They have their first target and will arrive within days. Clem."

By the time Rawk was done shouting about all the ways he'd like to kill, bash, and dismember Laroche, not necessarily in that order, Skullcrusher had decided the group would need to return to Clem through the mountains, in hopes of warning her people in time to prepare for the Lockewell legion. Laroche would be going with them, Skullcrusher proclaimed.

"Alive," she had told Rawk. Laroche had proven useful, she explained to the grizzled warrior, and there was no benefit in killing him anytime soon. Rawk accepted her orders; between the traitorous Laroche and the mysterious Acasta, however, he was growing more cantankerous by the hour.

Acasta was not keen on heading west to Clem, but he knew this was where he was meant to be. He pulled Jamie aside as everyone gathered their supplies for the trip to Kragon's Lair.

"I don't suppose big nasty will be training you and the other boy in the mornings anymore," Acasta said, motioning to Rawk, who was busy sharpening his ax blade.

"His name is Lukas," Jamie replied. "And no, I don't expect there will be time for deer-hunting lessons on the way to Clem."

Acasta nodded, appraising Skullcrusher's manservant. "Handles himself well for such a skinny boy. Though I guess that isn't rare in this group. From what I saw yesterday during the fighting, your friend Caldred also seems to have a knack for staying alive."

Jamie tossed a pack over his shoulder. He had taken it from one of the tents in the camp and stuffed it full of supplies the dead Lockewell mercenaries would no longer be needing: two shirts, socks, five different blades, and plenty of jerky, among other items. He was wearing claimed clothes as well, including new boots.

"Why are you coming with us?" Jamie asked.

"The same reason you're going."

"I'm one of Skullcrusher's soldiers. I don't have a choice," Jamie said.

"I don't have a choice either," Acasta said, mounting Jester with a smooth ease Jamie envied. "Until I hear otherwise from my queen, you're all stuck with me."

Acasta flashed a bright smile and urged Jester on, leading him toward Skullcrusher's horse. They would all be traveling on horseback, except for Rawk, who had commandeered a wagon and four steeds to shoulder the burden of his great weight.

Caldred struggled to direct his gray mare over to Jamie, who had climbed upon a black stallion that was giving him fits.

"He looks like he wants to throw you," Caldred noted.

"Because he does, and he probably will," Jamie said, patting the horse on the neck. It only seemed to annoy the animal.

"A couple weeks ago, if you told me we'd be riding on dead men's horses to save Clem from a secret army, after having crossed the sea on a schooner called *The Bitch's Roar*, I would've said you were a damn fool that smoked too much poppy," Caldred said.

"A couple of weeks ago, I was worried you stole the money I needed to buy flour for my aunt's blueberry muffins," Jamie replied.

Caldred laughed heartily at that. "I think I prefer soldiering to thieving."

"Says the guy sitting on a stolen horse wearing clothes he nicked from a corpse," Jamie said. He grabbed the reins and tried to control the stallion once more. "C'mon, Shadow, don't make me ask twice."

"Shadow?"

"Every horse needs a name," Jamie replied.

Final Days

The king's eyes fluttered open as he awoke from a deep sleep. He tried to rise from the bed, but his limbs felt weighted down, as if he were leagues under the sea. His heart was a mere whisper of its former strength, and his throat was constricted to the point of choking him.

"Water?" Arthur asked.

King Bane watched his young son put down a book and bring over a mug of water for him. Reading. He could scarcely remember a time when the prince didn't have his nose buried in a book or a set of maps, learning about the world instead of actually experiencing it. There was still time for him, the king hoped.

Time.

He used to have all the time in the world, now his life was finally ending. Even at three centuries old, he found himself dwelling on the regrets of his life. The loves he had lost. The adventures not taken. Now he was an old man being watched over by a child while his wife ruled the kingdom in his stead. He would never see Phaedra again, he knew. She had fled the island to escape her own mother.

"Drink, Father," Arthur said, putting the mug to the king's

lips and carefully pouring some water past them. "Did you dream about her again?"

"No," the king lied.

"Treat me as a child if you wish, but unlike your subjects and sycophants, I can tell when you are lying," Arthur told him.

"It's too early in the morning for such big words, son."

Arthur cast open the curtains, letting in bright rays of sunshine. The king squinted at the midday sun. "Oh," he said.

"Yes, oh," Arthur replied. "You sleep too long when you should be settling your affairs."

"Not a sentimental bone in your body, is there?"

Arthur shrugged. "I am not built that way. I do love you and wish you weren't dying, but I have no power to change that."

"And what makes you think a man of my age has not had ample time to settle his affairs?" the king asked.

"You left Mother in charge," Arthur explained. "Some would argue that is complicating your affairs, at least for your heirs and kingdom, if those are concerns of yours."

"What would you have me do?" King Bane asked. His son was only eleven summers old but possessed the wisdom of men five times his age. While the king didn't always listen to his advice, he usually enjoyed hearing it. Given his current condition, the banter with his son was bittersweet, but he waited patiently for Arthur to compose his thoughts, nonetheless. He knew the boy already had a plan in mind well before he was asked the question.

"Now? Nothing can be done. Mother never should have been put in power. She is a vindictive, selfish woman. Look at me like that all you want, but you know I am right. She loves neither me nor my sister. You should have named Phaedra the Queen-in-Waiting, as is the old custom. I read about it in Marder's Journals. There is plenty of precedent. But by naming Mother as your successor, you drove off the person you care about most in the world. Although …"

The king watched the boy's mind chew on something.

"Yes?" King Bane asked.

"Although perhaps that is what you wanted. Maybe you know something of the prophecy the rest of us do not. That Phaedra had another part to play before she could truly rule Skybane … and beyond."

The king forced himself to sit up in bed so he could look his son in the eyes. The boy shared few physical attributes with his father, save his silver eyes. Behind them, the king knew an amazing mind was at work.

"You know I love your sister dearly and believe she is destined for greatness," the king said. "But that does not diminish what a leader you could have been if you were the firstborn. Not a leader like me, or anyone that has come before me in the Bane bloodline, but a great ruler nonetheless."

The prince smiled and stepped closer to the king. "So, I'm right, then?"

With what little strength he could muster, the king laughed. "She must fight in many battles far from these shores, yes."

"I knew it!" Arthur exclaimed. "Does the prophecy say anything about me?"

"It says the second-born is too curious for his own good and must now fetch his father's advisers for him."

Arthur rolled his eyes and headed for the thick oak door, but it was already swinging open as he approached. Queen Perrin entered, followed by a flurry of servants. She regarded Arthur with cold eyes.

"Your father needs rest, Arthur," she said.

"Then his father would rather not be overrun," the king complained as he watched the servants set about cleaning and straightening his room.

"I look forward to talking with you more tomorrow, Father. I have much reading to do now."

"Of that I have no doubt," the king replied with a wink.

Queen Perrin watched the boy leave, then turned to her husband. "Sharing secrets, are we?" When she received no response, the queen harrumphed her displeasure. "At the very least, you should encourage him to undertake weapons training as befitting a prince of Skybane."

"I believe that is now your job," King Bane teased. "And I wish you luck in that endeavor."

Queen Perrin smiled and sat at the edge of the bed. She looked at her husband. When they had first met, he'd swept her off her feet; he was a strong, romantic man, and he'd stayed that way for the entirety of their marriage, up until the last few weeks, when his health rapidly deteriorated. As she considered his faint features and withering arms, the king smiled.

"What could possibly be funny?" she asked.

"I was remembering when you used to worry that I'd grow tired of you as you aged and I didn't," the king said. "It seems the gods had a different idea."

"You mention the gods? Now I know you're not doing well." The queen gave him a fresh mug of water to drink and waited for him to finish. "Better?"

The king took his wife's hand, feeling wistful. "Promise me something. Do not punish Phaedra or Arthur for any of my sins."

And your sins are many, the queen thought. She stood back up, and a coldness returned to her, the nostalgia gone.

"Phaedra cannot be allowed to wander the world. It is dangerous and an insult to my rule," she said. "I will see her back at my side here at The Falls."

"You must do what you feel is right, as a queen and as a mother."

"Do you doubt I would?"

The king sighed, the mere act of staying awake too much for him. He shook his head. "I did not think I would fade so quickly."

"I asked you a question, husband."

The king's eyes drooped as he tried to focus on her. His throat was constricting again.

"As you seem to be too weak to answer, I will answer for you," she said. "I will do what is necessary, always. Starting with restoring the belief in the gods to this realm. Too long have the people ignored the will of the gods, as have you. Now you let your daughter escape on the very night of my ascendancy."

King Bane tried to interrupt, but his speech faltered. He wheezed, grabbing for the water. The queen looked at the mug.

"Are you sure you want more of that?" she asked. Her meaning dawned on him as he struggled to breathe. The queen sighed. "I loved you once. Perhaps I still do. But I cannot let those emotions stand in the way of a path back to fealty and morality. The words of a witch and a false god will not determine our daughter's path—or mine."

The queen rose from the bed, not to leave the room, but to watch the king struggle. It gave her no pleasure to do so, nor did she feel remorse for poisoning him. It was merely what had to be done for the good of the realm. *For the good of all realms*, she reminded herself.

Reguirs

The winds from the west were unusually strong, whipping up sand and making the trials that much more difficult for the reguirs as they struggled to maintain their focus.

It was not such a bad thing, Amira decided.

These were troubling times for all, including those burdened with the pressure of being ordained mages of Tufthorn. Better to remain a reguir if a little sand or wind can keep one from performing their magic at a level befitting the title of mage. As the queen of Tufthorn and its chief sorcerer, Amira was responsible for all magic-born throughout the realms. Their actions reflected on her performance as a leader.

She stood on a dais above the holy arena, flanked by dozens of mages and hundreds of Tufthorn citizens, observing the five reguirs. Tradition dictated that a quorum of twenty ordained mages must be present, along with a contingent of citizens, to witness the Reguirvorn, when graduates of the Institute attempt to prove their worth as full-fledged sorcerers. Since the first Reguirvorn, about half of all graduates had passed the test. A reguir was allowed to participate in three such trials in successive years. If by the third attempt, they still cannot please the head sorcerer, they must have their magic burned away in a painful and tedious process, so there is no chance they misuse their talents.

A tall, lanky reguir stood in the middle of the arena, hurling fireballs at a moving target fifty feet away. Amira's pride in the young man's talent swelled as she watched him control the fire like a seasoned mage. The crowd roared as he obliterated the wooden target entirely with a final blast of force. He looked up to the dais for approval. Amira met his gaze and nodded. The reguir bowed and exited the pit. Moments later, a teenage, female reguir with flowing black hair walked to the center of the pit. Amira had spent a considerable amount of time with the young woman during her training, and while the queen hoped for the best, she assumed the reguir would need another year or two of practice before she mastered her talent.

As the girl prepared herself, Amira felt a chill run down her spine. *Strange.* It was not uncommon for the queen to sense the gathering of power by another mage—each sorcerer had a unique signature in their talent that skilled mages could recognize—but this reguir was gathering a magnitude of power Amira had not experienced since …

Amira's thoughts were interrupted by a terrible shriek of laughter. The queen looked down at the girl in the pit and saw her eyes gleaming with rage and delight. Instead of focusing her will toward the wooden target, she spun to face the queen and extended her hand. The last thing Amira noticed before a bright wall of flame shot toward her was the girl's hair morphing from black to white.

* * *

Amira opened her eyes, and the world was a blurry mess of fast-moving colors and smears of light. Everywhere around her, people shouted and cursed. The ancient dais beneath Amira buckled and cracked as it absorbed direct impacts, threatening to collapse. The only reason the queen was even alive was because she'd been able to muster a defensive charm in time to blunt the force of the attack from the reguir.

No. Not a reguir.

Osprey.

The evil witch had disguised herself as the young graduate to gain entrance to the arena, and she was now battling a score of Tufthorn's mages. Duty pushed Amira to her feet. Still wobbly, she scanned the destruction and strewn bodies, trying to locate Osprey amid the fires and mayhem. Her eyes came across men in light armor. They were dull-eyed and robotic in their pursuit and slaughter of Amira's people. Bewitched! Osprey not only dared to break The Code, she did so to kill innocents in Tufthorn's capital. Rage boiled in Amira's veins, and she unleashed a blast of energy so focused, it not only bored a hole directly through one of Osprey's men, it created a two-foot-deep trough in the ground twenty feet past him. The man's top half fell over, while his legs crumpled to the dirt.

One of Amira's personal guards, a stout mage-warrior named Halifor, arrived at her side. He wore chainmail under leather and carried a blood-soaked scimitar. "It is the White Locust. We must get you to safety," he urged. The queen pushed his hand off her elbow and continued to survey the ghoulish scene in the pit below.

"Until every one of my people in this arena is safe, I shall not shrink from the fight," she said. "Where is Osprey?"

"Last I saw, Tarnir and Soledad chased her into the catacombs beneath the arena. They are both dead now." Halifor knew the queen would not back down, and so he'd brought her weapons belt, complete with a pair of short swords, one on each side.

Amira struggled to control her anger as she strapped on the belt. "Follow me," she hissed. "And make sure this message gets to Acasta. Send our fastest raven."

The queen handed over a small scroll. As they left the room, Halifor passed off the message to another guard. "Do not fail," he commanded, and the guard immediately set off for the aviary.

Amira and Halifor stalked the tunnels leading to the ground floor. Spectators continued to flee the arena while Tufthorn's remaining mages fought Osprey's army of bewitched soldiers. The invaders looked to be rogues and nomads, trained in the art of killing. Halifor saw Amira doing the math and offered his assessment. "We have lost half the mages who were present at the trials, and the day is not done," he said, hoping to change her mind about confronting Osprey directly. A veteran of many fierce battles with outlaws, he was not a man who knew fear for himself. He was concerned for his queen.

"I shall stop her this night or I shall die trying," Amira said. With the next breath, she uttered a curse, flicked her hand, and the large ax-wielding man that had just appeared in front of her went careening backward into the wall with a sickening thud. Dead on impact. Halifor grunted his approval. Amira removed the twin short swords from her belt and picked up her pace.

"Where are we going?" Halifor asked.

"The Moonrise Garden," Amira replied. "That is where Osprey means to challenge me."

A five-acre oasis in the middle of Kanhara, Tufthorn's capital city, the Moonrise Garden was a sacred place where mages had sought respite from the vast desert surrounding the city. More than twenty types of trees and hundreds of species of plants and flowers dotted the garden. Just that morning, Amira had been meditating under her favorite poplar when she glimpsed Acasta's fortune; he had found the Promised Knight. He just didn't know it yet. She hoped her raven would get to him soon enough.

The chaos at the arena had been a diversion, of course. Osprey was here for one person and one person alone. While the mages battled the invaders at the arena, the garden was empty, save Osprey, standing among purple lilies in an open stretch between a dozen apple trees. She grinned at Amira as the queen rounded the corner, Halifor walking next to her.

"I'm impressed you showed up," Osprey said, her bright white hair gently blowing in the breeze. She was still wearing the simple garb of a reguir. "Not alone, though, so that makes it a bit less brave. Not that you became queen through acts of bravery. I see you still have your watchdog with you."

Halifor stepped forward, his face red with anger, but Amira held up a hand. "This is not your fight," she told him.

"My queen—"

"Has given you a command," Osprey interrupted. Before Halifor could react, Osprey had lanced his shoulder with a large rock from the pond near him. It happened so fast he barely had time to move his head out of the way. The flying rock knocked him off his feet, and he crumpled to the ground. Amira threw up a defensive globe around Halifor and turned to Osprey.

"Bitch," she uttered.

"Well, that isn't very royal and proper now, is it?" Osprey teased.

The two women slowly circled each other. They had sparred many times when Osprey was still recognized as a true mage of Tufthorn, and she had even taught a young Amira how to better channel her powers. Osprey had been cast out for her crimes when Amira was not yet fourteen; Amira lived her whole life in Tufthorn and rose through the ranks of the mages. Osprey considered herself the most powerful mage in all the realms; Amira felt the same way about her own talents.

The air crackled between them, thrumming with energy as the two sorcerers gathered their will and strength. A loud croak from above drew their attention. Amira's eyes went wide, but Osprey was too quick. The white-haired witch clenched her fist, and a raven dropped from the sky, its lifeless body splashing into a pond between the two women.

Amira used that brief distraction to send a flurry of blue fireballs at Osprey, who leapt fifteen feet into the air onto the branch of a nearby apple tree. Amira tried again, this time whipping her arm in an arc that expelled a thin slice of air that split the trunk of the apple tree in two. Osprey neatly hopped to the ground as the tree fell apart behind her.

"This is fun!" she exclaimed. "Even more fun than I had with your lover in the desert."

Amira grimaced at the mention of Acasta. They had never been lovers; Osprey knew that. "What do you want?" Amira asked.

"It's very simple, really," she said, sweeping her hand to clear the tree debris out of her way like it was a pile of leaves a little gust of wind had blown aside. "To destroy this city and its queen along with it."

"Oh, is that all?"

"No, it's not all by half. But rather than waste time explaining it to you, I'll just go ahead and make it happen," Osprey said, feigning boredom. Then she snapped her fingers and a dozen bewitched soldiers rushed in from the shadows, where they'd been lying in wait.

Amira cursed herself for falling into Osprey's trap, but her anger lasted only a moment, as she quickly centered herself and faced Osprey's followers head-on. She used one hand to throw up a defensive shield of compressed air, at the same time employing the rest of her talent to lift three of the soldiers high into the night sky, before making a fist and smashing them to the ground. Swords and axes pummeled the invisible, magic bubble around her. It blunted the blows, ensuring no blade cut her, but the force of those impacts knocked her sideways. She lost her concentration long enough for the magic shield to evaporate. The closest two fighters pounced on her, and each was quickly slashed with one of her short swords. Amira jumped to her feet and was about to attack the closest person to her when she saw Halifor's familiar face looking back at her. He withdrew his own sword from the opponent he just killed and went back-to-back with Amira.

"You didn't think I'd let you have all this fun without me?" he wheezed, raw pain in his voice.

They were outnumbered three to one by bewitched soldiers, and that wasn't counting Osprey, who was just enjoying the show for the moment. Out of the corner of his eye, Halifor saw the witch smiling at the scene in delight. He growled and stomped his foot on the ground, sending a shockwave in her direction that surprised her, knocking her over.

Amira dispatched a foe with her blade and then glanced at

Osprey, who was now running their way.

"Pissing her off. That's one way to handle it," Amira said.

"Better to fight them all together than to wait for her to find just the right moment!" Halifor yelled back. He grunted in anger as he blended his natural muscle speed with his magical force to kick a man twenty feet to his death.

Amira saw Osprey leap into the sky toward her and Halifor. The queen summoned all her strength and screamed loudly with her swords to the sky, calling down a bolt of lightning that electrified everyone but her and Halifor. The men collapsed to the ground, stunned, but Osprey was unaffected, coasting toward the defenseless Amira with both hands clutching a ball of flame. Halifor met the mighty sorcerer in midair and struck at her chest with his scimitar. Osprey's defensive magic was too great, however, and his sword snapped in half like a twig against stone. Osprey counterattacked with a flame-tinged punch to Halifor's head, and the veteran warrior tumbled to the earth, his face and neck charred beyond recognition. His final act was to protect his queen, who was now enraged at seeing his dead body. She spun to face Osprey once more, this time hurling one of her swords at the white-haired sorcerer like a huge throwing knife. It moved with the speed of Amira's anger and landed in Osprey's leg, burying itself six inches into the meat of her thigh. She went down, fury mixed with pain as she howled and got a defensive shield just in time to stop the follow-up attack from Amira.

Osprey sat up to face the queen, who held her short sword at the ready, waiting for Osprey to tire. The blood was leaking from her leg, and it was only a matter of time. Normally, Amira bowed to tradition, which in this case would mean sparing Osprey's life if she requested to be judged by a tribunal of mages. But Amira wasn't feeling particularly generous or bound by The Code at the moment.

"Osprey Sunbringer, exiled mage of Tufthorn," Amira said, pointing her sword. "For the lives you have taken here in the sacred city and throughout the realms, I, Queen Amira, Chief Sorcerer of Tufthorn and Judger of Oaths, sentence you to death."

"I knew you had it in you," Osprey hissed. "When it comes down to it, even the righteous and pious Amira sets aside the rules to mete out her own punishment."

Amira wavered for a breath, then looked at Halifor's ruined face and steeled herself. "Release your shield and receive your judgment. Witch."

"My queen," a voice said. Amira turned to see the tall, young reguir from the arena approaching. He saw her threatening Osprey with her sword, and he tried to reconcile that sight with the idea that the queen was above personal vengeance. "Has she not yielded?"

"I have indeed," Osprey said, waving her hand. The force around her dissipated with a brief puff of wind. She looked at Amira, daring her to attack. It would mean her life, but it would also mean the queen would break The Code in front of a reguir.

Amira took another step toward Osprey, her sword poised to strike. From somewhere inside of her, she found the will to stop herself at the moment. "You will be judged and put to death. Of that I am certain." Amira lowered her sword.

"I think not," Osprey chirped.

A pain bloomed in Amira's back and chest. She felt the dagger pierce her heart and looked over her shoulder to the reguir. He had stabbed her in the back. Amira struggled to a knee and saw the reguir's dull eyes staring back at her, devoid of emotion.

"The poor boy, he should at least know what he's done," Osprey said. Then she released him from her spell. His eyes turned back to green, and he looked at the queen, then at the bloody dagger in her back. As the realization of his actions dawned on him, Osprey used her powers to expel the dagger from Amira's body and fling it at him. It slid across the reguir's neck, and he clutched at the wound. It was of no use. He bled out in seconds.

Osprey yanked the sword from her thigh and placed a hand on her own thigh, using fire to cauterize the wound. She grimaced as she rose to her feet, hobbling to where the queen barely clung to life.

"Not to be a downer, but you should know I plan to sack the city as well," Osprey said. "I expect you already knew that, though."

Amira was too weak to respond, her eyes flitting as life left her body. Osprey had no more sarcastic remarks to share, so she simply watched and waited. Eventually, the queen's breathing ceased, and she was no more than a husk. Osprey shrugged and hobbled to the pond nearby. She held out her hand and searched the waters with her talent. She grabbed on to the dead raven and levitated it out of the water and into her hand. Osprey removed the scroll from the bird's leg and dried it out with heat from her fingers.

She unfurled the scroll and read the message to Acasta. Osprey looked to the west with an evil grin.

The Girl & the Serpent

Phaedra's best guess put Elok at four times the length of her boat. It was hard to get a true gauge in the dark water. Every once in a while, a portion of the leviathan's body crested the surface, reminding Phaedra that the creature was capable of swallowing her whole if she was ever so inclined.

The great sea serpent hadn't communicated to her since their first encounter, so Phaedra simply had to take it on faith that following her "to the home of her kin" was the right plan. *How could it not be? Surely being surrounded by leviathans is a good idea!*

Phaedra ate the last of the stale bread she had stolen back in Corcoran. It did little to settle her stomach; she could eat a feast and the nerve-induced rumbles would still be there. As she watched the moonlight-tipped waves rise and fall, something gnawed at her consciousness, a loss that was taking shape in her heart. She thought back to Lucian, lying on the beach, how he had used his final breaths to beg her to save herself. Phaedra gripped the trident, her knuckles white, caught in the memory. She did not know what twists of fate were in store for her, but there was one thing she knew for certain: Kywin would pay for killing her friend.

Elok slowed her pace until she was cutting through the sea alongside the boat. "We must fight now," the snake whispered directly into Phaedra's mind. Phaedra was still unnerved by the way the creature could effortlessly slip into her thoughts.

Phaedra didn't need to ask what fight Elok was referring to; two ships sailed on the water ahead of them, their lanterns forming an imposing shape in the distance. These were not small fishing boats. They were long, wide ships, most likely manned by pirates. Even if they didn't know she was the heir to King Skybane, a girl such as her was a nice prize. Phaedra looked to the moon in anger. On a darker night, she and her boat could have slipped away into the gloom undetected. But the bright moon meant the ships could easily spot her from their position.

"It has been many years since I've had cause to battle humans," Elok communicated. "I shall relish this opportunity. Be prepared, little princess."

"I am not a little princess," Phaedra retorted, rather child-ishly she knew. But Elok was already under the water and heading toward the oncoming ships. Phaedra removed her tunic and stood at the bow of the little boat in her pants and undershirt, equal parts scared and excited. She had seen fights before, but never a battle. And certainly never a battle involving a leviathan or herself.

The ships had black masts. It was pirates, then. Fittingly, the sky opened up, and it began to rain. Hard. Phaedra heard shouts and saw men pointing at the water, while others pointed at her boat.

No sense making it easy on them.

Phaedra dove into the cold water, the Sacred Trident in hand. Propelled by her fins, she cruised thirty feet under the surface. When she came up for air, the smaller of the ships was careening off course and tilted on its side. Elok! The huge serpent had half of her body on top of the deck, her other half still submerged in the water. The sheer weight of her was causing the ship to nearly capsize. Elok belted out an ear-piercing shriek that stunned Phaedra and made her cover her ears. She watched, dazed, as Elok bit a sailor in half with her massive fangs. Another pirate tried to stab her with a long spear, but Elok quickly turned her head and knocked the man into the water. Then she rose up ten feet above the deck and slammed back down, splintering the ship. The hull cracked under the force of her weight, and the vessel proceeded to list even further onto its side. Nothing would stop it from sinking now. Elok knew this and quickly slithered back into the ocean.

As impressive as the attack was, Phaedra knew the larger ship wouldn't succumb so easily to such a strategy. Phaedra bobbed in the water, waiting to see Elok's next move. Phaedra was so awed, she barely noticed the net that had been tossed at her before it was too late. She dove back under the water, eluding the large fishing net and its weighted hooks.

"Flee or fight, do not linger in between," Elok communicated.

Phaedra felt a burst of energy course through the trident. She dove deeper and circled around to the side of the ship that Elok was approaching from a different angle. Unsure of what strategy Elok had in mind, Phaedra sneaked to the surface to peek above the water. Elok blasted out of the sea, like a giant horse rearing up on its hind legs. The snake's head towered over the ship, and she bellowed another shriek. Some of the sailors were stunned, but others were ready. A whale harpoon sliced through the air and dug into Elok's body. Another followed and stuck just under the serpent's jaw. The pirates quickly anchored the thick lines to the boat's frame. The large ship tilted in the water as Elok thrashed, but the vessel was enough of a counterweight to keep Elok from submerging. As she continued to buck and fight, a third harpoon landed in her side, and the serpent shrieked again, this time in pain. They were trying to reel in the great beast.

Phaedra knew she had to help Elok. She climbed a rope ladder on the side of the ship and came aboard, where she was immediately spotted by a pair of burly pirates in black-and-red rags. The first pirate tried to rush her with a hand axe. The short weapon was no match for Phaedra's trident, which she used to skewer him at the neck before he could get in close enough to use his axe. The second man was quicker and kicked Phaedra into a barrel that was secured to the rail of the ship. In the scuffle, she lost hold of the trident. The pirate approached again, prepared to strike with his short sword. The boat suddenly rocked to the side as Elok tugged at the cables attached to the harpoons lodged in her flesh; the pirate was sent tumbling sideways. Phaedra tried to regain her footing, but she was off balance and unable to retrieve her trident. As the man started to bear down on her again, she yanked at a knot holding the barrel to the rail and kicked it with all her might. At the same time, the ship rocked and rolled, and the barrel catapulted at the surprised pirate, knocking him clear across the deck.

Phaedra grabbed her trident from the first pirate and moved toward the other side of the ship. She knew she had just killed a man, maybe two. There would be time for that to sink in later, she told herself. The air was filled with a cacophony of noises, from the thunder and rain to the screaming pirates and eardrum-splitting cries of Elok. Phaedra saw no fewer than a dozen men and women pulling on the cables with hooks, trying to draw Elok closer to the ship so they could continue slicing at her. Phaedra wasn't sure if they could overpower the snake, but they were certainly giving it their best shot. As Elok struggled, Phaedra saw another small group of pirates rolling in a contraption, some kind of long pipe on wheels. Heavy. Phaedra watched as they loaded an iron ball into the pipe and then set fire to the end of it. Nothing happened for a moment; then, in a burst of flame, the ball erupted from the pipe and struck Elok, tearing away a large swath of scales and flesh. It caused Elok to spasm, and Phaedra could see some of the creature's strength leave her.

Phaedra looked back to the contraption and saw the pirates loading another iron ball into the pipe. Then she looked at the harpoons and cables holding Elok in check. She tried to push away the fear, but she knew her next move could be her last. The raw blast of power she had somehow channeled back in Corcoran to kill the bounty hunter would be useful here. Figuring out how to use it was another matter.

They were about to light the pipe once more.

Phaedra sprang from her hiding spot and sprinted across the deck in full view of the pirates. She hurled her trident at the pirate holding the torch, the steel tips of the weapon slamming into the woman's back and bursting from her ribcage. In a fluid motion, Phaedra ripped the trident out and kicked at another pirate. Before they could react, she was running to the edge of the ship, pursued by half a dozen angry sailors. Someone caught her with a knife in the shoulder, and pain seared through her. She did not stop upon reaching the rail of the ship. She jumped onto it and then leapt into the space between Elok and the pirate ship. Somehow, she catapulted herself with inhuman strength more than twenty feet in the air, nearly overshooting her target: the harpoon cables. Luckily, her trident was just long enough to reach a cable as she passed by it, a mighty swipe of the weapon slicing the taut line neatly. She continued to arc in the air directly toward the second cable, which she also cut with a swing of her powerful trident.

Free of two of the cables holding her, Elok jerked away from the ship, snapping the third and final line. Phaedra splashed down into the water and swam away from the ship, arrows swimming past her on all sides. One landed in her calf, and she belted out a gurgled scream under the water.

"Leave the rest to me!" Elok screamed into her mind, nearly blinding Phaedra with the emotional force of her words. Phaedra surfaced again and turned to see the pirates searching the water for Elok all around the boat. There was no sign of her.

Then, nearly as fast as the iron ball was expelled from that pipe, the sea snake blasted from the water into the night sky—nearly fifty feet of her! The pirates watched in horror as Elok soared directly above the ship and then angled her body down to land flush on the deck, crushing five of her foes on impact. Three more she killed with a flick of her lower half, sending them to the water below, broken and bloody. One man tried to jump off the ship, but Elok caught him in her jaws and snapped off his legs. She rose up and slammed down on the deck again, splintering enough to cause a gash in the side where the tumultuous ocean water could rush in. Only a handful of pirates were left, and those who didn't jump to the water and their own lingering demise were quickly dispatched by the rageful serpent.

Sickened by the carnage, Phaedra found that she was not disgusted by Elok's actions; the princess had nothing but disdain for pirates. They traded in slaves; raped and pillaged all across the realms. Her father had told her many tales of pirates, none of them pleasant.

When the ship finally sank, Elok appeared next to Phaedra in the water, her enormous head twice the size of Phaedra. They floated next to one another, regarding each other. "It is true then," Elok communicated. "You really are the Daughter of Waves."

"I have never seen anything like that," Phaedra said.

"Nor have many humans that live to tell the tale," Elok replied. "But you are not just any human, are you?"

Phaedra wasn't sure how to answer that. She was also getting tired, and the wounds in her shoulder and leg were beginning to concern her.

Elok sensed this. "Do you trust me yet?" the snake asked.

Phaedra nodded.

"Touch my head," Elok said.

Phaedra extended a hand and touched the rubbery scales of the snake. They were smooth and spongelike, with a hardness underneath.

"Fascinating," Elok mused. "I secrete a toxin that is poisonous to humans, but it seems you are immune. Just like your father. Climb onto my back, and I will take you the rest of the way."

Phaedra looked at her hand, wondering what would have happened if she hadn't been immune to the snake's skin. One of so many questions. For now, she was too tired. She floated over to Elok, who dipped below the water so Phaedra could move onto her back. Soon, they were careening across the ocean together, rain pelting down.

Politicians

Henry slammed his fist on the table. "I was a fool to listen to you … fools!" he yelled, not caring who heard him through the thin walls separating their private room and the rest of the tavern.

"These things happen," Senator Farnosh said.

Modano sunk into his chair and took a long gulp of his mead. "I'm going to need something stronger."

"What do we do now?" Henry asked. He looked at the other men around the table, hoping for an idea that might mitigate this disaster. Somehow, their plot to kill Sir Grayfork had turned into a mass slaying of King Edward, his queen, and various members of the Lockewell court. As grotesque as that was, it had even more horrifying practical consequences: with the king dead, his son would assume power. The prince was notoriously close with Sir Grayfork and far more ambitious than his father. Instead of a potential ally on the throne to help keep the peace, Maldovar now had to deal with the very people looking to bring about the Republic's demise.

"*Nothing?*" Henry roared.

"I'm afraid our plan has failed, old friend." Modano sulked and sipped more of his mead. Senators Farnosh and Deguerrin did not dispute Modano's assertion.

"How could this happen?" Henry repeated, still angry at himself for getting involved with the Butcher. "And where is that bastard, anyway?"

"I wouldn't show my face if I were him either," Farnosh groused.

Henry grasped for any kind of silver lining in this mess but couldn't find one. Of all the people who had to be eliminated, Sir Grayfork was at the top of the list. Instead of removing him, they had made his job easier.

"Henry?" Modano had been speaking to him, apparently, but he was too deep in thought to notice.

"What?" he asked.

"We have no choice but to face the inevitable. Maldovar is lost. All we can do now is protect ourselves and our families," Modano said.

Farnosh and Deguerrin nodded along. Henry couldn't believe this was how their attempt to save the Republic would end—with a mead and a shrug. Henry's great-grandfather, the most influential first minister who ever lived, would be disgusted. Henry was disgusted with himself. He had been convinced that bloodshed was the only way to preserve the Republic. Now the situation was far worse, and it looked as if he would be alone in his bid to turn the tide. *Fine.* He would do just that. *This time, with diplomacy.*

He rose to his feet, full of purpose, when the door to the room opened. Henry expected to see Marco Belor, but it was a dark-haired, swarthy man wearing leather armor.

"This is a private room," Henry told the man, in no mood to deal with a drunken rogue. "See yourself out, or we'll have the barkeep do it."

213

The man smiled at that, his yellow teeth gleaming in the candlelight. He appraised Henry and the other men in the room, then stepped inside and closed the door behind him, locking the latch. Modano reached for a knife, but the armored man was much faster: he quickly unsheathed a sword and slashed it across Modano's throat. Henry watched his colleague and friend bleed out on the floor.

"With Sir Alan Grayfork's regards," the slayer said, before he made quick work of the other three men, saving Henry for last. Less than ten seconds later, Henry was staring at the ceiling, clutching the gash in his chest. The man knelt over him and grinned. "Politicians."

Kragon's Lair

"Maybe this is the boy that can fucking fly!" Wraggus shouted above the din, pointing at Caldred. Then he motioned to Jamie and Lukas. "How about we throw them all off Mount Farik and see which one goes the farthest!"

Anke held up her hammer to quiet the angry warriors packed into Kragon's Lair. Rawk stood next to her, jaw clenched, eyes fixed on Wraggus. They had traveled day and night to get back to Clem before the Fifth Legion arrived, and they paid a heavy price. Anke had slept a total of ten hours in the past four days. Even Rawk looked weary. The Red Bears had returned before Skullcrusher with news of the Clanright and resulting split from Clem. Now she showed up with a mage, a spy, and a few boys. It was hard to fault the gathered Clem warriors for their collective anger.

Undeterred by Rawk's glare, Wraggus continued, emboldened by the grunts of assent he received with his last few shouts. "Weeks ago, you said you left on a hunt! Now we learn you believe a prophecy spat by the assholes of gods we don't worship? And did you bring back the chosen pissant? No! Instead, you run off the Red Bears!"

"Enough!" Skullcrusher howled. "There will be a time for

complaints. And challenges. I welcome them. I will gladly step into the circle with any man or woman who raises their sword. But the next person who speaks before I say what I have traveled faster than a whipped horse to say will find themselves split in half by Rawk's axe."

The murmur in the hall died down. Acasta stood to the side, watching the proceedings. He had never been in the lair before. It met his expectations: dingy, cavernous, and filled with the smell of death. Enough blood had been spilled on these stones that the stain and stench would never wash away, if that was even the intention. Something told Acasta they didn't get around to scrubbing the grout here very often. Laroche was behind him, not in chains for the time being. Acasta had counseled Skullcrusher to either leave Laroche outside or remove his restraints; the last thing she needed was for people to question her judgment in sharing her bed with a confirmed spy. She had bristled at the suggestion but ended up listening to it, above Rawk's objections. He wanted to pummel Laroche and be done with it.

"Yes, it is true I left on a quest to find the Flyer. To claim him for Clem!" Skullcrusher roared in defiance. "That is our way! We do not wait for the gods of other realms to weave their fates. We intervene with axes and swords. We deal in blood and iron. And I did drive off the Red Bears, after I defeated their fiercest warrior in the circle. If they had not run, I would be returning with even more Clem brethren following our battle with the mercenaries of Lockewell."

Shouts went up demanding to know more about the battle. Acasta could see the anxiety building in Jamie and Caldred as the warriors' anger built to a crescendo. He studied the two young men. *Could one of them be the Promised Knight?* He had not heard from Queen Amira since he set out. Perhaps she would be able to tell if one of these boys was indeed the fulfillment of the prophecy. Acasta rolled his eyes at himself for getting caught up in the moment. These were just freed slaves. There is no Knight of War and Dawn. No Flyer. Just stories and whispers to keep the pious happy that their gods were planning something.

"We have an even bigger battle at our doorstep!" Skullcrusher yelled, trying to bring all of her presence to bear.

"After destroying the Lockewell fighters … with the help of this mage," she explained, "we caught a bird with a message. It told of a great army that would be at Clem within a week."

"A great army? From Lockewell? Let them come!" Wraggus laughed. "We will have their heads on pikes before our first pisses of the day."

The warriors laughed. It would have been a welcome release of the tension in the air, were it not for the very real chance that Lockewell was sending many thousands to their doorstep. Skullcrusher pressed on.

"These are no ordinary Lockewell soldiers," she said. "This is a special legion trained for one purpose: to destroy armies. They are fifty thousand strong."

That silenced the crowd. Even ten thousand would be a formidable number to repel from the gates of Kragon's Lair. But fifty thousand?

"Bullshit!" Wraggus exclaimed.

"Boss warned you!" Rawk yelled and began plodding toward the much smaller Wraggus.

"No!" Skullcrusher commanded, stopping Rawk in his tracks. He obeyed but was beginning to tire of being stopped from killing people. First Laroche. Now Wraggus.

Acasta smiled. *Save your anger, big man. There will be plenty of bastards to kill soon enough.*

"Wraggus the Gray, I challenge you to shut your mouth or meet your death in the Circle right fucking now!" Skullcrusher hissed. "Choose either way, I don't care."

Wraggus looked at the crowd, his pride wounded and his face crimson. His hand twitched to the hilt of his sword, but his senses got the best of him. He growled and bowed his head slightly.

"Perhaps it is Wraggus the Wise after all," Skullcrusher snarked, prompting some laughs from the assembled warriors. Wraggus remained stone-faced.

Skullcrusher looked around at her people. She swung her hammer into her hand and caught the heavy head of it with a slap. "Is this not what we were born for? Your leader comes home from a journey to tell you a great host of our enemies dares to enter our lands, and your honor is not challenged? They are from Lockewell, a nation our forefathers pounded into submission again and again!"

She surveyed the warriors. "You, Hulgar of Stag Clan! Do you not dream for a chance to destroy those who would doubt the power of Clem?"

Hulgar, a proud man with broad shoulders, nodded. "I do dream of this."

"Even Wraggus, whose heart burns with a hate for me that no bonfire can match. I bet he too would give his right bollock for the opportunity to maim these weaklings from the East."

Wraggus was forced to agree. "I might at that."

"So, I stand before you, warriors of Clem! Turn your backs on me another day. Challenge me another day. But on this day, link your arms in mine, and together we will show the dogs of Lockewell and the people of all realms what happens when you step foot on Clem soil and spit in our faces!"

Angry cheers filled the hall. Skullcrusher looked at her companions and nodded, then turned to her people. "Come, we have much to plan. They could be here any hour."

The next morning at dawn, the first scout returned with news of the Fifth Legion. The young man rode his horse right into Kragon's Lair and tossed the head of a Lockewell soldier at Skullcrusher's feet.

"There are eight thousand more where that came from," the scout said. "Maybe ten thousand."

The number was large, but not as bad as it could have been, Skullcrusher knew. "When will they be here?"

"By nightfall," said the young man, who now seemed more like a teenager to Skullcrusher's eyes. He was proud of himself, in a way that spoke more to duty than vanity. The teen instinctively patted his horse's neck. The animal was spent, no doubt a result of being pushed to the limit to deliver the news as fast as possible.

Skullcrusher bowed her head to the young scout. "You've done well," she said, turning to a nearby warrior. "See that his horse is given water and treated well."

Then she raised her war hammer high and roared the Clem battle cry of "Relhalla!" The other warriors echoed the cry.

In his chamber, Jamie heard the chanting. "So, the Lockewell army is here. Another battle." *More chances to die.* He had acted on instinct and adrenaline against the mercenaries; there was no time to worry about the fight beforehand. But there was plenty of time now.

"Maybe Acasta will just zap them all with his powers," Caldred joked, trying and failing to lighten the mood. "Probably not, though."

Jamie held his knife in his hands. The day he acquired the blade felt like a lifetime ago. In reality, it had been less than a month. Since then, he had been kidnapped, enslaved, trained, and conscripted into another realm's army. And he had killed—more than once. He looked from the knife to his friend.

"Do you believe in destiny?" he asked.

Caldred chewed on some jerky. "If it means I don't die today, sure."

"Laroche said our destinies are inevitable."

"The spy? That's who you get your advice from?" Caldred sneered. "Inevitable means like it has to happen, right?"

"Yes."

"So, a guy tells you things have to happen eventually, and that makes you think?"

Jamie opened his mouth to respond, then closed it. Caldred was right. *Of course, things had to happen.* "Well, I guess I hope my destiny doesn't involve me getting a sword in my neck today," Jamie said.

Caldred tossed him a piece of jerky. "Maybe we'll both get lucky, and they'll forget we're even here."

With that, there came a knock at the door.

"Destiny!" Caldred laughed.

He opened the door to reveal Acasta. Laroche was with him. Skullcrusher had decided the best person to keep watch over the spy was the mage. Caldred wasn't sure why such a powerful sorcerer was okay with being relegated to guard duty, but he opted not to bring it up.

"It seems our friend here was telling the truth," Acasta said, motioning to Laroche behind him. "The Fifth Legion is here, and there is no escape now. Come on. We're fighting with the rest of Clem today."

"How many?" Jamie asked.

"I've found it's best not to ask questions you don't want the answers to," Acasta replied. "Stay close to me, and I promise you'll be among the last to die."

"Nice," Caldred said.

"You were expecting lies? That's not my area of expertise," Acasta pointed out.

"Yes, yes, you're very clever," Laroche interjected, knowing Acasta was referring to him. "I still don't see why my participation is necessary here. I'm not a fighter. I'm a …"

"Businessman," Acasta interrupted. "You've made that perfectly clear. And I should think you'd be happy to even get the chance to swing a blade. If Rawk had his way, you'd have been dead days ago."

"Because the big lout is dumber than the boulder he was carved from," Laroche said.

"You're wrong," Jamie said. "He's actually quite smart."

"Good for him," Laroche snapped.

* * *

Kragon's Lair was nearly four hundred years old, and it looked every bit its age. The setting sun tried to cast a golden hue over the structure, but there was no masking its bleak, gray façade. The huge fortress took more than a decade to build, during which time thousands of slaves were worked to death under Kragon's watchful eye. The great Clem ruler was said to have personally overseen the construction of the wide, imposing castle. The outer walls were fifty feet high and ten feet thick. Kragon did not believe in moats, so instead of water, the first obstacle for an invading army would be the Valley, as the Clem warriors called it. It was a long stretch of open land on all sides of the great castle, depressed like a natural valley. The footing was made treacherous by centuries of digging and filling the earth. From the Lair's towers, bowmen could loose hundreds of arrows upon an invading force as their horses struggled in the muck below.

A strip of hard rock had been laid down the middle for returning Clem forces. In preparation for an attack, those rocks were slicked with oil to make them every bit as dangerous as the rest of the Valley.

Incredibly, Jamie found himself standing near Skullcrusher and her most trusted advisers atop the gate bridge tower, a massive platform that overlooked the main entrance to the castle. Jamie almost got vertigo as he glanced down at the ground more than a hundred feet below him. Slowly raising his eyes to the horizon, he saw the Fifth Legion approaching. Never before had he seen such a mass of humanity. They seemed to march in unison toward the Lair, their metal armor glinting, appearing slightly golden from the waning sun.

"That *inevitable* word comes to mind," Caldred said.

Jamie nodded. To their right, Skullcrusher was barking orders at the Clem contingency. Perhaps one thousand had come to defend the castle. *Outmanned more than ten to one*, Jamie thought. Despite its age and weary appearance, Kragon's Lair was supposed to be impenetrable. According to lore, no opposing army had ever set foot inside the outer wall. That would be tested this night, Jamie knew. He looked back to the horde of soldiers approaching. The first line reached the edge of the Valley and stopped, their fellow soldiers forming ranks behind them.

"They are many, but for their sake, I hope they have a trick or two up their sleeve if they hope to survive the Valley and somehow scale the wall," Acasta said.

On cue, the front lines broke open, and men from the back pushed forward carrying giant ladders on their shoulders. Acasta was not surprised.

"It will take more than a few ladders," he said.

Rawk grunted. "We meet them in battle. I will go!"

"It may come to that," Skullcrusher said, calming the big man with a hard look. "If it does, you and I will be the first to fight … if they get through the Valley alive."

Jamie saw dozens of archers along the outer wall, patiently waiting for the chance to start raining arrows down upon the Fifth Legion once they got close enough. Even with those tall walls and the bowmen ready, Jamie could feel a storm in his stomach. It would be too easy if the well-trained Lockewell army were simply turned back by the walls of the Lair. Surely, they had planned for those walls. They were famous around the world.

"What say you, spy?" Acasta asked Laroche.

"They didn't come all this way with nothing but ladders," he replied.

At some point during the last few minutes, night had finally taken hold. All Jamie could see of the army across the field were their torches. Those small fires moved aside as some kind of contraption was pushed to the front of the ranks.

"What are they doing?" Wraggus mused aloud. Between him and Laroche, Jamie wondered why Skullcrusher wanted to be surrounded by potential threats. Or maybe she was smart to keep them close.

Suddenly, three blue-flamed torches pierced the darkness. They were more intense and larger than the regular torches the other soldiers held. Acasta grimaced.

"Magefire," he hissed.

"How many?" Skullcrusher asked.

"At least two sorcerers, but the question is what are they up to?" Acasta said. He narrowed his eyes and focused on the flames. "Shit."

"What shit?" Rawk asked.

"Those walls might not be thick enough," Acasta said.

Skullcrusher turned in surprise, wondering if he was joking or serious.

A moment later, three loud cracks reverberated in the air, followed by deep thumps as three balls of fire shot out from the Lockewell army. In a second, they crashed into the outer wall of Kragon's Lair. They were huge boulders encased in magefire, and they crashed into the walls with such a force, the whole castle seemed to shake. The walls themselves broke apart around the projectiles, the boulders smashing through them like knuckles through teeth. Jamie looked down to see three massive holes in the wall, each one wide enough for three soldiers to run through at once. And that seemed to be the plan, based on the battle cry that preceded the rush of soldiers into the Valley.

Skullcrusher was still gawping at the damaged walls of her forefathers when Rawk screamed in anger. The big man's shout knocked her out of her daze, and she turned to the archers. "Loose!" she yelled.

A flurry of arrows, many of them fire-tipped, launched into the night sky. They would stop some of the attacking soldiers, to be sure, but with three gaping holes in the outer wall and thousands of soldiers sure to push through them, Clem's odds just went to shit, Jamie knew.

Skullcrusher barked more orders to her warriors, commanding them to defend the broken sections of the wall. Then she turned to the twenty or so warriors around her, including Jamie. "On me!" she yelled. Rawk slammed his axe into his metal chestplate so hard, it would have killed any other man. Jamie's knees went wobbly as he followed Caldred and Acasta down the steps toward the impending battle.

We're all going to die, he thought.

He could feel the energy pulsing through the castle. Rage. Fear. Excitement. Bloodlust. It was like every emotion had been blended together into a single *feeling* among the men and women. Jamie tried to tap into that for courage, but he couldn't trick himself into not being afraid. Sensing this, Acasta winked at him. "Remember what I said. Last to die if you stick by me."

It was so ludicrous Jamie actually laughed. Skullcrusher and Rawk looked back at him as they descended the stairs.

"Little Galantra thinks this is funny," she said. "You taught him well, Rawk."

Now Rawk and a few of the other warriors laughed as well, a slight breaking of the tension in the air. It only lasted a few seconds, however, as another boom sounded and more magic-laced boulders crashed into the outer wall.

Arthur

Arthur was no idiot. He was quite likely the furthest thing from an idiot in the realm, in fact.

So he understood the situation. His father had been alive and stable until his mother visited his bedchamber, and then he was dead. Were Arthur a normal boy his age, he might have believed the queen's lies and false tears. His own tears would have shrouded his judgment. He was not a normal boy, of course. So he didn't cry when he heard the news of his father's passing, nor did he cling to his mother in a tight hug, hoping for her to make it all better.

No, Arthur did what he always did in times of stress: he read books. He believed by filling his head with important knowledge, he would forget the things from life he didn't want to remember, whether it was because they were mundane or painful.

The library at The Falls was not the most extensive collection, but it was respectable. When Arthur was younger, his interest in reading and writing had prompted his father to acquire dozens of books as the prince became more and more "obsessed" with them, as his older sister often teased him. Arthur flipped through the beautifully illustrated pages of

Master Malten's History of the Sea, wondering where Phaedra was at that very moment. Probably in Maldovar, or perhaps sailing the open water somewhere off the coast of Lockewell. While he was tucked away in the dank basement of their family home, reading by candlelight, she was facing new dangers head-on. *Fitting.* He and Phaedra often debated whether there was more adventure to be found in his musty old books or out on the high seas. Arthur loved to poke easy holes in her arguments, until she was so angry she stormed away, telling him he would never make friends with that kind of attitude.

Arthur smiled. He realized he missed his sister. Now, with his father gone forever and Phaedra on the other side of the world, the only person he had left that meant anything to him was Tetria. Despite her stern edifice, she had always been kind to him. Flipping through the pages, Arthur found what he was looking for: tales of the sea serpents. Leviathans. He'd been drawn to them ever since hearing his father's stories about encountering them in his youth. In books, leviathans were monsters. But to hear his father talk of the creatures, they were more like ancient gods of the sea. Arthur had also noticed in other texts that they had some tangential relation to the prophecy about the return of the Flyer.

Arthur moved the candle closer to the page and leaned in, reading about legends of the sea kings of old who rode leviathans in battle. Arthur shook his head. Malten was always adding such hyperbolic flourishes to his supposed histories. It ruined the integrity of the book, in Arthur's opinion. He read on and learned about a queen who would one day bring the great serpents into battle. Arthur was prepared to dismiss this section as well, but then he read the description of the young queen, called the Daughter of Waves: "Cast aside by her family out of both love and hate, this queen shall ride a leviathan into the heart of the final war. The war that unites the realms. The war of the Flyer."

Arthur re-read that paragraph a dozen times. *Could it be Phaedra?* She was cast out, certainly, though it was not clear to Arthur what the part about love and hate meant. He knew his father had loved Phaedra, and it could surely be said his mother hated her. But was she cast out by both? Only if the king had his own reasons that were borne from love, Arthur surmised. The more compelling clue was the mention of the final war and the Flyer. According to the prophecy, Phaedra was to marry the Flyer. Which meant she could also be the Daughter of Waves.

It made him reconsider Malten, one of the more prolific historians of the era. The man had died thirty years ago and was known, depending who you asked, as a man with the gift of foresight, or a fine writer with a vivid imagination that often got the better of him. Some considered him a total fraud. Arthur had always felt Malten was an enigma; only after reading all his works could he decide if the Fidoran-born scholar dealt more in fact or fiction.

Still, if Phaedra was out there fulfilling prophecies and riding leviathans, Arthur wanted to be part of it. For the first time in his life, he found himself craving the kind of real-world adventure that would be written about in books. There was just one problem: he was trapped on an island with his murderous mother.

* * *

Slipping by the guard was easy. There were two entrances to

the seldom-used dungeon in The Falls. Really, Arthur thought, dungeon was a strong word for the small block of cells in the lowest level of the royal palace. As the guard slept at one end of the hall, Arthur snuck around the corner to the only occupied cell. He looked at the young man curled on the dirty cot.

"Lucian," Arthur whispered.

Phaedra's friend lifted his head to look over his shoulder. When he saw Arthur, he grunted a weak sound of confusion. Slowly, and painfully, the former member of the king's royal guard turned his body and sat up. He reached for his side, which was still grievously injured. The wound had healed enough to stop an immediate death, but Arthur gave Lucian one chance in three to last more than a couple more weeks without treatment. The internal damage would need luck or magic to heal properly, and mage-healers were in short supply in this part of the world.

"Artie? What are you doing here?" Lucian asked.

"Just out for an afternoon stroll," Arthur replied.

Lucian winced through a chuckle. "Your sister always said you had a wonderful sense of humor."

"Your sarcasm is not lost on me, but I'm not risking my mother's ire to trade barbs," Arthur said. "I'm here to make a proposal."

"By all means, I have nothing better to do," Lucian said. Then, realizing something, he sat up straighter. "I am sorry about your father. He was a great king, unmatched by any in the history of our people."

"What if I told you my mother was the one who ensured his quick death?"

Lucian darkened. "Your sister also told me you were smart. Too smart to say such things to anyone in this realm, even one

229

who might believe you."

"Yes, yes, do you want to hear my proposal or not?"

"You're a strange one. And sure … I'm all ears."

"Do you believe the prophecy about my sister?" Arthur asked.

His question seemed to exacerbate Lucian's pain. The young man sighed heavily. "I don't want to, for my own reasons."

"Because you love her. Yes. Everybody knows that."

Again, Lucian paused and then couldn't help but laugh.

"Am I that obvious?"

"You look at her like a puppy does at its master."

"Ouch. Good to know, Artie. Alright, do you believe the prophecy?"

"I do. And I wish to be at her side during these pivotal times more than I wish to be with my mother and her lecherous advisor."

"Kywin, that bastard," Lucian hissed.

"That's the one."

"What does it matter? You are a boy and I'm sentenced to be executed in a week's time, once the period of mourning for your father is over."

"I am a boy, true, which is why I need your help getting off this island."

Lucian looked at Arthur with fresh eyes. He was impressed by the boy's courage, but he knew the fatal flaw in his offer.

"Even if you could get me out of this cell, I am no use to anybody in this condition," he said, pulling up his shirt to show a festering wound. "By the executioner's ax or this godsforsaken gash, I am dead either way."

"I have a plan for that, too," Arthur said.

Lucian saw a second person appear from the shadows.

Tetria. The old woman had a small jar of paste and fresh bandages in her hand, and a defiant look in her eyes. She gave Lucian the supplies for his injury through the metal bars of his cell, then walked in the direction of the guard.

"She's a talkative one," Lucian noted.

He and Arthur listened for sounds of a struggle or raised voices, but heard neither. About a minute later, Tetria returned with the key to Lucian's cell.

"How did you do that?" Arthur asked. "Magic?"

"I am not blessed with that kind of talent, Artie," she said with a wry smile. "Though I did learn potions from a witch in my youth. Assuming I haven't forgotten what she taught me, the guard shouldn't remember a thing."

Once Tetria was satisfied that Lucian's wound was properly dressed, the three of them slipped out of the dungeon and into the main palace. Tetria took them to her chamber, where she told them to stay quiet while she packed items for their trip.

"Do I have time to go get a few of my books?" Arthur asked.

"No, boy." Tetria dropped a pair of knives and a small bag of dried fruits and nuts into the travel sack.

"Not that I don't appreciate being freed from jail, but where exactly are we going?" Lucian interjected.

"Stoneridge," Tetria said, as if it were the most obvious answer in the world.

Arthur and Lucian traded a glance.

"Other than an abandoned castle, what's in Stoneridge?" Arthur asked.

"If I have to tell you, perhaps this isn't a journey you two boys should undertake," she said.

"Phaedra ... and snakes," Arthur guessed, connecting the dots.

"Snakes?" Lucian chimed in.

Tetria grinned at the young Fin soldier, then paused, putting her finger to her lips. "Get under the bed," she whispered.

Lucian and Arthur heard approaching footsteps as they scurried under the bed. Tetria finished stowing the travel sack she was packing with supplies just as there was a loud knock at the door. She crossed the small room and opened it.

Kywin stood in the hall, flanked by two of the queen's royal guards. The cut on his neck from Phaedra's blade was still healing, and would someday be a nasty four-inch scar marring his otherwise pristine appearance.

"Does the queen require my services?" Tetria asked, perfectly composed.

"I can't imagine why she would, nor why you're still here at all," Kywin sniped.

"I serve at the pleasure of the royal family until I'm told otherwise."

"The prisoner has disappeared. Have you seen him?" Kywin growled, peering past the old woman at her chambers. She stepped aside and held her arm out, inviting him in.

"I assume you speak of Lucian, the one who tried to aid Phaedra in her escape," Tetria said.

Kywin scanned the small room from the doorway, not bothering to step inside. "The word you were looking for was flee, not escape. Escape implies she had something to run from, whereas only a coward flees."

Tetria's face turned dark after hearing Kywin disparage Phaedra in that manner. "A coward, you say. She is still your princess, is she not?"

"For now," Kywin said.

"In any case, if you seek help finding the prisoner, I'm afraid

I can't offer it."

Kywin wanted to strike her, but he restrained himself. He turned to the guards with him. "Check the grounds. He can't have gotten far."

As the two men left, Tetria began to close the door. Kywin stopped it with his foot and flashed an evil grin. "Enjoy these times of leisure, old woman, for they may be your last in this residence."

"The rumors of your charm have not been exaggerated, I see," Tetria snarked before shoving the door closed, pushing back his foot. She waited with her ear at the door until she felt comfortable telling Arthur and Lucian to crawl out from under the bed.

"That man deserves a sword in the eye," Lucian hissed.

Tetria nodded in agreement. She liked the boy's nerve. "It will have to wait. First, we have to get you two off this island." She pulled the shade from her window and motioned to the dock, where half a dozen ships were moored. "Let's hope you both fit in the same crate. I'm not sure I have enough money to purchase two."

Arthur looked at the smallest ship of the bunch, a merchant vessel being loaded with livestock and crates of dry goods. Being smuggled out of The Falls like chattel wasn't exactly a promising start to the type of adventure he had in mind.

Bloodlines

Phaedra had heard of such a place, but she always assumed it was a myth, a scary story parents told their kids about an island where leviathans lived and bred.

Now she was there.

On the back of a leviathan.

It was still the dead of night, so she was dependent on the moonlight when trying to pick out features of the landmass. It looked to be a few miles wide, dotted with coves and rocky beaches. She could understand why the great serpents would choose this isle to call home. Elok slowed in the water as they approached a small inlet surrounded by cliffs on three sides. Phaedra dipped a hand into the water; it was noticeably warmer than the open sea.

"Welcome to Marin, home of the Serpentium," Elok communicated. "You are protected as my guest. But be warned, princess: all who dwell here will not be enthused to see a human, even if she is the Daughter of Waves. Perhaps especially so, in fact."

"What? You said I'd be safe here," Phaedra replied.

"Did I? Or did I say you'd be safer than you were in the open water amongst pirates and other humans who seek to find you?"

Phaedra had no time to debate the issue with Elok, as other leviathans were already surfacing around her. Ten, at least. Whereas Elok was dark gray, the other serpents were various colors: white, pink, forest green, and more. They all had the same types of scales, and their bodies looked relatively similar in length. The most striking difference, Phaedra noted, other than the color of their scales, was in their eyes. Elok's eyes were oval, like giant silver eggs with dark spheres in the middle. Phaedra looked to the other snake eyes staring at her and saw gold, black, flecks of orange, and perhaps most chilling, milky white. Sensing Phaedra's fascination, Elok explained that a serpent's eye color was the clearest indication of their lineage. Her own scales were gray, while her father's were bright green. Their eyes were nearly identical.

A white snake lifted its head from the water and cast its slender, onyx eyes upon Phaedra.

"Hello," Phaedra managed.

"This is Mogar, protector of Marin," Elok said. "He cannot speak directly to you like I can. None of the other serpents have that ability."

"Why can you, then?" Phaedra asked.

"You are not ready for that explanation yet," Elok countered. "Perhaps in time you will be able to understand it."

Elok then turned to Mogar and spoke aloud for the first time in Phaedra's presence. The snake's language was more guttural than Phaedra imagined it would be. Mogar and Elok exchanged a series of grunts, growls, and hisses, then Mogar nodded his massive head and slipped back under the water, along with the other nearby snakes.

Phaedra breathed a sigh of relief. "Is everything okay?"

"For now," the great snake said, skimming the water toward a large cove. "I am going to present you to the leader of all serpents, Regodor. He is over a thousand years old, so mind your words around him. He will know if you are lying."

"He has been king for a thousand years?"

"We do not have kings and queens," Elok replied.

"But you're a princess."

"It is complicated."

As they entered the cove, it took Phaedra's eyes a bit to adjust to the darkness. When they did, she saw a large mass in the water, coiled near the edge of the rocks. Two gold eyes appeared in the middle of the snake's head. While the other serpents were roughly the same size, Regodor must have been twice their length, his head substantially larger than Elok's.

"Great Regodor, I bring you Phaedra Bane, heir to the throne of Skybane, Daughter of Waves," Elok communicated to Phaedra's mind as the snake also used her native language to speak to Regodor. It was a bit tricky to not be distracted by Elok's hisses and grunts, but Phaedra was grateful for the translation.

Regodor said a few words to Elok, who then translated for Phaedra. Apparently, the elder snake was expecting Phaedra to look more like her father. Phaedra wanted to question yet again how Elok and Regodor knew her father. She held her tongue, knowing it would be an offense to interrupt. For more than ten minutes, the two serpents spoke, with Elok providing Phaedra the highlights of their conversation. Much of it didn't make sense to her. Apparently, Regodor was wary of the prophecy and did not want to risk so many of their serpents in battle. What battle, Phaedra did not know. He also seemed to think Elok was biased toward Phaedra for some reason, and he believed she should know the truth. Finally, the discussion abruptly ended, and Regodor gave Phaedra one final look with his huge, golden eyes before coiling back into his body and blending into the darkness around him.

"What happened?" Phaedra asked Elok once they were out of Regodor's cove.

"He favors you," Elok replied. "It is not often he speaks with one of us for such a long time. Regodor's age requires him to rest almost the entirety of his days so he can be ready."

"Ready for what?"

"The Great Chaos. The war to end all wars among men and beasts," Elok said.

"Is that coming soon?"

Elok tilted her head to look up at Phaedra, who was still sitting astride her back. Phaedra thought she saw a smile on the serpent's face. "Regodor has also decided to provide six of my kind to escort you and me to the shores of Stoneridge."

"Stoneridge … the abandoned castle of the Flyers," Phaedra muttered.

"The very same."

"We need to find my father's boat," Phaedra said.

"I understand your connection to that boat, but our father would rather you and I travel together on this voyage," Elok said.

It took a moment for Phaedra to sort through the words. Before she could ask, Elok blinked at her with those big silver eyes. For the first time, Phaedra noticed the flecks of blue.

"Yes, the eyes tell the bloodline," Elok said.

"How could this be? My father spoke often of not having any children before me," Phaedra argued, her head swirling. Then it dawned on her. "No *human* children."

"You have much to learn about our family, sister," Elok said.

Sister. The word resonated with Phaedra. She had always felt something was missing in her life, even with Artie as a sibling. Now, as she rode the leviathan, she felt a deep connection to the creature.

Elok continued to slice through the sea, unburdened after revealing the truth of their shared lineage. With half a dozen serpents now following in their wake, the two sisters disappeared into the foggy night, leaving the home of the Serpentium behind them. Neither Phaedra nor Elok had any idea their father was dead.

Last Rites

Four mages and half a dozen members of Tufthorn's Royal Guard stood in a circle around Amira's body. The Moonrise Garden was quiet now; Osprey's soldiers had followed her back to the shadows once she was done with the queen.

An elderly sorcerer knelt down and touched Amira's lifeless arm, then her cold forehead. The old woman had gray, braided hair down to her waist, and the wrinkles on her face told the tale of many years of worry and pain. She closed her eyes and murmured some words as the other people surrounding Amira held their breath.

"Is it too late?" a mage asked.

The healer didn't respond. She remained focused on Amira, reciting incantations. Eventually, she exhaled deeply. She opened her eyes and turned to a younger mage, Na'il, with a mixture of sadness and relief. "It is time," the ancient sorcerer said.

"Mother, are you sure?" Na'il asked.

The healer smiled at her daughter for a few seconds, not needing words to describe her love for her; then she turned back to Amira and laid both hands over the queen's chest. A ball of light enveloped the two women, and the sorcerer's chanting grew louder. Finally, her words reached a crescendo, and she fell to the earth next to the queen.

A second later, Amira opened her emerald eyes and gasped a breath. Before she had even fully realized what was happening, that she had come back from the dead, she saw the sorcerer lying in the soft, dewy grass next to her. "No," the queen whispered.

"Queen Amira is alive!" a mage shouted, and the group cheered. "Dar Daria has given her life to save her!"

Amira met eyes with Na'il and bowed her head in gratitude, knowing the gesture was not nearly enough. But she also knew Dar Daria gave her life freely of her own accord and that her sacrifice must be honored. Surely, Na'il knew that as well.

The queen looked at the people around her and touched her wounds, which were already healing. She slowly rose to her feet. Smoke billowed from fires around the city, and the garden was scarred from her battle with Osprey. A memory flickered in her mind: her raven falling out of the sky into the pond. It was now on the ground, and the scroll was gone.

"We have to send a message on the wind," the queen said. "There is no time to delay."

The other mages linked arms with their queen. "We need to combine our powers and get word to Acasta Borro in the west," Amira said.

One of the men whose arm she held looked back in disgust at the mention of Acasta's name. Na'il reacted in a similar manner but swallowed the disdain and looked to her queen.

"If this task is what you ask, we shall see it done," she said. "On my mother's honor."

Amira bowed her head to Na'il once more. "Thank you,

Na'il. I will do my best to make your mother's sacrifice worth the price."

Queen Amira and her mages focused the power of their talents, amplified and bonded by their touch. Sending words on the wind to a specific person was no easy task, requiring the combined skill of multiple sorcerers trained in telepathy. Even then, the only way the task would be truly successful is if the mage on the receiving end of the communication was actively listening.

"What is the message, my queen?" Na'il asked.

"He has found the Knight of War and Dawn, though it is not clear he knows it."

Battle

Metal clashed all around Jamie. Axes dented shields. Swords struck chainmail. At close range, the warriors of Clem were fierce enough to take on whatever the soldiers of Lockewell offered. The problem was in the numbers.

For every Lockewell fighter who was cut down, nine more were ready to take his place. The only thing that was helping Clem was the bottleneck of the holes in the outer wall. Kragon's defenders stood shoulder-to-shoulder in the gaps, pushing back the horde of invaders.

For now.

Jamie was behind the front line with Caldred, Lukas, and scores of other fighters, finishing off any attackers who broke through. Given the danger of the battle overall, it was not the worst place to be … until the people in the front line fell and the second-tier defenders had to step in to replace them. Once that happened, it was only a matter of time before Kragon's Lair fell.

Jamie had just jabbed his knife into a stumbling Lockewell soldier when two more flew in the air and landed at his feet with a thud.

Rawk had sent them. The big man was swinging his axe

so hard, whoever wasn't hacked in two from the blade was launched into the air by Rawk's massive forearms. Dazed, the Lockewell soldiers tried to get to their feet, but Caldred cut one down with his short sword and Lukas bludgeoned the other with his war hammer before the man could raise his sword to strike Jamie.

"Thanks," Jamie said.

Lukas was already off down the line, swinging his hammer into the face of another foe. Jamie saw flashes of blue fire in the corner of his vision and knew that was Acasta using his magic to decimate scores of attackers.

"Replacement archers!" someone yelled from above. Jamie looked up to see a Halfmoon looking in his direction. Along with a few others, he and Caldred hustled up the stairs of the nearest gate tower.

"You good with a bow?" Caldred asked, taking the steps two at a time ahead of Jamie, who was trying to keep pace.

"Does one week of training with Rawk count?" Jamie huffed. "You?"

"Stole a bow once and had it for a couple months," Caldred replied.

They reached the top and saw a dozen men and women loosing arrows at the Valley below. They stood among the bodies of their fallen brethren. Nobody had to tell Jamie what to do; he picked up the bow from the nearest slain Clem archer and moved to the wall of the tower. It was a long way down. He tried not to think about that as he grabbed an arrow from a large crate next to him and loaded it into the bow.

He nocked the arrow and aimed toward the Valley. Jamie let it fly, and the arrow whizzed toward the mayhem below. His aim was way off, he realized, as the arrow lost height too quickly and landed among the front lines. He didn't think it struck a Clem, but he couldn't be sure.

Okay, higher this time.

He watched another archer loose an arrow and saw a much higher angle of release. Trying again, Jamie launched an arrow deep into the sky. It seemed to pick up speed as it descended into the maelstrom of Lockewell fighters in the valley. He was reaching for another arrow from the crate when something skimmed by his head. He turned behind him to see an arrow shatter on the wall. He ducked down just in time to evade another arrow.

"Yeah, you might not want to be such an easy target next time!" Caldred yelled as he let an arrow fly and then quickly took cover. "I guess Rawk didn't teach you about that part yet."

Jamie made a face. He peered over the edge of the wall, trying to find the source of the arrow strikes. It was useless. There were thousands of soldiers down there.

"I'd say it's all luck of the draw, but you know how I feel about fate," Laroche yelled. Jamie was surprised to see him skillfully send an arrow deep into the night.

"What are you doing here?" Jamie asked.

"Reciting poetry," Laroche snarked. "What does it look like, boy? I'm trying to not get killed. And maybe in the process prove my loyalty to Anke."

Jamie nodded. Laroche may have been a two-faced asshole, but he seemed earnest about his feelings for Skullcrusher.

* * *

Acasta did not enjoy killing, but he was certainly good at it.

He lanced the Lockewell lines with another barrage of fire, scorching a dozen men in a single attack. Next to him, Rawk grunted loudly as he split a man in half with his axe. The big man did not like being shown up on the field of battle.

"Good luck catching up, big guy," Acasta joked as he used his power to lift two nearby opponents and smash them back to the ground. Acasta had plenty of power in reserve, but he was human. As he tired or got injured, his magic would become harder to tap into. And with so many swords and arrows coming for his head, one would eventually get lucky. But for now, he was Clem's greatest weapon.

As the soldiers burned, fire lit up the sky around them, and Acasta could see the waves of fighters in the Valley pushing forward toward the Lair. He had to find the other mages who were helping Lockwwell's army. Acasta scanned the Valley yet again. Above the din of the battle, amid the grunts and cries of agony, Acasta heard something. It was a faint voice. A woman.

She sounded familiar. A searing pain interrupted Acasta's attempt to make out the words on the wind. He looked down to see a slash in his side. Across from him, a soldier was prepared to strike again. He never got the chance, as his head was removed from his body with a quick swipe of a large knife. Rawk looked at the wound in Acasta's side.

"Had worse. Don't be baby," Rawk said.

"I need your help. Can you defend me?" Acasta asked.

"What?"

"I need to focus for a moment. Don't let anyone kill me, please." Before Rawk could answer, Acasta closed his eyes, placing his faith in the Clem warrior. Confused, Rawk stepped between the mage and the Fifth Legion and continued wreaking havoc.

Acasta tuned out the screams and clangs of metal and found the voice again. This time he knew who it was: Amira. He listened to the words, then flung his eyes open and turned toward the tower above, where he'd seen Jamie and Caldred run a few minutes earlier. He started pushing his way back toward the steps leading up to the tower.

Rawk glanced over his shoulder and saw Acasta retreating. "You're welcome!" he yelled.

Acasta was almost to the base of the stairs when a pair of figures appeared in front of him, materializing out of thin air.

Mages. Acasta tried to surprise them with a blast of power, but they were ready, deflecting the gust of wind with magical shields.

"Hello, Acasta," one of them said in a mocking tone.

"Hello, traitors," Acasta greeted them, gathering his strength.

"Because we fight with Lockewell?" the mage mused. "Odd coming from a mage who fights for Clem."

"I just meant the clothes. You're wearing their uniforms. More of a traitors-to-fashion kind of thing. And also the mercenary part," Acasta said.

As he joked with the mages, he tried to crush them with a series of falling stones from the nearest wall, but their defensive shield held, the huge rocks bouncing harmlessly away. The mages grimaced and sent two bolts of lightning at Acasta, knocking him off his feet. He fell to the ground, dazed, just managing to get a shield up in time to stop another bolt from finishing him off.

"I have to ask, how did you know my name?" Acasta wondered aloud, stalling for time.

"We listen to the wind too. So, we know who is up there,"

the older of the mages said, casting a glance over his shoulder at the tower. "He will make a fine prize for the new king."

Acasta had worried about that. Amira knew other sorcerers might hear the message intended for him, but if it was a chance she was willing to take, it meant things were dire back in Tufthorn too, not just here in Clem. Acasta's shield held as the pair of mages advanced on him, pelting bolts of energy at it. Eventually, they would wear him and his magic down.

A Clem warrior saw the figures in Lockewell garb and tried to intervene; he was rewarded with a quick flash of fire and a gruesome death. Acasta sat up and looked just past the mages with a grin.

"I was wondering where you were," he said.

All nine hundred pounds of Jester slammed into the two sorcerers from behind, knocking them onto the ground. One turned and tried to cast a spell toward the horse, but Jester was already slamming down his hoof on the man's head, ending him in an explosion of skull and brain matter. Acasta used a gust of wind to slam the other mage back down to the stones, pinning him in place.

Jester snorted and moved to stomp on that man's head too. Acasta calmed him with a gesture. He looked at the mage.

"Why are you working for Lockewell?" he asked.

The mage sneered at Acasta. "For? The better word would be *with*, and I am not alone. She *will* come for you, Beasted One."

Crunch. The man suddenly turned into a bright-red grease spot on the stones under Rawk's giant hammer. "Less talk. More fight," Rawk growled as he turned back to repel another wave of invaders.

"We were having a conversation!" Acasta complained to

the big man's back. Jester whinnied in annoyance over Rawk stealing his kill.

"Go back to the inner courtyard and wait for me," Acasta told him. Jester responded with a shake of the head, but Acasta stood firm. "Go. And thank you."

On his way up the steps of the tower, Acasta heard a bevy of battle cries. It sounded like the Fifth Legion had broken through one of the wall gaps, which meant soldiers were beginning to flood the grounds. His thoughts were elsewhere. He knew who the knight was, and he knew mages were turning on Tufthorn, including Osprey, who he assumed the mage was referring to. *Great.* That's all he needed was for her to show up to this fight.

When he reached the gate tower, Acasta saw the bodies lining the walls. Nearly all the Clem bowmen were dead or injured. He tripped over Laroche, who was unconscious but alive. "Lucky fool," Acasta said before spotting Jamie and Caldred in a well-covered position, sending arrows into the sky. It was a pointless exercise at this juncture; Lockewell had broken the line in at least one spot. Acasta rushed over to their position.

"Acasta! Why are you up here?" Jamie asked, surprised to see him so far from the fray, where he could do the most damage.

"We must go," Acasta said. "Now."

"What? Go where?" Caldred asked.

"No time to explain," Acasta replied. He turned to Jamie. "You're not safe here, and you're too important to die in this battle."

The boys looked at each other, then back at Acasta.

"*I'm* too important?" Jamie repeated, incredulous.

Caldred couldn't help but grin. "Have you been hit in the

head, mage?"

Acasta whirled around and sent a blast of fire at the two Lockewell soldiers that appeared from the stairwell, so hot that it melted the metal of their armor as it disintegrated their bodies.

"Gods!" Caldred exclaimed.

"You're the one Skullcrusher has been looking for, Jamie," Acasta said. "And if she finds that out, not even I will be able to get you out of here. We have to go now."

"Hold on. He's the Knight of War and Morning?" Caldred asked.

"War and Dawn. And yes," Acasta said, getting impatient.

"You're not making sense. I'm just a farm boy who got kidnapped on the road home from the market," Jamie argued.

"I'm not going to argue about this, boy!" Acasta snarled. Then he ducked as Jamie suddenly loosed an arrow over his shoulder, hitting a Lockewell fighter. During their brief conversation, six soldiers had streamed onto the tower and were fighting the few Clem bowmen who were left. Summoning his full strength, Acasta held out his hands and focused on the Lockewell men; they were all lifted into the air and flung from the tower to their deaths below. The effort took it out of him, and he dropped to one knee, his body sagging, weary from exertion. For the first time, Jamie saw his blood-soaked tunic.

"I'll be fine," Acasta said, gritting his teeth. "I need a moment to rest, and then we are leaving."

Horns rang out from below. Jamie looked over the side of the tower wall and saw the invaders scurrying into the courtyard below. "We're not going anywhere," Jamie said, a note of defeat in his voice. Acasta dragged himself to his feet and surveyed the scene below. He grimaced.

"Fuck." Acasta winced. He considered his options, then came to a decision. He turned to Caldred. "Whatever happens to me, you will help him escape Clem and get to Tufthorn. Even if it means you leave me here to die."

"Tufthorn? Acasta, we are all going to die here. Tonight!" Caldred exclaimed, motioning to the battle below. "The castle is lost."

"Do it!" Acasta repeated, his green eyes glowing brightly as he grabbed Caldred's shoulder. When Acasta's hand touched his shoulder, he felt a surge of emotion, as if he was compelled to agree with Acasta.

"I promise," Caldred declared, sealing the spell Acasta had cast. It was an odd feeling. In his heart, Caldred knew he would do everything in his power to honor Acasta's request. "What now?"

"Now I do something very, very wrong. And equally as dumb," Acasta said. He stepped to the edge of the tower and spread his arms wide. Jamie and Caldred watched as the air around Acasta seemed to thicken, as if wisps of energy were gathering. Acasta leaned his back and closed his eyes, uttering words in ancient Tuftloria. Then Acasta pointed his hands to the battle below and bellowed a loud cry that seemed unnatural for any man. A soundwave washed over the fighters below, and Acasta fell to his knees again. Jamie caught him before he fell over onto the stone tower headfirst.

"I don't believe it," Caldred said, looking at the men and women below.

"Acasta, are you okay?" Jamie asked. The mage was not responding, his body a mere shell. He was spent and fell into Jamie's arms.

"You have to see this," Caldred said.

Jamie turned to glance at the Valley and saw scores of Lockewell soldiers fighting fiercely—with each other. They were slashing and hacking at their own kinsmen. The Clem warriors were stunned. It took them a full ten seconds to understand what was going on before they jumped in and helped the Fifth Legion tear itself to pieces. Jamie looked back down at Acasta and saw the mage was still muttering under his breath, despite being barely conscious. Whatever he was doing seemed to be draining the life from him. Jamie wanted him to snap out of it, but he also knew the mage was turning the tide of the battle.

"This is our chance," Caldred said, grabbing Jamie's arm.

"No, we can't leave him," Jamie countered in disbelief. "What are you thinking?"

"I made him a vow," Caldred said, unaware of the real reason for his sense of duty—like the Lockewell men below who had been bewitched into fighting among themselves, Caldred had been given a task he could not avoid. He had to get Jamie to Tufthorn.

At that moment, the strain was finally too much for Acasta. He passed out completely. His murmuring stopped. The boys looked down at the battle and saw the Fifth Legion slowly coming to their senses, realizing they'd been battling each other. Perhaps enough of them had been slaughtered to give Clem the chance to win. Perhaps not.

"He said to leave him," Caldred urged. "We have to go now."

"He's coming with us, or I don't go anywhere," Jamie insisted.

Angry, Caldred grabbed one arm, and Jamie grabbed Acasta's other, and they propped him up, his feet dragging between them as they made it to the stairwell. "Is that Laroche?" Jamie asked.

It was. The spy had awoken and was in a bleary haze, his head bleeding. "Going so soon?" he asked, his head bobbing. "I know a secret way out."

Jamie and Caldred stopped.

"You lie," Caldred challenged.

Laroche shrugged, standing. He used a wall to brace himself. "Often and well, but not this time. Help me escape, and I will show you the way."

"Help us get him down the stairs, and we'll consider it," Jamie said.

Laroche took some of Acasta's weight and smiled. "Deal."

The steps were littered with Lockewell soldiers who had most likely killed each other. Down the stairwell the three went, struggling with Acasta all the way. When they reached the ground level, they heard a whinny and saw Jester there waiting for them along with another horse.

"This keeps getting weirder," Jamie said.

They slung Acasta over the saddle, his head hanging over one side and his legs over the other. Laroche tried to climb onto the other horse, but Caldred stopped him. "You ride with the mage," he said.

Jester snorted in response and backed up a step. Jamie turned to the horse and patted his neck. "He's our only way out of here."

The horse lowered his head in agreement. Laroche blinked at that, then climbed into the saddle behind Acasta's body.

Jamie and Caldred climbed atop the other horse. Jamie went first, grabbing the reins, and Caldred followed. No sooner were they atop the animal than Jester took off, spurring their horse to do the same. They ran right over a Lockewell soldier as they retreated deeper into the fortress.

Inside the inner courtyard, Laroche pulled up on the reins. Both horses stopped. "We have to go through the stables and into the tunnels. We may encounter resistance along the way."

Caldred gripped his weapon. Jamie saw this and took a mental note of where his own long knife was. Laroche nodded.

"Good," he said, then spurred Jester into action.

They rode around the stables, blowing past the stablemaster. His apprentice gave chase briefly, but there was not much he could do as the two horses galloped away. Laroche led them to a metal gate with a Clem man standing guard.

"What the shit is this?" he yelled, drawing his sword. Caldred was off the horse and engaging him in the blink of an eye. The guard backed up a step and nearly tripped as he fought off a wayward parry from Caldred. That was the only opening Jester needed. Without any prodding from Laroche, the horse rammed into the guard and knocked him senseless against the gate. He crumbled in a heap.

"This horse is an odd one," Laroche noted.

Caldred leaned down and lifted the key to the gate from the guard's belt. "What are these tunnels?" he asked.

"Oh, didn't I mention? Sewage," Laroche quipped.

Hillhome

The capitol building in Genora was old and stately, built a century earlier to house the Senate. This structure in Ravinia, of Hillhome province, was a converted bathhouse at the edge of town next to a dairy farm. The smell of manure and livestock permeated the air.

The message was clear.

Philipa Black watched the bewildered senators as they milled about the plain, rectangular building. They had come to Ravinia with bold hopes of progress. A new era. A new seat of power. What greeted them was a city firmly under Lockewell's thumb. The smart ones had already realized which way the political winds were blowing before the capital switched cities, but many of the senators seemed caught off-guard by the meager accommodations.

"Is this really happening, Philipa?" a veteran senator asked.

"It's only temporary," Black responded. "We will have a proper place to gather once the Senate appropriates a bill to fund the construction of a building that meets all our needs."

"And when will that be?" the senator snarked. "This body is not exactly known for its expediency."

"A sad state of affairs I hope to address as first minister," she said.

"Shame about First Minister Martin," the man said, before quickly adding, "of course he couldn't have asked for a better successor."

"Thank you for your confidence," Black said.

"When it comes time for a new senate house, might I recommend allocating money to include more than one toilet?" the senator said, gesturing to the line of people waiting for their turn to use the lone bathroom.

The senator raised an eyebrow and walked back to grouse with his colleagues. Black didn't blame him. She also didn't care. She knew the Senate had been effectively relieved of its power. As acting and, eventually, permanent first minster, she reported to Grayfork directly, who in turn coordinated with the royals of Lockewell. Maldovar would be a fiefdom in practice for a few years until it was officially absorbed into Lockewell. Black felt a twinge of regret; in her youth, she had been an idealist. The Republic meant something to her. But those days were long gone, and she had risen to power by being a realist. Martin was unable to change, and he paid for that obstinance with his life. She had a hard time conjuring sympathy for him, however, as he had been given a very clear choice and he still decided on the road to self-ruin.

"Is he one of the problem children?" Dormond asked, motioning to the senator Black was just speaking to.

Black did her best not to look startled; the slayer had snuck up on her. She noted how well he fit in here, dressed just like the very men and women he'd been sent to eliminate.

"No," Black replied. "Now that Martin and Modano have been taken care of, you'll find many of these senators will think twice about raising too much of a fuss. Of course that doesn't mean they're above complaining about their new bathhouse."

"It is rather shabby," Dormond said. "Grayfork isn't one for subtlety, is he?"

Black remained stoic as Eliana Troy approached. She smiled wide at Black, extending her hand to shake. "Congratulations are in order," Troy said. "You are looking well."

"Thank you, Eliana," Black replied. "I only wish Henry were here to guide us in these times."

"Yes, I'm sure you do. You were close friends for many years. His death must weigh heavily on you," Troy said, shifting her gaze to Dormond. "And just who might this new and dashing friend be?"

Dormond bowed and took Troy's hand, kissing it. "Stockton Gilmore," he offered. Another new identity for him. "The minister's economic advisor."

"Charmed," Troy purred. "You'll have to join me sometime for lunch. I like to pretend I can still entertain men of your age with witty repertoire."

"I have no doubt you can," Dormond replied. "I'm free tomorrow if you'd like to try your skills over tea."

"That would be lovely," she said. "I'd invite you, Philipa, but I can imagine how busy you are now that you're in charge of this … transition, shall we call it?" Troy looked about the chamber, pretending to be impressed.

"Tea for two it is," Dormond chirped. He gave another slight bow as Troy sauntered away.

"That one is on the list," Black snarled.

"Pity. She seems quite fun," Dormond said. "On the bright side, the list comes from Grayfork, not you, so perhaps he has more interest in seeing some of your equals stick around. You know, just to keep things in the proper balance and perspective."

Dormond grinned at Black, then headed toward the senate floor to mingle with the officials from Maldovar. Black watched him with concern as he slipped into character and introduced himself to a pair of eager senators.

* * *

The cafe bustled with activity, owing mostly to the influx of officials, their families and the many hangers-on that had migrated from Genora to Ravinia in the last few weeks. As such, Dormond and Troy sat in the corner of the packed tea and coffee house at a spare, wobbly table with mismatched chairs.

Dormond sipped his drink and made a face. "Maybe in time, they'll learn how to steep tea properly here."

"It took the Eastern Maldovarians two centuries," Troy replied, sliding her own mug aside. "Let us hope these people of the west figure it out much sooner."

Dormond smiled at the elder stateswoman. She was somewhere in her fifties, he guessed, but she still had the demure confidence of a classic beauty. At nearly half her age, Dormond found himself attracted to her despite the years that separated them.

"People of the west? I'll have to remember that one. So you don't approve of the Lockewell influence in this part of the realm?" Dormond asked.

"Not as it relates to tea preparation or slavery, no," Troy said, not mincing words.

"Yes, well, I too find certain aspects of the slave trade to be regrettable," Dormond agreed.

"But only certain aspects?"

"I'm a man of commerce, after all."

Troy placed a hand on top of Dormond's, surprising him.

"I will call you Mr. Gilmore if you like," she said. "I will even call you Lord Gilmore if that is the alias you prefer. But we are both adults here, so let us speak truths now, shall we? You may present yourself as the economic advisor Stockton Gilmore to the rest of the Senate, yet it insults me when you try to perpetrate the same ruse on an old crow like myself."

Troy removed her hand from his and picked up her tea, steeling herself for a taste, then making a decent show of enjoying it.

Dormond liked this woman.

"Of all the words that come to mind when describing you, old and crow are very far down the list," Dormond said. "Your point is well taken. While I cannot reveal my actual name, I understand that a woman of your obvious political skills is not easily fooled by my thin veneer of a disguise."

"Thank you," she replied.

Dormond gave a slight bow and met Troy's eyes for a few seconds.

The moment was rudely interrupted by loud voices at a table nearby. Two senators were arguing about the price of cakes. Troy laughed.

"That's about the best metaphor I could imagine," she said. "They are angry about dessert when they should be worried about all the other things they're being forced to swallow in this godsforsaken town."

"Men with wounded pride tend to be very irrational in my experience," Dormond noted.

"And what kind of experience is that?" Troy asked.

Dormond didn't bite. "You tell me, wise old crow."

Troy made a tutting sound to gently rebuke him for using her own words against her. Then she hardened her eyes and looked at Dormond's hands.

"It's not often men of commerce have hands such as these," she said. "Rough and full of those little muscles you acquire over a lifetime of strenuous work. Not farm labor or long hours in the smithy, though. They bear none of those scars. This is more precise work than that. Coupled with the fact you've been installed as our new first minister's top advisor, I'd venture to say you solve problems. Or, more specifically, eliminate them. Considering your easy demeanor and charming looks, I'm guessing you're quite capable in that regard."

Dormond sat back and kept silent. She had the size of it. He instinctively surveyed the room; he had no intention of surreptitiously sliding a knife between her ribs and slipping away unnoticed, but years of doing just that had made him mentally make sure he could get away with it, nonetheless.

"Ah, it seems I'm not far off," Troy said. "I hope I'm not being too forward when I say I don't judge men in your line of work."

"That is most kind of you," Dormond replied, suddenly wondering if she was more adept at this game than he. "I have to ask. Why did you want to share tea with me?"

"Other than the unrivaled local steeping abilities?" she asked.

Again, Dormond laughed. It wasn't a feigned laugh, either. "Other than that, yes."

"To plot and scheme, of course," she said. "I get the sense you're a man who likes to play on the winning side, and I wanted to open a line of dialogue with you, as I'm not entirely sure that's the side you're on right now."

"Is that so?"

"Oh, there's no doubt Lockewell has a good hand to play," she said. "And momentum. That has value and cannot be underestimated. There is a wrinkle, though: the matter of one realm trying to conquer not just one, but multiple rivals at the same time. That is no easy thing, even for people of Grayfork's prowess."

"If I am what you think I am, are you sure you should be speaking so much truth to me?" Dormond asked. "We hardly know each other."

"We may not know each other, but I believe we understand each other perfectly well. I am a Maldovarian through and through, so if I don't say these words, I've already lost," Troy explained. "It seems only prudent to make sure you understand you have potential partners should the political winds change. And in my experience, the winds are quite prone to do so."

"You are not a fan of the first minister," Dormond said, making it a statement rather than a question.

"No more than you are, though my reasons are different. You see a puppet. I see a selfish traitor. But we agree on one point: she is inconsequential."

"And you and I, we are of consequence?" Dormond asked.

"Clever people are always of consequence," Troy said. "It's our curse and our blessing. Being a traitorous sycophant doesn't make Philipa Black clever. It just makes her a bitch, pardon my language."

"By all means, I enjoy such language. And I enjoy you, Eliana, if I may be so bold. This meeting was everything I hoped it would be and more. Alas, my current employer pays exceedingly well, so the best I can do is vow not to kill you for the words we've shared today."

Troy nodded. Fair was fair. "At least let me pay for your tea," Troy said.

"But then I would be a heel and in your debt, and we can't have that," Dormond teased as he stood up from the table and placed a few bits on the table. Then he tipped his hat and strolled out of the cafe. Troy watched him go, pleased with the outcome of this first encounter.

Aftermath

Skullcrusher walked through one of the giant holes in the outer wall of Kragon's Lair. She looked out at the Valley below. The morning was cool, and the breeze flicked at the few pieces of her hair that weren't matted together with dried blood.

Clem had repelled the Lockewell army, just barely.

It took the entire night, the lives of over half her fighters, and some kind of magic she'd never seen before from a mage who was nowhere to be found. The loss of so many Clem warriors was no reason to celebrate, but the victory was a sweet one. They had beaten a much larger force and held the castle at the heart of Clem's kingdom. The walls could be rebuilt; the warriors replenished. Had the Fifth Legion taken Kragon's Lair, however, it would have been a blight not just on Skullcrusher's reign, but Clem's aura of invincibility. This day, they remained the most formidable force in all the realms.

"There's no sign of the wizard," a warrior told Skullcrusher.

"Not dead," Rawk said.

Skullcrusher looked at the big man, covered in the blood of his enemies. *How many did he kill last night?* Anke wondered. *Fifty? A hundred?*

"What makes you say that?" she asked.

"No body," Rawk replied. "No horse, either."

Skullcrusher nodded. She took another swig of her ale and contemplated her next move. She had already sent riders to find the best builders in Clem to repair the outer walls. Once the dead bodies of the enemy were pillaged, they would be burned in the Valley. She doubted anyone would challenge her in the Circle anytime soon, not after a decisive victory such as this.

"The spy is gone, boss," Wraggus growled. He arrived with a younger Clem warrior who had a blooming bruise across the entirety of his face. The gate guard that Jester had rushed the previous evening. Skullcrusher was surprised at how well Wraggus represented himself during battle, and she was more than pleased to hear him addressing her as "boss" again. It was just the first sign of her renewed respect among her men.

Wraggus kicked the guard in the ass. "Tell her," he said.

"The mage escaped with the spy last night, boss," the guard said, nervous. "The mage was knocked out or dead, I don't know. They surprised me and went into the sewer tunnels. There was nothing I could do."

"The mage was dead ... and he surprised you?" Skullcrusher asked.

"Well, they weren't alone!" the guard argued. "See, the spy was on the horse, and the mage was dumped over the animal like he was dead or maybe passed out. I don't know. But there was another horse with two young boys ... er, fighters on it. I didn't see them coming."

"Your job is to see people coming!" Wraggus snarled, kicking the guard again.

"Did anyone find Little Galantra or the skinny one yet?" Skullcrusher asked Rawk.

"No," he said. "Could be under bodies."

"I think not," she replied. The wheels were spinning in her head as she wondered why Acasta would leave in the middle of the fight. Or maybe it was Laroche who kidnapped the mage; the guard had said Acasta looked dead or unconscious. Still more questions swirled, like how and why the boys she had picked up were involved.

"Wraggus. Your men served Clem well last night," Skull-crusher complimented. "I trust we can put our differences behind us?"

"Aye," he said, raising his axe. "We are united, Skullcrusher."

"Good," she said. "Take a few of your best men and go after them. Laroche cannot be allowed to make it back to Lockewell."

"And the mage?" Wraggus asked.

Skullcrusher looked back to the Valley, where she could see much of Acasta's handiwork in the form of bodies littered across the land. "Try not to let him kill you."

Secrets, Revealed

"I smell shit," Acasta said.

He was leaned up against a tree. Jester nudged his face and licked the back of his hair.

"That is most likely you," Laroche said. "Splashing around for a half mile in the waste produced by an entire castle will do that to a person."

Acasta looked down at his clothes. They were caked with mud and other brown and red smears. *Delightful.* Someone had dressed a wound in his side; the gash hurt each time he moved it. If he didn't get it treated properly, and soon, it would be trouble. Acasta reached up and patted Jester on the neck. "Hey, buddy."

"Horse hasn't left your side since we made camp," Laroche said.

"Friends are like that," Acasta replied. "Which brings me to my first question: why are you here?"

"You and I rode out of Kragon's Lair together," Laroche said, happy to possess more knowledge than Acasta of their escape. It made him feel like he was back in control, if only a little bit.

"Alone?" Acasta asked. The events of the previous night came rushing back. Jamie was the Promised Knight. He had bewitched thousands to save him. Or he had tried to, anyway.

"Little Galantra and Caldred are out gathering kindling for a fire. We rode all night and part of the morning. The horses needed a rest," Laroche explained.

"The battle?" Acasta wondered aloud. He didn't like asking Laroche so many questions, but he had to know what had become of his plan to defeat the Fifth Legion.

"We left before it was over, by many hours if I had to guess," Laroche said. "Was that you who … confused the Lockewell soldiers?"

Acasta didn't answer. He didn't have to. Laroche cracked a grin. "That is a neat and deadly trick, my friend. I can think of multiple realms that would pay well for such a weapon."

"Be careful what you suggest next, spy," Acasta warned.

"I am just a man speaking the truth."

A rustle in the bushes drew their attention. Jamie stepped into the clearing, holding a few sticks and branches. "I was worried you might not wake," he said.

"Sorry to disappoint," Acasta replied.

Jamie started placing wood on top of some rocks to prepare the fire. He and Acasta shared an unspoken look that suggested they talk about Acasta's revelations to him when Laroche was not in their company. Taking the hint, Laroche stood up.

"I think I need to relieve myself," he said.

"Go out of earshot," Acasta said. "If you don't, I'll know."

"I guess it would've been too much to expect a thank-you for saving your life," Laroche groused.

"Not at all. Thank you. Now make sure you go at least fifty feet into the woods to piss."

Laroche shook his head and made his way into the trees.

Once Acasta was satisfied the crafty spy was far enough away, he turned to Jamie.

"I told you to leave me," Acasta scolded.

"So, he gets a thank-you for saving your life, and I don't?" Jamie joked.

"Fine. Thank you. And thank the sun for shining. And the air for allowing me to breathe. And shit for making me smell like a boar's asshole. Am I done yet?"

"You forgot Caldred."

Acasta laughed, despite himself. He watched Jamie struggle with the spark for the fire, then took pity on the boy and sent a small bit of flame toward the pile with his magic, igniting the campfire.

"So, the Knight of War and Dawn can't even start a fire?" Acasta teased. "The gods do have a sense of humor, don't they?"

Jamie sighed and looked at the mage. "I don't know who or what you think I am, and I do not care."

"Nor does the prophecy care if you believe it," Acasta said. "That does not make it any less true. The only way we'll know for sure is to go to Tufthorn. My queen will be able to tell."

"I'm going home," Jamie said.

"No."

"You're going to stop me?"

"If I have to, sure," Acasta said. "Though I'd rather you go with me willingly, ideally once we've deposited our dear spy somewhere else along the way. Breathing or not, it makes no difference to me."

Jamie thought about this for a few moments. He had only heard pieces of the story from Laroche and the Clem warriors. It was not clear why being this "promised knight" was so important. "How could someone like me have such a big role in the fate of the world?" he asked.

Acasta looked at him with a smile. "Jamie. Do you really think I have any fucking idea?"

Now it was Jamie's turn to laugh. Something about Acasta's laid-back demeanor and straightforward nature made him very easy to talk to.

"If I heard the rumors correctly, I'm going to be the greatest fighter since, well, since Galantra," Jamie said. The nickname rang true now.

"There are no coincidences, kid."

"What about Caldred?" Jamie asked.

"Can't hurt having another friend along to watch our backs," Acasta said.

Jamie resigned himself to his fate for the time being. "So. Tufthorn. To see a queen."

"When you say it like that, it almost sounds boring. I assure you it will not be," Acasta promised.

Jamie looked off toward the woods. "Speaking of Caldred, where is he?"

* * *

Twigs and leaves snapped underfoot as Caldred raced through the trees. Were it a human chasing him, he would've lost his pursuer minutes ago. Unfortunately for Caldred, he was being followed by a jaguar. The animal had surprised him while he was tasting a wild fruit he'd found during his search for kindling.

Caldred puffed hard as he darted across a dried creek bed. He was hoping to tire the jaguar out; if he couldn't outrun the animal, he might be able to outlast it. He glanced back and saw the jaguar was still gaining ground and was maybe forty feet behind him now.

He was tempted to climb a tree, but his instincts told him the animal was also a better climber than he was. *Hell of a way to die.* Caldred was leading the jaguar in a wide circle, hoping to make his way back near camp, where Jamie or even Laroche might be able to help distract or scare the animal.

Caldred leapt over a fallen log and nearly lost his footing in the slippery moss on the ground where he landed, but he kept the pace. Still, the jaguar gained on him. *Shit!* He was approaching what looked to be another creek bed. The boy couldn't see the other side but took it on faith that it was merely a few feet below the boulder he was about to spring from.

Caldred planted his foot and launched himself from the boulder at the edge of a clearing. His heart sank when he looked down and saw the deep ravine below—along with the wide chasm between the boulder he just jumped from and the grass sprouting from the other edge.

It was one hundred feet across, if not more.

In that split-second after he leapt, Caldred knew his fate was sealed. His heart lurched in his throat as he soared into nothingness ... and kept soaring. Something buoyed him as his momentum continued. Twenty feet. Fifty feet now. Incredibly, he was not slowing down. If anything, it felt like he was speeding up as he continued to arc across the ravine.

Seventy-five feet.

Just now slowing down, though his heart was still racing.

He finally stopped running through the air, as it seemed pointless. It was not his legs that kept him afloat. It was some other force. As he neared the other side, he crouched and landed with a roll.

It took a few moments to steady his breathing and take in what had just happened. He felt the earth under his feet and knees. He was not dead, with his bones crushed and blood spattered all over the rocks. He was safe. Caldred looked back across the chasm and saw the jaguar standing at the edge, growling at him. Judging the distance again, it might have been 150 feet.

"So, that just happened," Caldred said to himself.

Fifty feet away from him, standing in the shadows of the jungle, Laroche gaped at the boy. He had just witnessed the Flyer. He was sure of it. A mischievous grin spread across his face.

Epilogue

King Cecil enjoyed being on the throne. Whereas his father was frequently annoyed with the trappings of ceremony, King Cecil spent hours sitting on his plush seat, giving subjects and sycophants an audience. Grayfork knew he didn't care about those people or their desires; he just enjoyed having his royal ass kissed.

Finally, after four hours of listening to dukes and lords grovel, King Cecil had had his fill and dismissed everyone but Grayfork from the chamber.

"Who knew the realm had so many problems?" the king joked.

"I trust you won't be indulging in this activity every day of your reign," Grayfork chided.

"Would you rather I spend my time being reminded of our great defeats?" the king snapped.

Grayfork grimaced. News of the failure at Kragon's Lair had reached the Silver Castle that morning. Given the covert nature of the Fifth Legion, the true scale of the loss would hopefully never be completely understood by more than just a few of the king's advisors. Cecil himself had taken the news surprisingly well for a man with such a volcanic temper;

Grayfork couldn't figure out if he was waiting to explode or simply cared less about the machinations of war now that he was finally king. That had been his life's ambition, fueled by a lust for power and hatred for his own father.

"We challenged their stronghold with a small portion of our army and nearly took the castle," Grayfork replied, trying to put a positive spin on it.

"Ah, nearly," King Cecil said. "I am sure if this doesn't work out, you will be satisfied with nearly keeping your head."

Grayfork bit his tongue. He'd like to see the king try to execute him. Grayfork was confident he had more allies in Lockewell than the king did. Perhaps sensing this, King Cecil smiled.

"Relax, old friend," he said. "We both want our own piece of the same thing. You seek the riches and I require the power. Together, we make a formidable pair. Though I would suggest next time you go up against Clem, you bring our full forces to bear."

Grayfork acknowledged the point with a nod. "I agree, your highness. We now know Clem is not as fragile as our spies suggested. That is a hard lesson, but a valuable one. We will deal with them after we take the forest kingdom."

"And what of Maldovar?"

"Diplomacy is progressing nicely there," Grayfork answered. "Combined with a few efforts from our new slayer that has decided to switch sides, we should have the Republic under our thumb in a year's time."

"Republic!" the king sneered. "Giving the people the power to rule? That's an ass-backward way of looking at the world."

"Agreed," Grayfork said.

"Fidora," the king mused. "I never liked trees, if I'm being honest. Cut them all down and make more ships, is what I say. When should we expect news of this victory? And a victory it better be."

* * *

Spiro looked out at the troops amassed at the treeline.

He'd known they were coming for days thanks to his rangers, but there was still nothing he could do to defend Arrow's Edge, the capital of his ancestors' kingdom. He shielded his light eyes from the sun and sighed at the sheer size of the army below. He had not known Lockewell had such numbers. *Could there be thirty thousand men down there?* It was not clear how many soldiers were hidden in the forest.

King Taldren Oak stood beside him. "How did we let this happen, brother?" he asked. Spiro had no answer for his older brother, though it was mostly a rhetorical question. Spiro looked at the king and saw the faintest hints of crow's feet at the corners of his eyes; he was nearly forty years old but had aged with the grace of the handsome and noble man he was. Spiro was handsome as well, but his brother the king possessed a certain quality that dazed men and women alike. His three Kingwives were equally attractive. Their beauty perfectly represented the forest kingdom.

At the moment, his brother's face looked weary.

"We were complacent, I suppose," Spiro said. "No war for a century will do that to a kingdom, even one as vigilant as ours."

King Oak nodded.

"We cannot fight them," he said. "Rather, we cannot survive the fight."

"No," Spiro agreed.

"Then we are forced to surrender," the king said.

"I will do it," Spiro offered. They were not the words of a coward; Spiro was one of the deadliest bowmen in Fidora. They were the words of a realist. Practicality was core to the Fidoran way of life. Like the forest itself, the kingdom had grown strong slowly and deliberately over time. A setback today did not mean collapse tomorrow.

The king gave his younger brother a hard look. Spiro returned it.

"Very well," he said, putting a hand on his brother's shoulder. "Do not give them any reason to kill you. We'll come for you, Spiro."

King Oak looked out at the invading force.

"They can't hope to hold Arrow's Edge, not with this army. Not even with a hundred thousand men," King Oak said.

The two brothers embraced and then the king headed back into the palace to gather his wives and children. They would be escorted through the Narrow Pass by the royal guard. The rest of the palace inhabitants would stay while Spiro negotiated a surrender with the Lockewell force. The thought of it made Spiro sick, but he knew his brother was right: they could sack the palace, but they could not hold it. Not in the forest. Thousands of Fidoran would soon know of this invasion and they'd cut off the routes for supplies in and out of the forest kingdom.

"What do you think they're up to?" Spiro's uncle, Japrin, asked as he arrived at Spiro's side.

"I don't know," Spiro said. That was what worried him. He'd heard that the Lockewell king had been killed and replaced by his petulant and ambitious son, but not enough time had passed for King Cecil to send this force. They must have been sent while King Edwin still sat on the throne; the same King Edwin that had abided by the peace accords his many years as ruler.

Something caught Spiro's eye.

He looked down at the treeline and saw a row of orange flames igniting. Arrows. A realization dawned on Spiro, kindling both anger and dread in his heart. The Lockewell soldiers had no intention of taking the palace. They planned to burn it to the ground.

* * *

About the Author

George Ellis lives in Austin, where he writes fantasy and science fiction books at night and runs an advertising agency by day. In addition to novels, he writes screenplays, viral videos and Internet memes.

Also by George Ellis

Wreckers

At 19 years old, Denver is the youngest wrecker in space. His only companion, other than his one-eyed cat, is an AI navigator based on classic 21st century sitcom personalities. That all changes when Denver meets Batista, a mechanic who claims to know what happened to Denver's missing father and brother. Soon, Denver is drawn into trouble with the various forces in the galaxy — bandits, feds and rival wreckers.

40+

Bill Remis retired at 33. He didn't save much money. And he never bothered having kids. But when a few people in the world start living past 40, Bill's predictable life is thrown into chaos. Could he be the next 40-something? Has he done everything wrong and wasted his life?

40+ is a fast-paced, witty sci-fi novella about age and how it shapes all our decisions. If you like smart dialogue, strong characters and some government conspiracies thrown in, then you'll love this unique story.